Prince
rendere

His first glimpse of Rory Kenilworth was one of those rare moments. With her outrageously brilliant dress in three varying shades of orange clinging to her generous curves, she looked aflame.

"I'm sorry I'm late," she said. He was disconcerted by the vulnerability in her blue eyes.

Laurent remembered his role and cleared his throat. "No need to apologize, Your Serene Highness," he said with a formal bow. "Allow me to introduce myself. I am Sebastian Guimond, royal deputy secretary." Laurent searched inward for the control he had mastered as a young boy.

"Pleased to meet you, Mr. Guimond."

Images tempted and tortured him. Her legs twined around his hips. Her belly swelling with his heir. He set his jaw as his body betrayed him by reacting to the images.

His mouth pressed into a thin line. He was honor bound to marry the woman standing in front of him. But he must never love her.

Dear Harlequin Intrigue Reader,

As you make travel plans for the summer, don't forget to pack along this month's exciting new Harlequin Intrigue books!

The notion of being able to rewrite history has always been fascinating, so be sure to check out *Secret Passage* by Amanda Stevens. In this wildly innovative third installment in QUANTUM MEN, supersoldier Zac Riley must complete a vital mission, but his long-lost love is on a crucial mission of her own! Opposites combust in *Wanted Woman* by B.J. Daniels, which pits a beautiful daredevil on the run against a fiercely protective deputy sheriff—the next book in CASCADES CONCEALED.

Julie Miller revisits THE TAYLOR CLAN when one of Kansas City's finest infiltrates a crime boss's compound and finds himself under the dangerous spell of an aristocratic beauty. Will he be the *Last Man Standing*? And in *Legally Binding* by Ann Voss Peterson—the second sizzling story in our female-driven in-line continuity SHOTGUN SALLYS—a reformed bad boy rancher needs the help of the best female legal eagle in Texas to clear him of murder!

Who can resist those COWBOY COPS? In our latest offering in our Western-themed promotion, Adrianne Lee tantalizes with *Denim Detective*. This gripping family-in-jeopardy tale has a small-town sheriff riding to the rescue, but he's about to learn one doozy of a secret.... And finally this month you are cordially invited to partake in *Her Royal Bodyguard* by Joyce Sullivan, an enchanting mystery about a commoner who discovers she's a betrothed princess and teams up with an enigmatic bodyguard who vows to protect her from evildoers.

Enjoy our fabulous lineup this month!

Sincerely,

Denise O'Sullivan
Senior Editor, Harlequin Intrigue

HER ROYAL BODYGUARD

JOYCE SULLIVAN

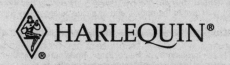

HARLEQUIN®

TORONTO • NEW YORK • LONDON
AMSTERDAM • PARIS • SYDNEY • HAMBURG
STOCKHOLM • ATHENS • TOKYO • MILAN • MADRID
PRAGUE • WARSAW • BUDAPEST • AUCKLAND

ISBN 0-373-22782-5

HER ROYAL BODYGUARD

Copyright © 2004 by Joyce David

This edition published by arrangement with Harlequin Books S.A.

® and TM are trademarks of the publisher. Trademarks indicated with
® are registered in the United States Patent and Trademark Office, the
Canadian Trade Marks Office and in other countries.

www.eHarlequin.com

Printed in U.S.A.

ABOUT THE AUTHOR

Like most little girls, Joyce Sullivan entertained a secret desire to be a princess. Princesses, she was sure, did not have freckles. She grew up in Lakeside, California, and often visited La Jolla, where this story is set.

A former private investigator, Joyce has a bachelor's degree in criminal justice. She credits her lawyer mother with instilling in her a love of reading and solving mysteries. The Lakeside library was their favorite destination.

Joyce currently resides with her own French prince and two teenagers in a Georgian home with an English garden and a secret garden in Quebec, Canada. You can write to her and visit her Web site at www.joycesullivan.com.

Books by Joyce Sullivan

HARLEQUIN INTRIGUE
352—THE NIGHT BEFORE CHRISTMAS
436—THIS LITTLE BABY
516—TO LANEY, WITH LOVE
546—THE BABY SECRET
571—URGENT VOWS
631—IN HIS WIFE'S NAME
722—THE BUTLER'S DAUGHTER*
726—OPERATION BASSINET*
782—HER ROYAL BODYGUARD

*The Collingwood Heirs

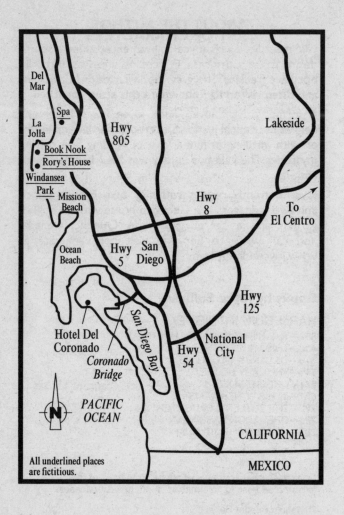

Del
Mar

Spa
•

La
Jolla

• Book Nook
• Rory's House

Windansea
Park
Mission
Beach

Ocean
Beach

Hwy
805

Lakeside

Hwy
8

To
El Centro

Hwy
5

San
Diego

Hwy
125

Hotel Del
Coronado

*Coronado
Bridge*

San Diego Bay

National
City

Hwy
54

N

*PACIFIC
OCEAN*

CALIFORNIA

MEXICO

All underlined places
are fictitious.

CAST OF CHARACTERS

Prince August of Estaire—He sacrificed his marriage and his daughter for the good of his country.

Sophia Kenilworth—She died before she could tell her daughter of her birthright.

Rory Kenilworth—Will this princess-in-training wed for love...or a crown?

Prince Laurent of Ducharme—He went undercover to protect the princess he was duty bound to marry.

Prince Olivier of Estaire—He was unable to father an heir for his country.

Princess Penelope of Estaire—Olivier's wife would go to any lengths to give birth to the next heir to the throne.

Heinrich and his merry men—Was one of these bodyguards involved in a plot to kill Rory?

Renald Dartois—How loyal was Prince Olivier's private secretary?

Odette Schoenfeldt—The palace press secretary's job was to nip scandals in the bud.

Claude Dupont—He blamed Prince Laurent for his sister's death.

Otto Gascon—Was Rory's elderly neighbor friend or foe?

To Julie, Lauren, Elise, Christine, Aubree, Isabelle,
Lysanne, Sophie and Gabrielle. The princesses in my life.

Acknowledgments

My heartfelt thanks to my editor Stacy Boyd,
and to the following generous people who came
to the rescue with this book: Ottomar Adamitz,
Claire Fried Huffaker, Teresa Eckford,
Dr. Stephen W. MacLean, Jake Gravelle, Jeannie Danyiel,
T. Lorraine Vassalo, Rickey R. Mallory and Judy McAnerin.

Prologue

Sophia Kenilworth couldn't put off the inevitable for too much longer. She'd lied to her daughter, Charlotte Aurora, about her birth, about her father and about her heritage. She'd have to tell Rory the truth soon, before her twenty-third birthday when that despicable marriage treaty would come into effect.

Her source in Estaire had informed Sophia that her former stepson, Prince Olivier, and his wife, Princess Penelope, were still childless after three years of marriage. Despite rumors that they'd been consulting with fertility specialists, there had been no announcement of a pregnancy that might save Rory from an arranged marriage to a crown prince.

Sophia was no fool. She knew Prince Olivier was as much a martinet as his father, Prince August, had been—always placing the principality and what was best for Estaire above the needs of his own child's happiness. Sophia's deceased ex-husband had viewed the treaty as a brilliant political and economic move that would settle a three-hundred-year-old feud with the neighboring country of Ducharme and ensure that Estaire had a suitable heir apparent in the event that his son Prince Olivier was unable to provide one.

With no sign of an heir on the horizon, Sophia knew it was futile to hold out hope that Prince Olivier would rescind the contract. During her two-year marriage to Prince Olivier's father, Sophia had become well-versed in the stifling complexities and obligations of royal life. But that damn marriage treaty had been the breaking point of her tolerance.

Sophia had cried, ranted and threatened divorce for months. She couldn't believe that her beloved prince, who'd chosen her—an American bride without a family trust fund or an ounce of nobility in her veins—had heartlessly consigned his daughter to a loveless marriage.

But at least she'd succeeded in giving Rory a normal childhood away from the spotlight in exchange for the sacrifice Prince August expected his daughter to make for her country. Under the terms of the separation agreement, Sophia had no obligation to tell Rory of her birthright until her twenty-third birthday. If Rory happened to fall in love and marry in the meantime, well then, *c'est la vie.*

Sophia frowned worriedly and stirred her tea. Unfortunately, Rory wasn't seeing anyone, despite Sophia's urgings that she go out more often.

Sophia consoled herself with the knowledge that she had done her best to prepare Rory for the future that awaited her. She'd encouraged her daughter's love of knowledge and had given her a broad range of experiences. She'd insisted Rory study French and had carefully chosen the small private college that would encourage Rory to find her strengths.

And Sophia would be there to guide her daughter through the transition to palace life. Provided, of course, that Rory forgave her for keeping this secret.

With a shaking hand, Sophia carried her mug of raspberry tea out to the cliff-side garden of their La Jolla home that overlooked the Pacific Ocean. The water was lazy this afternoon, the waves jiggling and lifting like huge rolls of blue-green gelatin topped with whipped cream. Surfers in wet suits bobbed among the waves.

Sophia settled into the wooden swing that perched on an outcropping of sandstone at the rear of the sun-drenched garden. It was Rory's favorite place to dream and read, with the world and the ocean at her feet.

Sophia kicked the swing into motion. How was she supposed to tell Rory she was a princess? Or explain that her father had betrothed her to a prince?

Sophia never had time to find the right words. With a sickening lurch, the cliff beneath the swing gave way. Crying out in horror, she plummeted to the rocky beach below.

LA JOLLA WOMAN Killed in Fall.

The ten-day-old newspaper headline made the reader's pulse thrum with excitement. Was Princess Charlotte Aurora dead? There was mention of a cliff and a swing. This had to be it. The reader eagerly devoured the details: "Neptune Place…erosion…the dangers of building homes on cretaceous sandstone along the California coast… The victim was pronounced dead on arrival."

Dead. For the paltry sum of one hundred thousand American dollars.

There was no mention that foul play was suspected.

The thrill of having successfully gotten away with murder buzzed in the reader's brain like the finest champagne. Prince Laurent would not be marrying Princess Charlotte Aurora after all.

Slowly, as if relishing the last bites of a delectable meal, the reader read the final sentence of the article. *The victim was identified as Sophia Kenilworth.*

No! This could not be! The reader gouged the news-print with the ornate silver-plated letter opener from the desk. The wrong woman had died. Princess Charlotte Aurora still lived.

Chapter One

Eight Months Later

It was her first birthday without her mother.

Rory Kenilworth felt the raw ache of loss squeeze her throat as she stuck a birthday candle in her morning cranberry muffin—just as her mother, Sophia, would have done.

She was *not* going to cry.

She sniffled. Okay, maybe she was. *I miss you, Mom. I wish you were here singing off-key and giving me a birthday card announcing this year's bonding adventure.*

Her mother's birthday presents had always taken the form of memorable moments spent together rather than the exchange of material objects—a trip to Egypt to see the Great Pyramids of Giza, an Alaskan cruise, backpacking in the Grand Canyon, a tour of Thailand. Rory's favorite had been the trip to Prince Edward Island to see Green Gables—the home of Anne Shirley, one of her favorite fictional heroines, who had the enviable ability to express herself in a way that Rory rarely had the confidence to mimic.

Even the less agreeable aspects of those birthday adventures, such as having a fifty-five-pound pack strapped to her back, her fear of horses or her tendency to get motion sickness, couldn't dampen her fond memories today.

Following in the footsteps of tradition, Rory lit the candle and stared into the leaping yellow flame.

Tears collided in her throat.

"'Happy birthday to me,'" she sang quietly. "'Happy birthday to me—'" She broke off with a choked sob as pink wax dribbled down the candle onto her muffin.

Rory covered her mouth with her hand and blinked rapidly to stem the tears stinging her eyes. She could hear the echo of her mother's soft alto singing in her ears. See her mother's proud smile.

Rory was not going to fall apart. She could share her birthday with her mother in spirit. She sighed, causing the candle to flicker. Okay, what to wish for?

Usually she wished to meet her father, but since that hadn't happened on her twenty-two previous birthdays and she hadn't found any information about him in her mother's belongings after her death, Rory wasn't going to waste her wish again. If she could have anything in the world it would be to have her mother back.

But wishing wouldn't make that happen.

She frowned. How about the miracle loss of ten pounds in a single day?

Those kinds of diet never lasted.

A good hair day?

She grabbed a fistful of amber curls. Another miracle request that had no chance of ever coming true.

How about someone tall, dark and handsome who had read the classics?

Hmm…now *that* had potential. She rolled her eyes

heavenward and laughed. "Bet you never thought I'd make a wish like that, Mom." But then, she'd never been lonely while her mother was alive. Her mother had been her best friend, as well as her parent and her only family.

Rory upgraded her wish to a tall, handsome male under thirty-five who knew that the classics referred to literature, not cartoons featuring a smart-aleck rabbit or a roadrunner, and blew out the candle.

The doorbell chimed over the muffled roar of the surf.

"Okay, that was freaky." Rory ran her fingers through the riotous curls that slipped out from her ponytail no matter how hard she tried to contain them and tightened the belt of her mother's red silk kimono that she'd donned over her sleep shirt. Not for a moment did she really think she'd find a tall, dark and handsome man on her doorstep at 8:27 a.m. on a Saturday morning, but it was *her birthday* and she was keeping her options open.

Her stomach lurched as she peered through the glass door and recognized the sleek silver bob and Ann Taylor wardrobe of her mother's steel-magnolia lawyer, Marta Ishling.

Was it a coincidence that Marta had chosen today to drop by? She opened the door. "Marta, this is a surprise."

The lawyer's surgically perfected face stretched into a taut smile as she held up the briefcase clutched in a manicured hand. "Happy Birthday, Rory! I'm here this morning at your mother's behest. May I come in?"

Rory's hand faltered on the doorknob. A fresh spate of tears stung her eyes like dust. "Of course. Can I offer you some coffee or a glass of orange juice?"

"No, thank you, dear. Perhaps later, after we talk."

Rory stepped back to let the lawyer enter, her palms damp and her stomach churning. Marta's heels clicked on the marble slabs that formed a compass on the floor of the foyer as she crossed to the sunset-red-inspired great room. She settled on one of the white ultramodern sofas.

Rory sank into a nearby armchair and tried not to appear anxious as Marta laid her briefcase on the bubble-glass coffee table from which a bronze mermaid arose.

"I confess I feel somewhat like a fairy godmother this morning." Marta laughed as she removed a black portfolio embossed with an unusual seal from her briefcase. She held the portfolio on her lap as if guarding its contents. "How much did your mother tell you about your father, Rory?"

This was about her father? Curiosity tingled in Rory's chest. "Not much. I know he was a European businessman."

Marta arched a thinly plucked brow. "That's an interesting way of describing your father's occupation. Your father was August Frederick Louis Karl Valcourt, the tenth ruling prince of Estaire, a small European principality located along the Rhine. Your mother was the prince's second wife for just over two years. You were the only child of the marriage."

Rory gaped at the lawyer, stubbing her toe on the coffee table as her knee jerked in reaction. Valcourt was the name on her birth certificate, though she'd never used it. She rubbed her toe. "My father was a prince?"

"Yes, and you're a princess. Her Serene Highness, Charlotte Aurora, Princess of Estaire, first in line to the throne." Marta beamed, preening.

"The throne?" Rory felt dazed. She'd imagined

many things about her father, but not this! Why hadn't her mother said anything? Her fragile self-esteem immediately provided the most logical answer. Her father hadn't wanted her, of course. "You said my father *was* a prince?"

Compassion softened Marta's hazel eyes. "I'm afraid he died seven years ago. But you *do* have an older half brother, Prince Olivier, who is currently ruling Estaire. He is Prince August's child by his first marriage."

Rory's crushing disappointment over the loss of her father warred with the elation of discovering she had a brother. An older brother! She'd always wanted a sibling.

Her mother's lawyer studied her. "Your brother has arrived from Estaire for your birthday and wishes to meet you for dinner tonight. He's sending a car at seven."

"Tonight?" she squeaked. "But...I need time to prepare. I don't have a thing to wear, and look at my hair!"

"You'll do fine," Marta said.

Panic broadsided Rory. "Why didn't you tell me any of this after my mother died?"

"Under the terms of your parents' separation agreement, you were not to be informed of your birthright until your twenty-third birthday when it was expected that you would assume certain responsibilities. Your father left you a five-million-dollar trust fund that will provide you with a generous allowance as of today. You'll find documents concerning the trust fund and the first monthly check in the portfolio, plus some photos your mother intended to give to you on this occasion."

Rory nodded, her knees shaking. She and her mother had been comfortably well-off, but five million dollars! She struggled to think through the layers of shock numbing her brain. Something Marta had said had raised a red flag.

"What do you mean 'certain responsibilities'?"

Marta's smile faded a notch. "Your brother will explain that to you this evening." She handed Rory the portfolio. "I'll leave you to look at this in private. Call me on my cell phone if you have any questions. Happy Birthday, Princess Charlotte Aurora."

Princess Charlotte Aurora.

Rory nearly fell out of her chair. "Wait! What do I do? Should I curtsy? Should I address him as Your Highness? How do I act?"

But Marta just waved as she left.

Rory's mouth opened and closed in soundless protest. This had to be a mistake. She could *not* be a princess. She had her life all planned out. She was going to open a children's bookstore and marry a nice handsome man who loved literature as much as she did. They'd have four children in a house overflowing with books, a dog and her cat, Brontë.

Unease furrowed her brow. She hadn't liked the sound of her parents' separation agreement that Marta had mentioned. It sounded like a contract. And most contracts, she knew from the business course she'd taken, were difficult to break.

Was that why her mother hadn't told her about her father?

Rory felt sick to her stomach. She and her mother had always been close. Having this news dropped in her lap mere months after her mother's death felt like a betrayal. Her mother had been the one person she'd trusted most in her life to be honest with her. Why had Sophia lied to her?

Hoping to find answers, Rory opened the portfolio.

Papers, documents and photographs tumbled onto the coffee table.

But Rory only had eyes for one photograph. Tears blurred her vision. She'd waited a lifetime to see the handsome blond man wearing regal gold robes and a ruby-studded crown. The father who hadn't wanted her until now.

"Hi, Dad. Your timing sucks."

BY THE TIME the doorbell rang punctually at 7:00 p.m., Rory had drawn blood with her toenail clippers as she'd trimmed her nails, ripped two pairs of nylons and decided to do without them, and rejected as impractical the possibility of disguising herself as a paper bag princess. There wasn't a shopping bag large enough to contain the volume of her hair.

She stared at herself in the full-length mirror, her stomach churning with doubts. The dress she'd bought looked great, thanks to the cleavage that came courtesy of a water-filled bra that her personal shopper had convinced her to purchase. She just hadn't realized in the dressing room that the dress would be so snug across her backside or that the narrow skirt that was so slimming would be so difficult to walk in. But the gorgeous fabric made her feel special.

She might even order champagne to celebrate the gift of a newfound brother and drown out the wounded, angry voice in her head that kept asking why her mother had never told her the truth about her father or her heritage. The French and English newspaper articles she'd found in the portfolio along with her parents' wedding pictures had only told her that her parents had had a whirlwind romance. There were no details about their divorce.

The doorbell rang again. Rory reached for her mother's black evening bag. It looked hideously conspicuous against the brilliant orange tones of the gown. Whoever said black went with everything was wrong.

She teetered toward the foyer in her high heels, feeling more awkward than elegant. Why had she believed the sales clerk's promise that strappy sandals were sexy? She felt strappy enough, but not the least bit sexy.

The bell rang a third time before she could reach the door. "Coming," she called out, hurrying forward. To her dismay, she heard fabric rip.

She looked down. The right side seam of the skirt had torn a good two inches. The doorbell chimed impatiently, accompanied by an authoritative knock. No time for needle and thread, she needed duct tape. Shuffling to the kitchen, she scavenged some duct tape from the junk drawer and repaired the torn seam. Praying that her hair still looked decent, she finally jerked open her front door, blowing at a curl that flopped over her left eye.

The man waiting on her doorstep, whom she presumed was her half brother's chauffeur, was her birthday-wish fantasy come to life. Tall enough to be imposing, he fit the image of the dark hero in every romantic novel she'd devoured in her youth. Dark brows winged over eyes that were full of intelligence and capable of great arrogance. The refined strength in his full lips and aquiline nose made her shiver with appreciation.

Though broad in his shoulders and obviously athletic, she had a feeling this man had cracked the spines of dozens of books in his lifetime. Hundreds even.

He did not, however, look friendly. She tucked the curl away from her eye. Did her hair look worse than she'd originally diagnosed? With the duct tape rubbing against her leg and the water-filled chambers of her bra pressing against her breasts, she felt like a fraud. And she suspected this man knew it.

PRINCE LAURENT OF DUCHARME rarely found himself rendered speechless. His first glimpse of Princess Charlotte Aurora was one of those rare moments. By the time she'd opened the door, he'd been about to summon Heinrich, his bodyguard, fearful that she had come to harm.

Mein Gott, what was she wearing?

With her outrageously brilliant dress in three varying shades of orange clinging to her generous curves and her golden skin dewy with heat, she looked aflame.

And that hair. Amber curls corkscrewed in wild abandon around her head and shoulders, seizing him with an insane desire to catch one in his palm.

Feeling aflame himself, Laurent searched inward for the control he had mastered as a young boy while he took in the ripe, golden cleavage that should only be revealed to her husband on their wedding night. *To him.*

Sharp talons of frustration and grief curled into his heart. His first—and only—love might have deliberately ended her life three years ago because he was honor bound to marry the woman standing in front of him.

The never-ending questions about Marielle's death had been the reason he was embarking on this charade of posing as his own deputy secretary. He would never be convinced that she'd died by her own hand, no matter how deeply he'd hurt her that night by breaking off their relationship. Marielle had had too much self-esteem to dabble in recreational drugs.

No, Laurent was convinced that someone had slipped

her the drugs and that her death had darker political roots; to ensure his infatuation with her wouldn't threaten the marriage treaty between Estaire and Ducharme, or to implicate him in her death and cause a scandal that might induce Prince Olivier to rescind the treaty. Laurent was determined to keep his presence in California and his identity a secret to protect Charlotte Aurora. He would never forgive himself for failing to protect Marielle.

"I'm sorry I'm late," Princess Charlotte Aurora said, her cheeks pinking becomingly.

"No need to apologize, Your Serene Highness," he said with a formal bow. "Allow me to introduce myself. I am Sebastian Guimond. I hold the position of deputy secretary. Prince Olivier dispatched me to escort you to his hotel. The car is waiting out front."

"Pleased to meet you, Mr. Guimond."

Her eyes were an unusual shade of violet blue, like the hyacinths—a gift from the Netherlands—that bloomed in the spring in the royal gardens of Ducharme.

The fate of two countries and the resolution of a three-hundred-year-old feud hung in the balance of his union with this woman. Three hundred years earlier Charlotte Aurora's ancestors had purchased land from a bankrupt member of his family and had formed the country of Estaire. That land had previously been under Falkenberg rule for four centuries.

Laurent's father and Charlotte Aurora's father had hoped that the marriage treaty would put an end to the feud between their two countries and improve economic and diplomatic relations. But now that Prince Olivier had confided to Laurent that his passion for mountain biking had rendered him sterile, the treaty would change Estaire's history. The tiny principality would one day return to Falkenberg rule under the reign of Laurent's firstborn son.

With rumors of Prince Olivier's infertility circulating in the tabloids, Laurent feared that Princess Charlotte Aurora's timely reappearance and the announcement of their engagement would be greeted with suspicion and resistance.

Laurent and Olivier were both agreed that they had to protect Charlotte Aurora from possible threats against her life and prepare her for the future that lay ahead of her.

Laurent remembered his role and cleared his throat, disconcerted by the vulnerability gleaming in Princess Charlotte Aurora's blue eyes. She wore very little makeup, applied inexpertly, not that she needed much with her flawless skin. "Permit me to say you look lovely, madame."

While he'd hoped to put her at ease, his compliment appeared to make her more nervous.

"Thank you." Ducking her head, she lifted her skirt with one hand, wrinkling the delicate fabric as she stepped timidly onto the cobbled front stoop, closing the door behind her. She dug her house key out of her evening bag with shaking hands, then promptly dropped it at her feet.

"Allow me, madame."

Laurent gallantly pretended not to notice her clumsiness. When he bent to retrieve her keys, he noted that her toes were as erotically golden as the rest of her, and one of them was encircled with an inscribed gold band.

He locked her door, then offered her his arm, first checking with Heinrich to ensure it was safe to proceed to the car. Heinrich signaled that all was clear. As they walked down the cobblestone path, Laurent felt the quivering of Charlotte Aurora's fingers on the sleeve of his jacket. Fresh doubts overtook him as he tried to imagine sharing his life with this awkward creature. His stomach tensed at the thought of those amber curls tumbling across the cool linens of his bed. Curling around his fingers.

She was not as polished nor as sophisticated as he had hoped. She moved unsteadily in her shoes as if walking on ice. He would have his work cut out for him training her to be a proper princess to her people, and his.

Prince Olivier had informed him that the princess had been unaware of her title and her heritage until this morning. No doubt it had come as a shock, he thought with a large measure of sympathy. He could only imagine what her reaction to the news of their arranged marriage might be. He'd been spoon-fed the importance of their betrothal along with his morning porridge.

"Who's that?" the princess whispered timidly when she saw Heinrich. At six-three, Heinrich was solid imposing muscle. His head, which Heinrich kept razored in a brush cut, reminded Laurent of a boulder.

"That's Heinrich. One of the prince's bodyguards," he said simply. "Your brother wanted you to have protection."

Heinrich opened the rear door of the limo for them. Although Heinrich's vigilant presence drew unnecessary attention, Laurent was not taking any chances with his princess's safety. There was too much at stake. A second car containing four other bodyguards would follow them at a discreet distance.

As Princess Charlotte Aurora endeavored to seat her royal person, an awkward movement to be sure in that tight-fitting gown, Prince Laurent heard the ominous tearing of fabric.

"Shoot!" A deep flush spread from the princess's face to her generous cleavage as she gazed in dismay at the damage to her gown. A slit the width of his hand revealed the delicate shape of her ankle. And there appeared to be a peculiar object dangling from the hem of her gown. Prince Laurent saw no need to embarrass her further by drawing her attention to it.

The sheen of tears dampened her eyes. He touched her arm in the lightest of caresses and attempted to salvage her pride, remembering the many occasions in his life when he'd felt suffocated by his title and his duties and wished he were anyone but a crown prince. "Take me at my word, madame. You look so radiant in that gown, no one will be paying attention to the hem."

"Really?" A tremulous smile budded on her lips. A smile so filled with naiveté that he feared the machinations and the frustrations of life in the royal court would destroy her fragile confidence in a week's time, if not sooner. Her mother hadn't lasted more than two years in Estaire.

"Indeed," he assured her, catching the tropical scent of her hair—coconut, mangoes and pineapple. "You will be dining privately with your half brother in his suite."

"Well, in that case…" To his amazement she leaned over and removed what appeared to be some form of shiny adhesive tape from the hem of her skirt. Then she grasped the torn edges of her skirt and ripped it up to a point just below her knee. She peered up at him through her lashes. "Now I'll be able to walk without breaking my leg."

Prince Laurent should have been appalled by her lack

of decorum—a princess tearing off her clothing in the back seat of an automobile…and in full view of the hired chauffeur whose integrity could no doubt be sold to the highest bidder. This was exactly the kind of situation that made salacious headlines in the press. But oddly, he felt like laughing. She was such a study in contrasts. Her forthright ingenuousness and the provocative glimpse of her tanned calf were a fascinating combination.

His princess possessed lovely legs.

As he walked around the limo he visualized her golden legs twined tightly around his hips. Her belly swelling with his heir and their children playing in the palace garden. He deliberately set his jaw as his body betrayed him by reacting against his wishes to the images filling his mind. Images that both tempted and tortured him.

His mouth pressed into a thin line. He would do his duty to his country and marry Charlotte Aurora. He would produce an heir. But he would never love her.

Not the way he'd loved Marielle. Or his mother had foolishly loved his father.

He of all people knew love had no place in a royal marriage.

Chapter Two

Rory's heart was locked in her throat by the time they arrived at the Hotel Del Coronado. The San Diego hotel on North Island had a long history of receiving royalty, including King Edward VIII who'd met Wallis Warfield Simpson here, the divorcée whom he'd loved so much that he'd abdicated the throne of England to marry her.

From the curve of the Coronado Bridge, Rory saw the majestic hotel lit up for the evening. Its distinctive turrets traced in white lights resembled diamond-studded crowns. A shiver worked over her skin.

Overwhelmed by Sebastian Guimond's commanding presence and the prospect of meeting her brother—a prince!—for the first time, she nervously soaked up every word as the handsome deputy secretary instructed her how to properly address the prince.

"Okay, I curtsy and call him Your Serene Highness. After that I address him as sir or monsieur—unless we're alone. Then I can call him by his first name. But I never call him Olivier in public," she repeated.

"Excellent."

Her knees trembled as the limo pulled up at a rear entrance to the hotel. The steely strength of Sebastian's fingers was the only thing holding her up as they stepped out of the limo and were instantly surrounded by several dark-suited men.

Rory felt as if she were in the middle of a cloak-and-dagger movie.

"More bodyguards?" she murmured to Sebastian.

He gave her an enigmatic smile. "Protection against the paparazzi and other undesirables. You will become accustomed to it. Keep moving inside the building. You are at your most vulnerable in those few exposed seconds whenever you are arriving or departing from a vehicle."

Vulnerable to what? Rory wanted to ask. Not to mention, what were other undesirables? But they were quickly ushered into an elevator and she felt too self-conscious to say anything that could be overheard by the bodyguards. Anxiety and anticipation multiplied inside her. She was about to meet her brother!

The elevator doors finally slid open with a soft ping, and she and Sebastian were whisked down a corridor.

"Smile, madame," Sebastian commanded as he escorted her into a luxuriously appointed suite. The sensual charm of his German-accented British English raised goose bumps on her arms. "You are Princess Charlotte Aurora of Estaire, and *that* is a great deal to smile about."

She shot him an uneasy glance. "Easy for you to say. You're not trapped in strappy sandals."

"Pardon?"

"Never mind." She forced an obedient smile and prayed her brother would like her. The presence of the grim-faced security guards was unnerving. Two of them took up posts outside the door of the suite. But Heinrich and two other merry men accompanied them inside. She didn't think she'd ever become accustomed to being surrounded by guards.

Sebastian bowed to her. ''I will leave you now. The prince will be joining you momentarily. *Bonne soirée.*''

Rory wanted to plead with him not to leave, but there was something buried in the recesses of his intelligent eyes—a level of expectation—that made her draw a deep breath and square her shoulders. She glanced pointedly at the bodyguards. ''Are you taking Heinrich and his merry men with you? I don't want an audience for my first meeting with my brother. There aren't any 'undesirables' here.''

Sebastian hesitated, then he said something in French to the bodyguards. They followed him down a hallway, but Rory had a feeling they wouldn't be far away. She shuddered. Being surrounded by bodyguards didn't look like a fun way to live.

''Charlotte Aurora.''

Rory whirled around, joy and uncertainty bubbling into her heart as she came face-to-face with her brother. He looked older than his thirty-two years. She could immediately see the resemblance to their father's picture in the angular shape of his jaw, the slight flare to his nostrils and his thinning blond hair. His eyes were a paler blue than hers. In his finely cut black tux, he was a model of decorum and perfection—the antithesis of her.

She curtsied inexpertly. ''Your Serene Highness.''

''Olivier,'' he corrected her kindly, his accent distinctively French. ''We are alone, *ma petite soeur.*''

Rory understood his French, *little sister.*

A faint smile curved the serious line of his mouth as he took her hand and kissed her on both cheeks. ''I was nine years old when you were born. Your hair is much as I remembered it.''

She resisted the urge to hug him, not knowing whether it would be considered a breach of protocol. ''I'm so happy to meet you! I've always wanted a brother or a sister—I just assumed I'd be younger when I got one.'' Rory knew she was gushing, but she couldn't stop. She had a big brother, and he wasn't acting as if he disliked her on sight.

Her brother bowed slightly, formally. ''I agree, it has been too long. I understand your dear mother passed quite recently. I am sorry for your loss. I remember her well.''

Rory's grief surged within her like a wave about to crest. She closed her eyes, blocking the picture that wanted to form in her mind and replacing it with a pleasanter image of her mother strolling along the beach at sunset, the foam-tipped arcs of the waves lapping upon the shore and erasing her footsteps.

She hugged herself. ''What happened between them?'' she bluntly asked Olivier. ''Why didn't they stay together?''

He waved his hand in a regal dismissive gesture.

''I will endeavor to answer your questions while we dine, *ma petite soeur*. But first, some champagne. It is your birthday—a reason to celebrate.''

She hadn't noticed the bottle of champagne on ice in a silver bucket. Easing herself onto the sofa in the ridiculous dress, she hid her evening bag behind a pillow and watched in a haze of happiness and awe as her newfound brother popped the cork from the bottle, then pressed a crystal flute bubbling with champagne into her hand.

He raised his own glass to hers. *"Bonne fête,* Charlotte Aurora. And welcome to the Valcourt family."

Rory awkwardly clinked glasses with him. She was so happy she forgot to tell him she preferred being called Rory. She took a sip of the golden liquid and felt the bubbles dance over her tongue and swirl in her belly.

Olivier set aside his glass and produced a box covered in royal-blue velvet from the breast pocket of his tuxedo jacket. An insignia in gold and red thread—identical to the crest she'd seen on the portfolio—was stitched into the velvet. "This is for you. A gift from our father. It originally belonged to his great-grandmother, Princess Anne of Greece, who wore it on her wedding day. He had it redesigned especially for you for your twenty-third birthday."

He had? Rory was moved beyond words. The idea that her father had given any thought to her feelings or needs was alien to her. A child's wish that never came true. Until now. Her heart tapped a nervous rhythm like a finger on a pane of glass as she fumbled to open the box.

Oh, my word. The delicate necklace of diamonds with a heart-shaped diamond pendant was exquisite. Rory forgot how to breathe.

Olivier lifted the necklace from its velvet bed. "The heart was part of the original necklace. The twenty-two diamonds on either side were added to signify each year he thought of you, waiting for you to turn twenty-three."

A painful lump formed in Rory's chest. "Th-thank you," she blubbered, self-consciously aware of how awful she looked when she cried. But she couldn't help it. She was a princess and she had a brother, and the necklace was proof that her father hadn't conveniently forgotten about her existence. She held still, lifting her wayward hair off her neck while Olivier fastened the necklace around her throat.

He stood back and looked at her with a measuring gaze that gleamed with approval. "*Magnifique!* Now you look like a princess."

He held out his arm to her, "Come, *ma petite soeur,* your birthday feast awaits."

"HAPPY BIRTHDAY TO ME," Rory sang to herself, hiding a tiny hiccup behind her hand. After sipping two glasses of champagne and a glass of white wine, she was feeling completely pleased with herself and less conscious of the rigid formality of the wait staff and the bodyguards in her brother's suite. Under Olivier's questioning she had already confided that she had attained a bachelor of arts in the humanities from Sarah Lawrence College. She'd told him she was working in a bookstore to learn the business so she could achieve her lifelong dream of opening a children's bookstore once she had found the perfect location and formed a business plan.

"You promised you would tell me about my parents," she reminded him as the appetizer course of pan-seared sea scallops was cleared from the table and the entrée served. "The newspaper articles my mother left me said that they met at a European trade convention."

"That is correct. I believe our father was fascinated by your mother's business acumen, as well as her beauty. At the time, Estaire's economy was struggling. During her first visit to the palace, your mother suggested we entice Hollywood producers to use Estaire's fortress city of Auvergne and the surrounding country-side to film period pieces. The movie industry is now our second major industry after tourism."

Rory glowed with pride. "That sounds like my mother—she was always able to see possibilities no one else could see. She worked as a trendsetter for a department store, traveling the world for the latest fads in home decor."

"I'm not surprised. I remember when she moved into the palace she was eager to redecorate."

"She hated antiques."

Her brother looked up from his plate of grilled pacific swordfish, amusement lighting his pale blue eyes. "I remember that, as well. She created a furor when she suggested commissioning a new set of china for the palace. The plates were to be an appalling shade of yellow stamped with a red crown. She did not succeed in her request."

Rory tucked some stray curls behind her ear, feeling slightly defensive and ill at ease. She suspected that the plates her mother had wanted to replace were dreadfully ugly and still in use. "My mother's lawyer told me they were only married two years. What happened?"

"Your mother left when you were eight months old, citing irreconcilable differences. She was perhaps too American. Too independent. She wasn't accepting of our ways."

Rory flushed, not too giddy to hear the note of censure in his voice. She toyed with a spear of asparagus and wished Sebastian hadn't abandoned her so quickly. She still hadn't decided what color his eyes were. Could intelligence be considered a color? Maybe she shouldn't have drunk so much. Or eaten so many scallops. "What ways?"

"To marry into a royal family involves great personal sacrifice, a willingness to put the needs of one's country above one's own personal needs."

Rory stole another glance toward the bodyguards hovering in the hall. Her mother had been a creative and fiercely independent woman. She'd probably hated being hemmed in by guards and rigid rules. "So it was more than yellow china?"

Olivier nodded. "Much more, Charlotte Aurora." A haunting sadness touched his aristocratic features. He placed his fork on his plate. "A disagreement over the path of your future led to your parents' separation and divorce."

"My future?" Rory frowned. Her brain was muddled from the effects of the alcohol. "I don't understand."

"I've known my duty and my destiny from the time I was a toddler. My only desire has been to carry out my responsibilities to Estaire to the best of my abilities. Unfortunately, I have failed in one regard. Princess Penelope and I have been married three years. Recently we have learned that I am incapable of fathering children and that I can not provide Estaire with an heir to the throne."

Rory was at a true loss for words. She found her older brother intimidating, but she could see that his admission caused him great pain. She reached out and touched his arm, not caring if it broke some rigid protocol. "I'm so sorry."

He looked at her fingers, but instead of reprimanding her as she expected, he covered her fingers with his own. "Just as my destiny was predetermined for me, so was yours." The gesture brought tears to her eyes. Olivier squeezed her fingers, then removed a folded sheet of paper from a pocket of his tuxedo jacket. "I don't suppose you read French?"

"Not well," she admitted with a hiccup. "My mother and I traveled to France occasionally and she insisted I study French in college, but all I can do is find chicken on a menu and read street signs.''

Olivier showed her the document. ''This is a photocopy of a marriage treaty. Shortly after your birth, our father entered into negotiations with King Wilhelm of Ducharme, the ruling prince of the neighboring country. He promised your hand in marriage to Ducharme's Crown Prince Laurent. It was a political move to encourage trade and cooperation between both countries. And it was hoped that the marriage would put to rest the ill feelings of a three-hundred-year feud over the purchase of land from a member of the Falkenberg family, which became the country of Estaire. The Falkenbergs are the royal family of Ducharme. They did not take kindly to having a sizable portion of their country sold beneath their noses.''

Rory tried to make sense of the piece of paper and the story her brother was telling her. In a way it sounded like a fairy tale, but she didn't think she was going to like the ending. In fact, her stomach felt queasy.

''Your mother left your father when she found out about the treaty,'' Olivier continued gently. ''She brought you back to America with her. Our father allowed you to leave with her on the condition that you return to Estaire on your twenty-third birthday to assume your title and your responsibilities to your country and to marry Prince Laurent.''

Rory stared at him, horrified. The father she'd fantasized about, made innumerable excuses for and dreamed she'd someday meet had bartered her away as if she were a piece of property. Her stomach dipped and rolled.

''That's sick!'' she exclaimed, indignant. ''It's so medieval. No wonder my mother left him.'' And no wonder her mother had kept the secret to herself all these years. Her mother had been a shrewd businesswoman, and she'd bargained for her daughter's life. Well, her childhood anyway.

Rory didn't know who to be more angry with. Her father or her mother. The elegantly papered walls of the suite seemed to close in on her; the candles burning on the table seemed suffocatingly warm. "I don't want to be a princess. I can't marry a prince. What if I refuse?"

"Then you place the future of the Valcourt family's rule of Estaire at great risk. You are the heir apparent. If you resign all rights to succession then the principality would revert back to France upon my death—unless you have a child who can be appointed as the heir. I would ask you to consider that decision carefully. Prince Laurent is an honorable man, who, like me, has been raised to assume the responsibilities of his position. He is as devoted to the well-being of Ducharme as I am to Estaire. Your firstborn son, or a daughter in the absence of a son, will one day rule both countries."

Rory gulped. Put that way it made her personal wishes seem childish and insignificant. Had her mother really expected her to go through with this wedding? Why, then, had she told Rory that she wanted her to marry for love?

Rory was royally confused. "I don't know anything about being a princess. Women more qualified than me have tried and were terribly unhappy—look at Princess Diana and Fergie!"

"I have taken that into consideration, as has your fiancé." Olivier lowered his gaze. "You've already met Sebastian Guimond. He is Prince Laurent's deputy secretary. He will train you in royal protocol and etiquette. When we feel you are ready to embrace your duties, we will make a formal announcement of your impending nuptials.''

Sebastian was her royal fiancé's secretary?

Rory lurched to her feet. She needed some air and a powder room. She was never, ever, ever going to make a wish on a birthday candle again. "S'cuse me."

Olivier tried to stop her, "I know this must come as a surprise, but you have a duty to your country…''

She tuned him out as she ran toward a door she hoped would lead to a powder room. A bodyguard was hot on her trail. Her stomach had coiled into a monstrous cobra that was rearing its ugly head. She yanked open the door and ran full tilt into Sebastian Guimond.

She had the fleeting sensation of being captured and held against his solid chest by arms that were strong and unexpectedly comforting. He smelled wonderful—an erotic combination of wool, linen, sandalwood and warm male flesh.

She lifted her eyes to his face. She hoped that he would tell her that this was all a sick joke. Her parents would never force her to marry a stranger.

Sebastian's eyes, she finally noted, were black as ink on a page and as bluntly revealing. His gaze summed her up and found her lacking.

Something rebellious rose in Rory. All those years of feeling that if she were only prettier or smarter, her father would have wanted to love her. To be with her. Her silent entreaty turned to a mutinous glare. Then, she clutched her stomach and threw up on Sebastian's shoes.

THE PRINCESS'S HOUSE was silent and dark, the incessant pounding of the surf outside the only pulse of life.

The hit man toured the vast shadowed rooms, seeking to redeem himself for failing to kill her and earn the rest of his reward. There was a security alarm system, but the princess had not activated it before she'd left. He nearly jumped out of his skin when a black cat with yellow-green eyes wove around his ankles, meowing raucously.

He kicked the annoying creature away from him, hard enough that it struck the wall with a howl and slunk into the shadows. He only had a few hours to accomplish his task before Princess Charlotte Aurora returned. A few precious hours to arrange her death.

Chapter Three

Rory splashed cold water on her face and groaned at her reflection in the powder room mirror. Her non-smear mascara had smeared, and her hair resembled a clump of snarled wool.

She'd never been so embarrassed in her life. She'd ruined Sebastian's expensive leather shoes. He'd behaved like a perfect gentleman, whisking a pristine handkerchief from his pocket to offer her, one arm curling around her waist as he ushered her to a powder room. He'd dispatched a maid to her aid who'd provided her with a robe, a toothbrush and toothpaste. Rory accepted the maid's offerings, then sent her away. She wanted to wallow in her misery alone.

Some birthday. The dress she'd bought to give herself confidence was as ruined as her pride. She'd completely humiliated herself. Olivier was no doubt shaking his head, regretting that she'd ever been born. She couldn't imagine what Sebastian Guimond was thinking. Yes, she could.

Well, she thought mutinously, rubbing at the mascara smears on her cheek with a facecloth. She hadn't asked to be a princess. *Mom, why didn't you tell me? Why did*

*I have to find out like this? Why couldn't you have let
me meet my father at least once?*

A discreet knock sounded on the door. Probably the
maid again. Rory gave an exasperated sigh. "Please
leave me alone. I told you I'm fine."

She just needed a few minutes to work up the courage
to face the carefully disguised censure in her brother's
and Sebastian Guimond's expressions.

A knock sounded on the door again. This one imperious in manner. "It's Sebastian. You will open the
door, Your Serene Highness."

Something in his tone warned her she could not refuse. Rory took one look at the pink splotches on her
face from her vigorous rubbing and threw the facecloth
into the sink. What was the use? No amount of scrub-
bing would turn her into an elegant, composed princess.
Not when she was wearing a bathrobe over a phony
water-filled bra.

She yanked the bathroom door open. "Yes?"

He looked so arrestingly debonair, perfectly groomed
without a hair out of place, his feet shod in a pair of
glistening black leather shoes that seemed identical to
the pair she had ruined.

Her heart thudded with uncertainty. His inky-black
eyes raked over her, as if taking in every curve beneath
the robe's soft material and counting every pink splotch
on her face. "We will begin our lessons now, madame."

Before she could protest, he entered the powder room,
closing the door behind him. She instinctively took a
step back as his imposing presence filled the small
room.

Rory flushed red with acute embarrassment. He ex-
uded a dangerous aura of power and savoir faire. She

didn't like the hard glint in his eyes as if he'd accepted an impossible challenge.

She hiked her chin a notch and glared at him. "Don't take this the wrong way, but no thanks. If you'll just call me a taxi, I'll see myself home."

"You will do no such thing." His eyes softened with what might have been compassion. "You will be living in distinguished circles. You will meet presidents, kings, prime ministers and their representatives. Their staffs will do their utmost to see to your comfort and security. And the first lesson you must learn is how to conduct yourself when the unexpected happens and things go wrong. No matter how awkward the moment, you ignore the gaffe and continue as if nothing has occurred."

His voice hardened. "Princess Charlotte Aurora of Estaire does not leave a dinner half-clothed with her head down. The lady's maid is well trained. I suggest you make wise use of her services. You will hand her your soiled gown to be properly cleaned and request her to have something in the same size sent up from the hotel's boutique. You will allow her to offer you some cosmetics and assistance with your hair. When you are presentable, you will make a simple apology to Prince Olivier and inform him that you are not feeling well. Then I will escort you home. Is that understood?"

Rory braced her hands on her hips. "No, I don't understand any of this! Do you think I asked to be lied to my entire life? I didn't even know my father was a prince until this morning—and I found that out from my mother's lawyer." Her chin wobbled. "Frankly, I don't want to be told the proper way to act by a big intimidating male secretary who—" She stopped before she could say he made her insides tremble like the aftershocks of an earthquake. Oh, God, this was embarrassing!

She yanked her gaze from Sebastian's shocked expression. The diamonds around her throat winked back at her in the mirror.

Grief prickled like needles in her throat. She touched the heart-shaped stone with a tentative finger. Was the necklace proof her father had missed her over the years?

"Did my father really have this necklace made for me?" she demanded. "Or is it some trick that my brother and Prince Laurent dreamed up to get me to do what they want?"

Sebastian frowned, the guarded fierceness of his dark eyes sending a warning rippling through her.

Oh, God. Were her brother and Prince Laurent trying to manipulate her? Bitter disappointment seeded in her breast. Was it too much to expect her brother to want an honest, loving relationship with her?

Sebastian stepped toward her, dwarfing her with his size, yet his eyes warmed with a protective compassionate air that made her want to seek the fortress of his arms again. "You are wise not to be so trusting, Princess. Palace life has its share of machinations to be sure. There are always factions who would seek out a royal's vulnerabilities and use them for their own purposes. I can assure you that Prince Laurent has the highest of intentions for this marriage. While I owe my allegiance to him, you have my word that my only purpose is to assist you in fulfilling your destiny."

He touched the heart-shaped pendant with a long supple finger. The moisture in her mouth evaporated and her stomach twisted and clenched like clay being kneaded.

She licked her dry lips as she noted the dusting of

dark hair on his fingers. She'd never noticed that a man could have sexy, arrogant fingers. Sebastian wasn't wearing a wedding band. Did that mean he wasn't married?

"As for the necklace," Sebastian continued in his German-accented English, "I am not personally aware of its history, but there are ways to obtain information. Discreetly, of course."

Rory's eyes widened. "You would do that for me?"

Determination settled on his handsome features. "That, and more, madame. Prince Laurent would trust no other with your concerns. Can you not do the same?"

Prince Laurent. Her fiancé.

Rory's face flamed at the reminder. Could she really trust Sebastian? Whether she was being played for a fool or not, the unanswered questions she had about her father lay in Estaire. As did the possibility of a relationship with her brother, Olivier. Could she completely turn her back on what they offered? Would she be a coward if she didn't even try? What would her mother say?

Knowing her mother's aversion for confrontation, Rory suspected her mother had hoped to avoid the whole sticky situation until the last possible moment, then tell Rory she was capable of making her own choices. When Rory was twelve, she'd found a bag of feminine products on her bed along with a magazine article describing how to use them. There'd been no embarrassing mother-daughter talk.

Anger and confusion battered Rory's emotions. She had no intention of rushing into a marriage to a stranger. She retreated two steps from Sebastian's disturbing presence to regain her equilibrium. Her fingers curled into her damp palms. "I would appreciate it if you could find out about the necklace, but let's get one thing straight. You can teach me how to be a princess, but you can tell your prince that I won't be marrying him unless he meets my standards.''

Sebastian's nostrils flared. ''Indeed,'' he said, a trace of wry amusement curving his lips. ''I will convey the message. And I look forward to discovering what standards those might be.'' With a slight bow, he left her.

Rory sagged against the sink. She'd insulted his prince and made him angry. Well, that was too damn bad.

''HOW IS SHE?'' Prince Olivier inquired, tapping his fingers worriedly on the arm of a gold brocade wing chair as Prince Laurent strode into the suite's sitting room.

Laurent flashed his future brother-in-law a confident smile. ''Nothing a good night's sleep and some aspirin won't cure. She'll be joining us shortly.''

But inwardly he was concerned about Charlotte Aurora. Turning her into a proper princess would not be what Americans termed a walk in the park.

The princess could barely walk in the shoes she was wearing. And he found her refusal to marry him unless he measured up to her standards preposterous. Americans placed far too much emphasis on the romance and completely ignored the more practical issues of sharing a life together.

Charlotte Aurora's mother had disgraced herself and made a public fool of her husband when she'd ended their marriage. Laurent's commitment to Charlotte Aurora would be built on honor and mutual trust and the devotion of duty to both their countries. Members of the Falkenberg royal family did not divorce, nor did they attract scandal.

Laurent routinely used his influence and contacts in the media to maintain a low profile in the press. He exercised discretion in his intimate relationships. But evading the paparazzi and overzealous fans was no easy feat.

Last year a fashion designer he'd dated had stopped seeing him after she was attacked in the ladies' room of a bar by an obsessed woman wielding a knife. Fortunately Nathalie suffered only a mild cut to her arm and Laurent had managed to whisk her to a hospital without making headlines. But he hadn't been so fortunate after Marielle's death. His name and his heart had been trampled in the press after she'd died at a party on her family's yacht.

While the authorities had concluded that her drug overdose was accidental, the gossip rags had pumped out rumors that Marielle had committed suicide after a violent argument with him. There were rumors she'd been pregnant with his child. Other articles had claimed he'd given her the drugs. The facts feeding the articles supposedly originated from an unnamed source inside the palace, but neither Laurent nor the palace press office had been able to identify this mysterious source.

Tension tightened Laurent's body. Losing Marielle and coping with her death had been the most devastating experience of his life. He'd loved Marielle the way his mother had loved his father. As if she were a rare treasure that had been entrusted to him. But Laurent had taken to heart the last conversation he'd had with his mother before her death from renal cancer when he was sixteen. His mother had tearfully confided that her deepest regret was falling in love with her husband. She would have spared herself much suffering over King

Wilhelm's lifelong affair with his mistress if she had kept her heart intact.

Laurent had known about his father's mistress. In fact, upon his entry to puberty, his father had detailed what was expected of him, including the advisability of keeping affairs private.

Laurent had always known that Marielle could never be his wife. Nor would she have been happy relegated to the role of his mistress. The heiress to a shipping fortune, she could have had any man in the world. As soon as he'd realized she was assuming he would propose, he'd told her about the marriage treaty and explained his duty to his country.

Laurent took a chair opposite Olivier.

Olivier sighed, frowning. "I'm not sure what I expected, *mon ami,* but she is so young."

Laurent understood Olivier's sigh. He knew well the mantle of responsibility that rested on his shoulders to ensure his country had a suitable heir. Despite the rivalry between their countries, he considered Olivier to be an honorable man and a strong ally. Although Olivier had been two years ahead of Laurent at Oxford, they'd traveled in the same royal Euro brat pack, partying on yachts, in castles and in ski chalets across the continent.

Doubts registered in Olivier's eyes. "Sophia should have told Charlotte Aurora about the treaty years ago. Today was too much of a shock for her."

"I'm afraid it will be the first of many shocks she'll have to deal with," Laurent said, alluding to the numerous precautions he and Prince Olivier had taken to travel to California in secret to prepare the princess for her future and to keep her safe from any political cells who might wish to prevent the marriage from taking place.

Laurent didn't plan to reveal his true identity to Charlotte Aurora until he judged she was ready to meet her fiancé and discuss the complexities their marriage would entail. "We have to prepare her to cope with the public and the media and to recognize the risks to her personal safety—"

"At the moment I think I'm my own worst enemy," Charlotte Aurora said, interrupting them.

Laurent rose, pleased that the princess had accepted his instructions and joined them so expediently. She looked presentable—and demure—in a simple black dress that shadowed her curves and rhinestone-studded sandals. Instead of repairing her makeup, she'd scrubbed her face and tied her hair into a knot at her nape.

She clutched her evening bag, and to Laurent's consternation, he noted that she'd removed the necklace. Her eyes carried the hint of a rebellious streak. She'd carried out his order just so far.

Still, she'd made a beginning. And the fact that she'd removed the necklace suggested she was not going to let herself be vulnerable to lies. He approved.

And he planned to continue earning her trust even though he wasn't yet ready to tell her his real identity.

Her gaze raked past him as she looked at her brother. Rarely had Laurent been so ignored. He felt a rather primitive desire to fist his hand in her hair and loosen the knot. To spread the abundance of amber curls out about her shoulders and whisper in her ear that she was far more entrancing that way. Earthy. Sensual.

"I'm sorry to end the evening so soon, Olivier," she said softly. "But I need some time to digest all this. Thank you for the dinner—and for coming all this way to meet me." Moisture misted in her hyacinth-blue eyes, and her sincerity and vulnerability etched a mark on

Laurent's heart. He couldn't imagine what his life would have been like had he been denied a relationship with his father. "I really am so glad to have a brother."

"*Bonne nuit,* Charlotte Aurora." Olivier kissed her on both cheeks. "We'll talk again tomorrow, *oui?*"

Her head jerked up. Her face reddened as she stammered, "I don't mean to be rude, but I prefer Rory. No one has ever called me Charlotte Aurora."

Rory? Laurent frowned, imagining the undignified headlines the press could create with her nickname.

"*Non?* That is what I called you, *ma petite soeur.* You were named after your grandmother, Queen Charlotte. She was a very fine woman. Aurora was your mother's contribution. It came from a storybook. I remember Sophia holding you in the nursery and telling me the story of a sleeping princess with several fairy godmothers."

Charlotte inelegantly sniffed back tears. "The story was *Sleeping Beauty.*"

Olivier patted her shoulder. "When you come to Estaire I will show you a portrait of your grandmother. You resemble her."

"Really?"

"Indeed," Olivier assured her. "There are many things I wish to share with you about our family and Estaire."

Laurent experienced a cinching tightness in his chest at the wistful yearning in Charlotte Aurora's tone. What had her mother been thinking to deprive Charlotte Aurora of her heritage for all these years? Instead, Sophia had encouraged her daughter to dream of fairy tales. Sophia had enjoyed her fairy-tale wedding to Prince August, but she had run the moment she was faced with the daunting responsibilities of royal life. Only time would reveal if her daughter was cut from the same cloth.

At least the princess hadn't immediately objected to the idea of visiting Estaire to learn about her family.

Olivier nodded. "With your permission, I would like to continue calling you Charlotte Aurora."

"Of c-course."

"*Bien.* You rest now. Sebastian will see you home. And, *ma petite soeur,* you must be very careful to keep this news to yourself until you are ready to accept your duties as a princess. The press can be relentless in their pursuit of a story. You must learn to be guarded about your personal life and your activities."

"Are you kidding? My lips are sealed. No one would believe me, anyway."

"With your permission, I would like to assign you a team of bodyguards."

"No," Charlotte Aurora said firmly.

"It is for your protection," Olivier insisted. "Being a royal makes you a target. I'm concerned that there may be some resistance to your marriage to Prince Laurent."

"Well, it's nice to know I'm not the only one who has concerns about the wisdom of the arrangement. But my answer is still no. I've had enough shocks for one day without suddenly taking on two stern-faced roommates."

She marched toward Laurent, her sandals slapping ominously against her heels and a glint of hostility embedded in her eyes. "I'm ready when you are."

Laurent bowed to Olivier. "Your Serene Highness."

He felt the stiffening of the princess's body as he politely took her elbow. He suspected it would be a very long walk in the park.

RORY BRIEFLY CONTEMPLATED ways to ditch Sebastian as they stepped into the hallway with Heinrich, the stony-faced human tank. She didn't know where the other bodyguards had gone. She'd much prefer to take a cab home alone than to put up with Sebastian's arrogant, disturbing presence one second longer than necessary. But his strong, uncompromising fingers cupped her elbow, preventing her from dashing into the elevator without him. Her skin resonated with his touch like a single clear note picked out on a piano keyboard. Every nerve of her body was attuned to the slowly fading sound and made her feet forget where to put themselves.

She jerked her arm free of his grasp, then almost wished she hadn't when the sensation abruptly ceased, leaving her feeling unbalanced and disoriented. Any thought of running away fled when Sebastian studied her with the inky-black fires of his eyes carefully banked and his firm, sexy lips pursed thoughtfully. A shiver inched in slow motion through her limbs.

"You're angry," he commented. "It shows."

"Well, duh! My whole life has been mapped out for me without my consent. Wouldn't you be angry?"

His eyes gleamed with faint amusement. "Duh?" Rory almost giggled at the sound of the word in his odd accent.

"This is a strange American word. As for your question, madame, I would be honored to be in your position where my actions could positively impact so many lives. I would consider it a privilege."

"Then, *you* marry Prince Laurent and spend the rest of your life surrounded by bodyguards," she snapped. "I have plans for my life that don't include becoming a princess."

Sebastian raised an eyebrow and regarded her dubiously.

"What do these plans for your life include?"

Rory suspected he was mocking her, but she wasn't sure. She narrowed her gaze on him. "It's none of your business."

"If it concerns your reasons for not wishing to marry Prince Laurent, then it is most certainly my business."

Rory swallowed hard and wished he would stop looking at her so intensely.

She wet her lips and told him her plan to open a children's bookstore. She expected him to peer down his arrogant nose at her and assume a patronizing smile. But he didn't laugh at her.

"So you are interested in literature and education and promoting literacy. I applaud you, madame. That is a very noble endeavor. Think what you could do on a grander scale to further those worthy causes. That is what I meant about positively affecting lives. Prince Laurent shares those interests, as well. He believes a society is formed on the education of its children. Ignore the needs of children and society suffers for it."

Rory eyed Sebastian suspiciously. Was he telling her what he wished her to believe? Or was it the truth?

Sebastian lowered his head over hers. "What other dreams do you have, Your Serene Highness?" he asked, his rich husky voice filtering into her ears like a caress. He touched her cheek with the back of two fingers. "Do you want a partner? A companion? Children? That is what Prince Laurent desires."

Rory disentangled herself from the disturbing touch of his hand. She knew exactly what she wanted. Someone who thought she was the center of his universe, who loved her unconditionally. "What about love?" she challenged him.

"*Love?*" He spat the word back at her. "You Americans talk of love and the importance of it, yet your divorce rate suggests you discard it at the first hint of incompatibility. Prince Laurent does not so easily disregard his promises or his responsibilities." He glanced down the hallway as a door opened. A middle-aged man in a navy suit stepped out into the hallway and gave them an interested glance. Rory noticed Heinrich close ranks in front of them and keep a trained eye on the man. Did the bodyguard really think the man with the bad comb-over might pose a threat to them?

Rory glanced back at Sebastian. He was smiling at her.

"Prince Laurent would most certainly not approve of my discussing him in such a venue. You make me forget myself."

"I do?" Her heart spun dizzily in her chest. She told herself it must have been a mistranslation. He couldn't have intended it to come out the way it had sounded. Not for a moment did she believe that Sebastian felt anything toward her more flattering than disdain. He was her supposed fiancé's deputy secretary. She'd never met another man like him. One who fascinated her as much as he did, whose touch set her nerves jangling with warnings and fantasies and whose dark, disapproving eyes instilled her with a curious desire to earn his approval.

Sebastian took her arm again, and Rory's hypersensitive nerves reacted like wind chimes caught in a breeze, twirling and playing out a melodious song that echoed through her bones. Rory attributed it to the combined effects of the champagne and the wine she'd drunk.

He smiled down at her, a smile that made him seem younger. Less intimidating. "You do not appear so angry now. That is good. You never know when the paparazzi might take an unflattering photo and create an unflattering story to accompany it. You must learn to conceal your emotions."

Rory sighed as he guided her toward the elevator. The navy-suited man who'd arrived before them was holding the elevator for them. Heinrich entered the elevator first, positioning himself between them and the man. Rory wondered if the bodyguard truly thought that harmless-looking man would pull a knife or a gun on them. "Give it up, Sebastian. This is as good as I—"

The toe of her beach sandal wedged in the crack between the floor and the elevator cage.

"—get," she huffed, bruising her toes as she pitched forward.

She cried out, accidentally smacking the gentleman in the face with her purse as she tried to catch her balance and keep from landing nose-first on the elevator floor. The man reached toward her. Heinrich grabbed him.

Rory could see the headlines: Clumsy Princess Assaults Man and Breaks Toe in Elevator Incident.

Fortunately, an arm that felt like iron clamped around her waist and stopped her inches from disaster. "Oomph!" she exhaled.

Sebastian helped her to her feet. "Are you all right?"

Rory wanted to snap that she obviously wasn't—her toes were shrieking with pain. But before she could complain, she noticed Heinrich had the poor man pressed up against the elevator wall, his forearm burrowed into the man's throat. Her purse print was clearly visible on the shocked gentleman's face.

She was mortified. "Heinrich, let him go! I'm so sorry, mister! I didn't mean to strike you. It was an accident. I tripped."

"No harm done, young lady," the man gasped. Alcohol oozed from his breath. Rory wondered if Heinrich had smelled the alcohol in the hallway. "What are you, a pop star or something? I'm having a party in my suite tomorrow night. You're welcome to come."

"The lady says no, thank you," Heinrich said, reluctantly releasing his hold on the man.

The bodyguard extracted her sandal from the gap and passed it to her. The toe strap had torn off and rhinestones dribbled forlornly onto the floor.

Rory felt as pathetic and tawdry as the ruined sandal. Heinrich pushed the button for the lobby. Rory's stomach lurched all the way down with the elevator's descent. She couldn't look at Sebastian, but she felt the humiliation of his nearness and the wrath of that iron-hard arm still circling her waist. Even the refined scent of him—wool, linen and sandalwood—rebuked her.

Mindful of Sebastian's warning about the paparazzi, Rory jerked free of Sebastian's grasp and hobbled out of the elevator to the limo as gracefully as possible.

She ducked into the limo's secluded rear seat. It wasn't a closet to hide in, but it would do.

Clenching her ruined sandal and her purse in her lap, she braced herself for another lecture as Sebastian slid onto the spacious black leather seat beside her.

But Rory was in no mood to talk. She threatened him with the sandal. "*Do not* say a word."

NOT SINCE MARIELLE'S DEATH had Laurent been at such a loss for words. How could one articulate Princess Charlotte Aurora's predisposition for faux pas? He ig-

nored the sandal she was brandishing like a dagger and
withdrew a handkerchief from the breast pocket of his
blazer. "Your foot is bleeding."

"It is not."

He illuminated the lights in the rear compartment. "I
suppose that's not blood on the carpet, either."

He heard her small sigh of surrender. "When I wake
up tomorrow, will this be a bad dream?"

He found himself smiling. Gently. The day—especially this evening—had the makings of a nightmare.
She looked so out of sorts brandishing that sandal that
he couldn't bring himself to offer more constructive crit-
icism. He gestured for her to lift her foot, so he could
bandage it.

"It hasn't been all bad," he mused as she offered her
foot up for examination. "You've discovered who you
really are. Some people spend all their lives without
accomplishing that feat."

"I already knew who I was. Who I *am,*" she groused.

He raised an eyebrow as he gently took her narrow
foot between his hands. It was an exceptional foot;
finely arched, the skin golden and smooth. The toes perfectly formed and unvarnished. She'd cut the tip of her
big toe. She winced as he dabbed at the wound. "Perhaps I misinterpreted the expression on your face when
Prince Olivier confided that you resembled your grandmother."

"Ouch!" She attempted to pull her foot away. Laurent held it firmly, curiously aware of the intimacy between them. Of the tempting golden curve of her calf.
Of the sweet mermaid scent of her hair. Of the lights
shimmering on the mirrored surface of the bay beneath
the Coronado Bridge and the salty tang of the ocean
permeating the air.

"I'm sorry. I didn't mean to hurt you."

Her chin jutted up. "The fact that I resemble a grandmother I never knew doesn't have anything to do with who I am. I want to know who my father was. What's wrong with that?"

"You don't see a connection between who your father is and who you are?"

Her foot tensed in his hands. He sensed the resistance building in her and knew she wasn't going to admit to any such thing. "What's the connection between you and your father?" she asked.

Laurent paused for an instant, considering. "He's my teacher. I see myself as the continuation of everything he taught me."

"What does your father do?"

Laurent debated how to best answer the question. "He's one of King Wilhelm's most trusted advisors."

"He's still living, then?" Envy traced her tone.

"Yes."

Charlotte Aurora tilted her head against the leather headrest, her hair cascading over her shoulder in a fragrant waterfall of curls. Her lashes slowly lifted and her eyes pierced him. "Was it your choice to follow in his footsteps or was the decision made for you?"

Laurent avoided her gaze and stared down at her slender foot. "Both. We always have a choice to act or not to act." He deftly tied his handkerchief around her toe.

Charlotte wiggled her foot free and stretched her leg out like a sleek golden cat desiring to be stroked. She eyed the neatly folded bandage critically. "Do you always do everything so perfectly?"

"I suppose so. It's how I've been taught."

"By your father?"

Laurent shrugged and extinguished the overhead

light, cloaking them in shadows. "My father is often too...busy. I've been taught by many people." For some peculiar reason he was certain that he would remember this odd conversation for the rest of his life. He felt as if he'd revealed more to this woman he was fated to marry than he'd ever revealed to anyone before. Even Marielle.

He realized how freeing it was to be Sebastian Guimond and not Prince Laurent. He felt light, as if the world were a simple place and not complicated by his responsibilities of being a crown prince. If only that feeling could last.

Her hand crept onto his on the seat, fragile and trusting. "I'm sorry."

Laurent was puzzled. "Sorry? Whatever for?"

"That your father was too busy. At least you know him."

Laurent squeezed her fingers, not knowing how to reply.

She sighed. "I wasn't cut out to be a princess, Sebastian. Tonight was proof of that. Why don't you give me a call if an opening comes available for a court jester?"

He lifted her hand to his mouth and pressed a kiss on the back. A tremor rippled to his soul at the exquisite softness of her skin and the knowledge that his behavior was entirely inappropriate for a deputy secretary toward a royal. But tonight had been an extraordinary night.

"As I recall," he said softly, "Cinderella arrived home without one of her shoes and riding a very large squash."

"It was a pumpkin, not a squash."

"The point is, she wasn't a princess to begin with,

but she still went to the ball. All I can ask is that you choose to try. The future will take care of itself.''

He heard a quiet sniff. Was she crying?

He couldn't be sure, but he continued to hold her hand until the limo pulled into her driveway.

"I'll escort you inside," he offered. "Walking will be difficult on those cobblestones with only one shoe." The roar of the surf thrummed in his ears.

Down the street Laurent heard a car door slam and an engine start. Heinrich was aware of the other vehicle, too. Laurent knew that the bodyguard would wait until he received the all-clear signal from the detail in the car following them before he'd assist the princess out of the limo.

It was all clear. Heinrich opened the door for the princess and Laurent scooped Charlotte Aurora up in his arms.

It seemed a surprisingly natural gesture.

"What are you doing?" she yelped in surprise.

"Carrying you," he murmured against the fragrant cloud of her hair as her soft curves grudgingly relaxed against his chest. "I don't wish you to injure yourself further. This seemed the safest option."

"Oh. I thought that might be the bodyguard's job."

A smile flickered to Laurent's lips. "I outrank him." True, his princess was far from what he had expected. But his heart pounded with a curious combination of wonder and desire as he carried her up the cobblestone path that curved through lush, blooming shrubbery to the striking stained-glass front door with its unusual pattern of flowing water. Her home was distinctive—as if it had artistically evolved from its coastal setting—an architectural triumph of gray weathered shingles and beams, stone and stained glass.

"Pass me your key," he ordered brusquely.

Charlotte dutifully dug the key out of her purse. "I can unlock the door. I think I can do that without creating another disaster." Proving her words, she slid the key into the dead bolt lock and opened the door.

Laurent shouldered the door open and entered the darkened foyer. "Where's the light switch?"

"On the wall to the right."

He turned and nudged the stained-glass door with his foot. The door closed with a solid thud, shuddering in its frame. A split second later something struck him from behind and glass shattered all around them.

Chapter Four

Laurent fell to the floor, shielding Charlotte Aurora with his body.

Had they been shot at?

He couldn't tell in the dark. Piercing arrows of pain in his shoulders led him to fear he'd been hit. His heartbeat thundered in his ears. Where was the shooter now? He had to protect Charlotte Aurora.

She was Estaire's only heir. If Laurent were killed, he had a younger brother who could rule Ducharme.

He ran his fingers over her, checking for signs of injury. Relief surged in his heart when he felt the rise of her chest. Good, she was breathing.

"Are you all right?" he demanded harshly. "Heinrich!" Where was the bodyguard? Had he been shot, too?

"I can't breathe," she responded in a strangled tone. "You're crushing me—"

The door to the house burst open. Laurent saw the imposing broad-shouldered silhouette of a man holding a gun. Heinrich.

Gott sei Dank! Thank God. "Watch out, Heinrich," he warned in a low tone. "There's a shooter. I've been hit."

''Stay down, sir.'' Heinrich ordered him, conducting a physical sweep of the darkened foyer.

Laurent couldn't have risen if he tried. He was aware of the excruciating darts of pain in his back and the inviting softness of Charlotte Aurora's body beneath him.

Heinrich moved stealthily to check the rest of the house. Laurent could hear him issuing instructions, via the communications headset he wore, to the team of bodyguards who'd followed them back to the princess's home.

Charlotte Aurora's fingers curled against his cheek. Her voice trembled. ''Sebastian, have you been shot?''

''Nowhere vital, Princess. I fear you will not escape your lessons that easily.''

Her laugh sounded suspiciously like a sob. She wiggled beneath him, making him acutely aware of her enticing curves. ''Let me up. You're hurt. You need an ambulance.''

''I cannot do that, madame. My duty is to protect your person and your safety above my own. The shooter may still be present.''

She shoved at him, and he heard the fear in her voice. ''Don't be ridiculous! You might be seriously wounded! Get off me right now!''

Laurent groaned as pain arced through him. ''I've never been more serious in my life, Princess. Humor me.''

He gripped her hair in his fingers, holding her fast. Holding on to his future.

His mind raced with questions. Had someone followed him and Prince Olivier to California despite the security measures they'd taken to avoid the possibility of leaks? Had the threat to Charlotte Aurora originated from an Estairian faction or from within Ducharme?

The lights suddenly blazed on in the living room off the foyer. "It's all clear," Heinrich said. "There's no one in the house. Or outside."

Laurent blinked, taking in his surroundings as light filtered into the foyer. Shards of glass lay scattered across the inlaid compass pattern in the marble floor. Charlotte Aurora's eyes were frightened blue pools in her delicate face. She pointed at the ceiling.

"Oh, my God, Sebastian. The ceiling fixture fell. That's what hit you."

Laurent's breath whooshed out in a grateful sigh. It was a light fixture, not an assassin's bullet. "I'll take your word for it." He gritted his teeth against the pain and eased his weight off Charlotte Aurora so she could scramble out from beneath him.

"Heinrich, please carry the princess to the other room. She only has one shoe. She'll cut herself again."

The princess crouched beside him. Her fingers lightly stroked his hair. "Don't you dare touch me, Heinrich. Call an ambulance. Sebastian has glass embedded in his back."

"No," Laurent countermanded her. He shot a look at Heinrich, who looked uncomfortable at the conflicting orders. "How bad does it look, Heinrich?"

"Tweezers and rubbing alcohol should take care of it."

"Do you have tweezers and rubbing alcohol?" Laurent asked Charlotte Aurora.

Her mouth dropped open in disbelief. "Yes, but you can't be serious. Does Heinrich have a medical degree?"

Laurent gave her a crooked pain-filled grin. "I

thought we had previously established that I am always exceedingly serious. Heinrich is trained in first aid and I trust his judgment. Please, bring the items. I have no wish to go to a hospital where it might draw attention that a Ducharmian official is in San Diego.''

Her reluctance to forgo an ambulance was stamped clearly on her face. Laurent was oddly pleased by her concern and by the trembling touch of her fingers at his temple. Perhaps she was not as immune to him as he believed. ''Please, Princess, there is nothing to be gained by taking such a risk.''

''All right,'' she finally acquiesced. ''But I'm going on record that I disagree. I'll be back in a minute.''

Laurent watched as the bodyguard carried her down the hallway. When Heinrich returned, he retrieved the light fixture's hardware from the glass-strewn floor and peered up at the wiring at the ceiling.

Laurent knew exactly what he was thinking.

''Do you think it was an accident?'' he said.

The burly bodyguard shook his head. ''I'm not an expert, sir. But *ja,* it looks suspicious.''

RORY WAS SHAKING as she searched the bathroom for the first-aid kit. It was a miracle Sebastian hadn't been killed. What would have happened if she'd arrived home alone and the chandelier had hit her? Was it even an accident?

Heinrich and his band of merry men were making her see death threats around every turn. Her hands trembled as she grabbed cotton balls and tweezers. Sebastian had been sure she'd been shot at. He'd been willing to die for her. He'd protected her with his own body. Had he anticipated that something like this might happen? Was that why her brother had wanted to assign her a team of bodyguards?

Rory suddenly viewed her brother's tactfully worded warning about resistance to her marriage to Prince Laurent in a whole new light. This arranged marriage was supposed to mend a feud that was three hundred years old. Three hundred years was a long time to hold a grudge.

She tried to tell herself that she was being ridiculous. She was in no danger. The chandelier's falling was an unfortunate accident—just like the tragic accident that had killed her mother. She thanked God that Sebastian had been there to protect her tonight. With the exception of her mother, no one had ever treated Rory as if she were special and needed protection. Or said she was beautiful as if they really meant it.

She reminded herself that it was Sebastian's job. But it didn't matter. From the moment she'd met him, she'd felt an awareness burrow under her skin like a cactus needle, invisible to the eye but impossible to ignore.

She closed the cupboard door and hurried out of the bathroom. She knew she shouldn't be entertaining these feelings for Sebastian. Not when she was officially engaged to his employer. Treaty or no treaty, she and Sebastian were from different worlds.

Rory scrounged two plastic bowls from the kitchen and hobbled back to the foyer in a pair of slippers.

Sebastian lay on his stomach on the white leather ottoman in the great room. The bodyguard had moved a floor lamp so that it shone on the deputy secretary's back like an operating room light. Rory's stomach knotted in dismay at the bits of crystal piercing his blazer.

"Oh, Sebastian, this doesn't look good."

She dumped the first-aid supplies onto the coffee table. The plastic bowls bounced to the floor. She hurriedly picked them up.

Sebastian turned his head toward her, his dark eyes soothing her. "Charlotte, it's all right. I promise I'm not going to expire."

Charlotte. He'd called her Charlotte, not Charlotte Aurora, not madame or Your Serene Highness. So, the man was capable of the occasional blunder in protocol. That, or he was in great pain.

Rory decided it was probably the latter and quickly splashed some rubbing alcohol into one of the bowls. "If I find one piece of glass that looks deep we're going to a hospital. I took a wilderness first-aid course once, and I'm not going to run the risk of you bleeding to death if an artery's been punctured. I don't care who you are."

"Why would you take a wilderness first-aid course?" Sebastian asked, his dark eyes on her face.

"My mother made me. We were going backpacking in the Grand Canyon."

Sebastian muttered something in German. One of the words sounded like mother. Rory sterilized both pairs of tweezers in the rubbing alcohol, then handed one pair to the bodyguard. "Let's pick out the glass first, then we'll remove his clothes and disinfect the cuts."

Rory pinched a piece of crystal between the tips of her tweezers. Oh, God, she'd never liked blood. "This might hurt," she warned.

"It will hurt much worse if you *don't* remove it."

Rory eased the shard of glass from his skin and dropped it in the second bowl. A dot of blood seeped through the black wool of his coat. Sebastian muttered more German under his breath. By the time she and the bodyguard had removed all the bits of glass, she'd realized he was reciting something, *"'Und das hat mit ihrem Singen die Lorelei getan.'"*

Lorelei? Why did that name sound vaguely familiar?

"There. Can you take off your jacket and your shirt?"

Sebastian sat up gingerly, his mouth so compressed that she saw a white ring around his lips. She helped ease his coat off, experiencing a peculiar urge to hug the finely tailored garment to her breast. It was warm and smelled of his luxuriously male scent, and blood.

When she moved to help him with his tie, his dark eyes bore into her, carrying a warning. "I can manage, madame."

Okay, they were back to that again. She was not a virgin, but she had never witnessed firsthand a man of Sebastian's caliber remove his clothing. He tugged free his tie with mastered grace and made rapid work of the buttons.

Her breath caught in her throat as he eased the black silk shirt off his shoulders. Muscles that the exquisite cut of his clothes had only hinted at were revealed in their finest glory. Rory had always found the descriptions of the male body in books more fascinating than the real chests she saw at the beach. But Sebastian's chest completely captured her attention. An inky patch of hair matted his chest with an air of mystery, tempting her fingers to explore the flat dusky nipples and the springy, curling hair. His skin was lightly tanned, the ridges of muscles and ribs as sculpted and defined as ridges in the sand at low tide.

Below his left pectoral she saw a four-inch-long horizontal scar. And another puckered scar beside the sexy trail of hair that dipped past his navel.

Her mouth turned as dry as a Santa Ana wind with

lust, embarrassment and concern. Had he received those scars while protecting his prince? God, she hoped not. An image of Sebastian being attacked rose in her mind. She stared at the shards of broken glass on the foyer floor that had been her mother's treasured sea-spray chandelier. Was this what her life was slated to be like? One narrow escape from harm after another?

Prince Laurent had trusted Sebastian to protect her. For the first time, Rory considered the kind of man Prince Laurent might be. She knew he was educated, noble and considerate. Would she like him? Would she love him?

"Turn around," she ordered Sebastian. "Please," she added more gently. Her heart winced at the bleeding cuts marring his beautiful shoulders. She dabbed at the cuts with alcohol-soaked cotton balls, searching for pieces of glass they may have missed. Sebastian's shoulders twitched at the sting of the alcohol.

It was all she could do not to cry out or press tiny comforting kisses near the worst of the wounds, but she knew Sebastian would be affronted...especially if she kissed him. Not that she would.

How could she go from disliking him to wanting to comfort him in the course of a few hours? Her only explanation was the champagne and the wine she'd drunk.

She sneaked a sideways glance at Heinrich to see if he was as appalled as she was by Sebastian's injuries. The gruff, unsmiling bodyguard gave her a discreet nod. At least none of the cuts necessitated an emergency room visit.

Sebastian sucked in a breath as she wiped another cut.

"Almost finished. You just need some bandages and a clean shirt. I can loan you a T-shirt." Rory and Heinrich taped at least a dozen bandages and several large gauze pads to Sebastian's back.

Rory excused herself to find Sebastian a T-shirt. When she returned, Heinrich was sweeping up the last of the shattered crystal chandelier shards with a broom and dust pan and depositing them in a double-thickness garbage bag, and Sebastian was fitting the dented metal frame of the light fixture into another bag. They were talking in German. Judging by their stubborn expressions and their curt tones, Sebastian and Heinrich were arguing.

Heinrich shrugged his shoulders. *"War das ein Unfall? Oder vielleicht ein Mordversuch?"*

Mordversuch? The word reminded Rory of the word in French for death. Murder.

She hesitated in the hallway. Did they think someone was trying to kill her? Or was she just being paranoid?

Why did Sebastian look so disapproving? Did Sebastian and Heinrich think she would be an embarrassment to Prince Laurent? An embarrassment to their country? Tonight had been a complete disaster.

Rory felt a void open up inside her. She was eight years old again with skinned knees, and no one wanted to pick her for their dodge ball team because she was such a klutz.

She swallowed hard, battling confusion, anger and the deeply rooted childhood hurt that her father hadn't thought his daughter worthy of his time and his love. She'd told Olivier and Sebastian she wasn't princess material, and Sebastian had responded that all he asked was that she try. He'd sounded so sincere. On some elemental level she couldn't fully explain, she'd wanted to trust him. Wanted to believe him.

Rory cleared her throat. She wanted the day to finally

be over and Sebastian gone from her house so she could crawl into bed and try to make sense out of the unexpected turn her life had taken. Try to figure out what she wanted.

"Thanks for cleaning up the mess." She tossed the black T-shirt she'd found in her drawer to Sebastian, knowing that it would annoy him.

He caught the shirt easily with his left hand, his intelligent dark eyes telling her he knew that she was deliberately baiting him. "Thank you."

He pulled the T-shirt on over his head without so much as ruffling his hair. The soft cotton fabric stretched taut over his chest and biceps. He tucked his ruined shirt and jacket in the garbage bag with the light fixture.

"Heinrich, if you will be so kind as to leave us a moment. I will join you outside momentarily." He gestured toward the garbage bags. "Take this with you."

"Leave it. I'll take it out in the morning," Rory objected, but Heinrich followed Sebastian's orders.

Her insides quivered and trepidation raced over her skin like the trace of a feather as the bodyguard left. Sebastian stepped toward her, his jaw locked tight and his inky eyes unfathomable in their intent. He touched her chin with his thumb, his voice surprising her with its gentleness. "Will you be all right here alone?"

"Yes, of course I will," she said waspishly. "I'm not a helpless female. Besides, I need time to think."

He nodded. "Good night then, Princess. I hope you remember this day fondly for the rest of your life."

He was kidding, wasn't he? But no, she saw that he wasn't. His eyes dropped to her lips and for the craziest moment Rory thought he was considering kissing her. Her pulse kicked up into a frenzied state of alarm.

She waited expectantly. "Oh!" A soft sigh—half disappointment, half relief—escaped from her lungs when his strong fingers encircled her hand instead and he brushed a warm, electrifying kiss over her fingers.

"Happy birthday," he murmured huskily. He didn't immediately let go of her hand.

Rory forgot about the gaffes she'd made this evening. The warmth of Sebastian's fingers, his imposing presence and the secrets banked in his eyes held her spellbound. How could the closeness of a man's mouth be so distracting?

She inhaled, feeling her ribs expand at the swift intake of oxygen filling her lungs. She held up a finger. "Promise me one *little* thing before you go?"

One corner of Sebastian's mouth quirked. A skeptical line creased his cheek. "Just one?" he teased.

Rory blinked, flustered. Was he flirting with her?

"Put your mind at ease, madame. I will inquire at the hotel for a doctor to make what you Americans call a house call."

She smiled gratefully up at him. Even though she was wearing a pair of fuzzy yellow smiley-faced slippers and a water-filled bra, she felt more confident. More beautiful. "Wise decision, because wilderness first aid is a far cry from medical school. But seriously, promise me you'll never call me Princess Charlotte Aurora when we're alone. I'm not going to be able to do this if I lose myself."

She saw the objections mount in his eyes, but she wasn't up for another protocol lecture tonight.

"I can't, Sebastian. I won't," she said mulishly.

To her relief, he nodded solemnly and squeezed her hand. "*À demain,* Rory. Tomorrow is a new beginning."

Rory. One tiny victory in a day marked by mishaps. She'd settle for that. "*À demain,* Sebastian."

Rory closed the door after him, taking care to throw the dead bolt and set the security alarm. It couldn't hurt to be a little bit more conscious about safety. She usually only set the alarm when she was working.

On the abalone-inlaid table near the front door she noticed the ruined beach sandal resting beside her black evening bag. A tiny band of rhinestones hung precariously by a thread from the sandal. Had Sebastian left it there?

Rory reached for the broom that Heinrich had leaned against the wall to give the floor another sweep. She didn't want Brontë, her cat, to get a sliver in her paw. Her gaze shot back to the beach sandal. Funny, this wasn't how she remembered Cinderella turning out.

BRONTË'S PLAINTIVE CRIES roused Rory just before noon. The wooden shutters in her room were closed against the bright glare of the California sunlight. Rory blinked in the shadowy interior of her room, trying to orient herself as the whole embarrassing sequence of her birthday played through her mind like a half-baked comedy. The visit from her mother's lawyer. Meeting her brother. The gift from her father. Had she really thrown up on Sebastian's shoes?

Yes, she must have. Her stomach still felt unsteady, and a headache buzzed in her brain. Her fingers curled into the sheets as she remembered the way Sebastian had shielded her from flying glass last night. She yanked the sheet up over her head. Had he debated kissing her when he'd said good-night? Or was that only a fanciful flight of her imagination?

Brontë meowed again, the sound oddly muffled.

Rory sighed. "Brontë? Here, kitty. Did I lock you out last night?" Her cat usually slept curled up at the foot of her bed. She lowered the sheet and checked the door. Bad move. Her brain sloshed inside her skull like the gyrations of a lava lamp.

The bedroom door was open.

Brontë meowed again. Her cry sounded closer. Maybe she'd trapped the cat in the closet when she'd gone hunting for a T-shirt for Sebastian.

Dragging herself out of bed, Rory slid open the white shuttered door to the closet. "Sorry, baby," she crooned. "I didn't mean to lock you in."

Rory waited for the black long-haired Persian to appear and twist around her ankles, seeking a good-morning petting. "Come on, girl. Don't be shy." But no cat. Rory climbed into the closet to make sure Brontë wasn't curled up in her dirty laundry hamper.

She stubbed her cut toe on a shoe. *Ouch.*

Brontë was not in the closet. Rory listened for cries. "Come on, girl. You've got to be somewhere. Did the glass falling scare you? Come on out. Everything's fine now."

Rory peered under the bed. The space was jammed with books and magazines she'd read but didn't have room for on her bookshelves. "Hey, Brontë, are you under there?"

"Me-ow."

"You are under there." Rory pulled out several stacks of books and lay belly down on the hardwood floor. Brontë's yellow-green eyes gleamed from a cavern of books beneath the center of the bed. She stretched out a hand, shoving piles of books aside to clear a path. "Here, kitty."

Brontë didn't move. There was a pitiful sound to her

cry that wasn't right. Rory forgot about her headache and her sore toe. "What is it, sweetie? Are you stuck?"

Rory debated shoving the bed to one side, but was worried she might inadvertently topple some books on her pet. Poor Brontë was obviously frightened enough.

Shoving books out of the way to make a narrow passage, Rory wriggled under the bed until her fingers finally found Brontë's sleek head.

"Meow," the cat cried piteously, licking Rory's fingers with her sandpaper tongue.

Rory scratched her beloved pet behind the ears and murmured coaxing words. Brontë started to purr but made no effort to move. Hooking her arm around her pet's body so she could draw her out gently, Rory scooted backward the way she'd come—and came to an abrupt, painful halt when her hair got caught in the metal frame supporting the mattress. She tried to pull her right arm up to free the snared lock, but the passageway she'd made through the books was too narrow. Her phone started to ring.

Her head jerked at the jangling, pulling her hair. "Ouch! I'm coming, hold your horses," she muttered at the phone as she tugged her head to one side, hoping to free herself. But she succeeded only in yanking her hair taut to the roots. "Ow!" The phone rang again, insistently.

Brontë wailed pitifully.

It was probably her brother, Olivier, calling to arrange another meeting. Or maybe Sebastian wanting to book a time for her princess lessons.

Rory's heart raced at the thought of facing Sebastian again after last night. Would she still feel that undertow of attraction to him today? Or had that been a byproduct of nerves and too much to drink?

Rory jerked at her hair again, trying to free herself and the cat and get to the phone. "It's okay, girl. Just another minute." Her eyes smarted as the hair pulled at her tender scalp. Damn, it was no use. She was stuck. She gave up and collapsed, sneezing at a dust bunny.

Why did these things always happen to her?

RORY WASN'T ANSWERING her phone. Laurent hung up when her voice mail came on, choosing not to leave a message. He'd try again in an hour. The princess had told him last night she'd needed time to think. Even though he'd instructed Heinrich to assign two bodyguards to watch over her home last night, Laurent was worried.

Was she safe? She could have been killed or horribly wounded if the heavy chandelier had struck her. Laurent's back throbbed. The hotel's doctor had recommended X-rays to ensure that glass wasn't embedded under the skin, but Laurent had declined. The doctor stitched three of the wounds and put antibiotic ointment and bandages on the rest. He'd told Laurent he would have a few scars. Scars were the least of Laurent's concerns.

Ignoring the twinge of protest in his bruised shoulders, he clasped his hands behind his back and paced in front of the windows of his suite. A panoramic view of the Pacific Ocean stretched toward a horizon shrouded with haze. The sun was burning through a layer of cloud cover, and seagulls dived over the waves. What were the chances of a light fixture crashing to the floor like that? Was it a coincidence? Or had it been an attempt to kill the princess under the guise of an accident?

Laurent had immediately alerted Prince Olivier of the incident when he'd returned to the hotel.

Prince Olivier had been shocked and concerned. They'd discussed the possibility of moving Rory to the hotel or hiring female bodyguards to protect the princess twenty-four hours a day. Olivier had approved of Laurent's forethought in bringing the fixture back with him so they could have an electrician examine it for signs of tampering, which Laurent planned to accomplish today.

A discreet knock sounded on the door of his suite.

"Enter," he commanded.

"Good morning, Prince Laurent," his royal press secretary, Odette Schoenfeldt, said to him in German. "You wished to see me?"

"Yes." Laurent cast an appraising eye on Odette who looked cool and elegant in a pale-lavender suit that accentuated her willowy figure and her high cheekbones. Her ice-blond hair was twisted into a knot at her nape and her gray-green eyes held a measure of calm that Laurent always appreciated when chaos threatened. He gestured for her to be seated. She demurely crossed her legs at the ankles, the hem of her skirt short enough to be sexy, yet well within the confines of propriety.

Laurent had known Odette since they were children. Her family, with their blood ties to the royal houses of Greece, the Netherlands and Great Britain, had always been part of the Falkenberg royal circle. Laurent could not remember a birthday when Odette had not been present. He'd even kissed her once on one of her birthdays. He couldn't remember how old they'd been, but they were young enough to hide in a coat closet and she'd been wearing braces.

He trusted no other with the diplomacy of his mission to California. He was counting on Odette to assist him with tutoring Rory in how to act and dress the part of a princess and future queen. And to deal with the press.

"How are the arrangements coming along?" he asked her.

She smiled. "Nearly finished. I've booked a top Beverly Hills hairstylist and a makeup artist to give Princess Charlotte Aurora a complete makeover at a nearby spa—appointment time to be confirmed. They've both signed confidentiality agreements. And I'm negotiating with a Hollywood stylist to attend to her wardrobe. The press will go crazy when they discover they've had a princess living in their midst. We want her looking and feeling her best."

"What about the French and German lessons?"

"Handled. A tutor is on retainer."

"Excellent. There is one other small matter I would like you to attend to—immediately."

"Certainly, Prince Laurent."

He gave her an abbreviated account of the incident and showed her the skeleton of the light fixture that he'd salvaged. "I'm quite all right," he assured her when she paled. "But I would like you to find an electrician. Have him examine this for signs of tampering."

"Tampering?" Odette frowned delicately. "Are you suggesting someone tried to harm the princess?"

"We both know that there are factions within Estaire—and within Ducharme—that may be opposed to this marriage."

Reproach rose faintly in the calm gray-green wash of her eyes. "Why did you not inform me of this last night?"

"It was late. The princess was not injured and I was assured by the hotel management that the doctor who examined me is the soul of discretion."

"Very well, then." She rose and curtsied. "I will locate an electrician immediately." She slid the fixture back into the bag to take with her.

Laurent delayed her on her way out. "Odette, be careful. Don't mention this to anyone on Prince Olivier's staff. There may be a leak."

"Understood."

OOOMPH! RORY BRACED one arm on the floor and lifted herself onto her toes, taking the weight of the bed onto her back. All she had to do was lift the mattress and box spring high enough so that she could wiggle her right arm free and untangle her hair from the metal crosspiece supporting the box spring. She was never going to use the space beneath her bed for a bookcase again.

Brontë mewled as the box spring rose. Rory freed her right arm and tugged viciously at the lock of hair that was caught in the crosspiece, hearing strands break. But hey, at least she was free. She lowered the bed down, then hooked her arm around her pet and slid out the rest of the way. Brontë hissed and sank her claws into Rory's arm.

Rory felt sick to her stomach when she saw Brontë's right front paw. It was swollen and misshapen. Definitely broken.

Her phone rang again as she was rushing Brontë out the door to the cat hospital. Rory ignored the summons. She put Brontë's carrier in the back seat and revved up the engine. Being a princess would have to wait.

THE LISTENING DEVICE had been worth the investment. Prince Olivier's personal secretary, Renald Dartois, frowned with concern as he eavesdropped on the private conversation between Prince Laurent and his press secretary taking place in the suite across the hall. So, Prince Laurent feared a plot was afoot to kill his intended bride.

Renald was not surprised. Why should Estairians embrace as their princess an uncouth American who'd been raised on a beach and who clerked in a bookstore? Renald shuddered at the very idea. Equally appalling was the prospect of Estaire's return to Falkenberg rule after three centuries of independence.

Renald had been groomed all of his life for a position of importance in the palace. His mother had been a close friend of Prince August's first wife. When Renald had finished school with high marks, he'd been singled out for an entry position on Prince August's personal staff. While Renald had held the prince in the highest regard, the treaty he'd negotiated with King Wilhelm of Ducharme was proving as disastrous as his marriage to that hussy Sophia Kenilworth.

Estaire must remain under the rule of the Valcourt family. Despite Prince Olivier's fears that modern technology would not be able to help him father a child, Renald was confident that Prince Olivier and Princess Penelope would soon be the proud parents of a Valcourt heir. He had researched everything—including DNA. The clinic had provided him with detailed information about its procedures, and he knew exactly what to do if the first cycle failed to prove successful. DNA would prove the child was a Valcourt.

"I will locate an electrician immediately," he heard Odette Schoenfeldt assure Prince Laurent, followed by the sound of plastic being rumpled.

"Odette, be careful. Don't mention this to anyone on Prince Olivier's staff. There may be a leak."

Renald smiled to himself and hurried to the door to

his suite. He waited, listening. The door to Prince Laurent's suite opened and footsteps passed by his room. Renald eased the door open a crack. Odette was leaving. She was carrying a large green garbage bag.

He slipped into the hallway after her. He would make sure there was no evidence. Then he would call Princess Penelope in Estaire and ask for further instructions.

Chapter Five

It was late afternoon before Rory zipped into her driveway in her red convertible with Brontë in her animal carrier on the back seat. She'd bought a fish taco and a soda from a fast-food drive-through on the way home, but she was exhausted and worried sick over Brontë's broken paw and cracked rib. She'd thought her beloved pet might have fallen or been hit by a car, but the veterinarian believed Brontë had been kicked.

What kind of sick person kicked a cat?

Rory was furious. She hated to think one of her neighbors capable of such an act. It must have happened after she'd left for dinner because while she was dressing Brontë had been fine. The curious cat had jumped up onto Rory's dresser and attacked the tissue in the shoe box.

The more she considered the warning her brother had given her last night about keeping her princess status a secret, the more worried Rory became that Brontë's injuries had not come from a neighbor. What if someone had entered her house while she was out and had tampered with that light fixture? Rory planned to call an electrician to have a look at it first thing Monday morning.

She climbed out of the car and lifted Brontë's carrier from the back seat. Now that she was home she planned to make herself a cup of herbal tea and snuggle with Brontë on the kitchen windowseat. They could both have a snooze.

As she headed up the cobblestone walk, Rory paused. An eerie sensation prickled over her scalp and spread down her back. Her front door was standing open.

Had she forgotten to close it when she'd raced out of the house earlier? Or had an intruder broken in while she was gone? She'd been too worried about Brontë to bother setting the alarm.

And her birthday necklace was in her evening bag, in plain sight on the table near the door! Rory hurried forward. How could she have been so careless? She'd never forgive herself if the only gift she would ever receive from her father was stolen.

She'd almost reached the door when the distinctive double tap of hard-soled shoes on the marble floor in the foyer froze her in her tracks.

Oh, God, someone *was* in her house!

What should she do? Go next door and call the police?

She didn't have a cell phone; she didn't have anyone in her life whom she could call from the grocery store to ask if she should bring home milk or lunch meat. Clutching Brontë's carrier protectively, she backed down the walk. She'd cut through the shrubbery to the Krugers' house—

''Aaah!'' Rory screamed, nearly dropping Brontë as a hawk-nosed, dark-suited man appeared in her doorway. His stone-cold eyes narrowed on her. Fear catapulted to her chest and hammered at her heart. Brontë hissed. The man could be one of her brother's bodyguards, but Rory wasn't taking any chances. For all she knew she was facing down the person who'd kicked her cat and had rigged that light fixture to kill her.

"Stay away from me," she warned, her voice shaking. "I've just called the police."

Her heel hit a stone as she retreated another step. She stumbled, but quickly regained her balance as a second man appeared in the doorway.

Sebastian.

Rory's body sagged with a different kind of unease. Sebastian looked as fierce as a warrior en route to the battlefield, his brows bold strokes of charcoal on the tense planes of his face.

Uh-oh, this wasn't good, she thought as his gaze swept over her. She flushed, remembering that she'd snatched her Hawaiian print capris and halter top from the floor before she'd dashed out of the house to the vet's. And she hadn't bothered to comb her hair or put on lipstick.

Her hair. Rory cringed. She'd driven with the top down on the convertible. Okay, she was not going to punish herself by picturing a mental image. Sebastian had no right to show up without calling first.

Suppressing a sigh of annoyance she marched toward him. "What are you doing in my house?"

Sebastian bowed to her. "Your Serene Highness. I was concerned about your welfare. I phoned several times—"

"So you just came dashing over with your bodyguards? Didn't it occur to you that I might not have felt like talking?" She rudely nudged him out of the way so she could enter her home. Why was he glowering at her? "What did you do, have your muscle men pick the lock?"

"No, I—the door was unlocked when I arrived." He glanced down at the carrier, his expression puzzled. "Someone saw you load a suitcase in your car and drive away like a madwoman this morning. I thought—" he faltered.

She glared at him. "You thought what, that I'd run away?"

He had the grace to look uncomfortable. "Quite honestly, yes."

Rory told herself that she shouldn't feel hurt. Sebastian was a stranger to her. His opinion was irrelevant. "Thanks for the vote of confidence, teacher."

"You evaded the two guards I'd posted on the house."

"You posted guards on the house when I specifically told you I didn't want them? I don't believe this!" Rory whirled away from him. Her purse slipped off her shoulder and slapped against her legs.

"It was necessary. For your protection."

"Argh!" Rory clenched her teeth and marched through the foyer to the kitchen, Brontë's carrier still in her arms. Oh, she knew exactly why he thought it was so necessary that she had protection! That little snippet of conversation she'd overheard last night between Heinrich and Sebastian was proof they thought someone was trying to kill her.

But first things first. She wanted to get Brontë settled on the windowseat. The vet had told her that her pet needed plenty of rest.

Heinrich was in the kitchen, studying her address book and her calendar, which he'd spread out on the soapstone-topped island. He jerked up guiltily.

"Don't mind me, Heinrich, you go right ahead and

invade my privacy,'' she snapped. ''I've got nothing to hide.'' But apparently Sebastian and her brother did.

Sebastian dogged her into the kitchen. ''Leave us, *bitte,*'' he said to Heinrich, snapping his fingers.

''That's a neat trick, Mr. Secretary. I'll have to try it. Snap my fingers and watch people disappear. Will it work on you?'' She gently set Brontë's animal carrier on the cushioned windowseat and opened the door.

''Here, we go, girl. Home sweet home,'' she said, settling Brontë in her favorite sunny spot on the pillows. The cat purred contentedly and swished her tail.

''What happened to her?'' Sebastian leaned over her shoulder. Rory inhaled the distinctively rich scent of sandalwood combining with his clothes, with him.

She swallowed hard and gazed out the window. A stiff breeze ruffled the broad fronds of the palm trees. A kidney-shaped pool, its form softened by silvery mounds of ornamental grasses, dwarf evergreens and flamingo-pink geraniums, was tucked close to the house in the cobbled rear courtyard. Beyond the pool, the exotic orange flowers of birds of paradise and sprays of blue plumbago created pockets of color against the glossy dark-green leaves of lemon, orange and grapefruit trees. Ruby-red impatiens blazed in the shelter of an enormous avocado tree.

Rory let her gaze travel to the spot at the back of the garden where her swing had once stood.

''Rory?'' Sebastian prodded gently, his fingers brushing her bare shoulder.

Her heart pulsed with an acknowledgment of him that was overwhelming. Her gaze remained rigidly fixed on the spot where her swing had once stood. The spot where her mother had died.

Hot, stinging tears blurred her vision. Rory told herself she was not going to cry. She was too angry and horrified by the suspicion that was fraying the edges of her control. She wanted to know the truth.

She rubbed Brontë behind the ears. "According to the vet she was kicked, Sebastian," she said tightly. "It happened last night—after I left for dinner. I think there was an intruder in my home who fiddled with the chandelier. That's really what my brother was trying to warn me about last night, isn't it? You're not just worried about the paparazzi. You think someone wants to kill me, which explains the bodyguards and sneaking into the hotel through the back entrance—and the tense words you had with Heinrich when you were cleaning up the glass. Admit it."

Her intelligence was commendable. He cupped her bowed shoulders. "It's a possibility," he admitted.

"Why?" she asked. "Because of the feud?" She tilted her head back, her fragrant curls tumbling over his hand, her blue eyes sharp. "Don't even think about lying to me, Sebastian."

Laurent was relieved to see the firmness surfacing through the wounded visage that her body language projected. "Ahh, the truth. 'It takes two to speak the truth—one to speak and another to hear,'" he quoted.

"That's Thoreau."

"Yes. For far too many years the people of Estaire and Ducharme have been unwilling to truly speak to one another, and to listen. They compete against each other in a world market rather than working together to foster opportunities that would benefit both countries. Had you grown up in Estaire, your marriage to Prince Laurent might have been viewed with more tolerance. A Romeo and Juliette story.

"But your long absence from Estaire and your

brother's inability to provide Estaire with an heir complicates matters considerably.''

Laurent allowed an amber curl to twine around his finger. ''Estaire has been independent from Ducharme for three hundred years. I'm sure they view the prospect of being forced back under Falkenberg rule in much the same way that Americans would embrace the concept of accepting Queen Elizabeth as their sovereign.''

''What if I just refused to marry Prince Laurent?'' Rory asked. ''The worst that could happen is he would be insulted and the feud would continue.''

Laurent frowned, but he didn't take her comment personally. One of his tasks was to teach her to evaluate the repercussions of her actions. ''Your brother views this treaty as a means of preventing the worst from happening. If he were to die before you were properly trained to rule Estaire, your country could be plunged into political unrest. Prince Olivier has trained since birth to be a ruler. It would be strategic on his part to see you married to Prince Laurent who has been similarly trained.''

Tension bunched in her shoulders, giving away her emotions. ''You don't think I can do it on my own?''

''It is too soon to tell, madame. It is a formidable undertaking.''

''Rory,'' she reminded him softly, her voice choked.

''Rory,'' he corrected. He caressed her shoulders, fighting the urge to hold her and reassure her that he would be with her every step along the way. She needed to find her own core strength, her own confidence. ''You will have to win your people's hearts and earn their loyalty.''

''Provided someone doesn't kill me first.'' Her gaze

remained rigidly fixed on the horizon. Beneath her fingertips, her cat licked at the cast covering her paw.

"I will do everything in my power to keep you safe," Laurent promised, trying to interpret her thoughts. Was she scared? Would she run from her responsibilities as her mother had? He hoped she would commit herself to her duty, and to him.

"Then stop shielding me from the truth. Do you think whoever tried to kill me last night killed my mother?"

He stilled. Her mother? "What do you mean?"

"Didn't my brother tell you? She died eight months ago." Rory touched the windowpane. Laurent saw a tear course down her golden cheek. "Out there. On my swing. At the rear of the garden—overlooking the ocean. It was set back from the cliff by six or eight feet. It was my favorite place for dreaming and reading. My mother never sat there, but that day she did and—"

A shudder racked her thin shoulders. "The cliff gave way beneath her and she fell. The police said it was erosion, but now I don't know what to think. How could a swing be a murder weapon? But then I never thought of a light fixture as a weapon, either." She twisted around to look at him, the horror in her eyes reminding him of the sleepless nights he'd lain awake questioning Marielle's death. "Sebastian, do you know something I don't?"

"Mein Gott." His heart filling with compassion for her, Laurent lowered himself onto the windowseat and pillowed her head against his chest. The fragrant cloud of her hair tickled his nose.

She felt as soft and vulnerable as a child in his arms.

"I am so sorry. I was not made aware of this." But gut instinct was clamoring that it might have been staged—just like the light fixture that had fallen last night. No questions. Just another tragedy on the evening news. He had to protect Rory no matter what the cost.

Rory sniffed, her voice muffled against his shoulder. "Maybe my brother didn't know. Maybe my mother's lawyer didn't tell him." She choked back a sob. "I loved her so much. If she was killed, I want to know."

Laurent caressed her back. "I'll find out," he promised.

"Do you have evidence the fixture was tampered with?"

Laurent told her the truth. "I have someone looking into it. I'll inform you of the results." When the bodyguards had called to say that the princess had evaded them, his first priority had been to find her. He hadn't checked with Odette yet.

Guilt pricked his conscience that he was withholding his identity from her. But telling her now would only apply more pressure and make the situation more awkward. She had so much to learn before she could decide what was best for her, and for her country. And he hoped, too, that by then she would see what a partnership their marriage could be, based on common goals and concerns.

"Would it upset you too much to show me where the swing was located?"

She drew away from him, moisture glistening on her cheeks as she wiped at her face. "I can handle it. If someone killed my mother, I want them punished."

He handed her his handkerchief. "I'll get Heinrich. He trained with Interpol."

By the time he had returned to the kitchen with Heinrich, Rory had washed her face. A resolute air was stamped on her delicate features.

He remained close by her side as she unlocked the sliding glass door and walked out into the courtyard.

The blistering heat of the July afternoon seared his head and shimmered like stars on the surface of the pool. The surf clapped like sporadic applause as Rory silently led them to the back of the garden where the ocean and the sky merged into an enormous canvas of azure. The vegetation ended abruptly where soil became rock. Laurent's stomach knotted when he saw the jagged scar in the sandstone cliff that resembled a bite taken from a cookie.

Sunbathers dotted the boulder-dotted beach below, and Laurent prayed that her mother's end had been swift, without suffering. It could have been Rory.

Keeping a tight rein on his emotions, he cautiously took a step closer to the edge of the cliff.

But Rory restrained him, fear riddling her eyes. "Be careful," she pleaded.

Laurent tucked a stray curl behind her ear. Whether she knew it or not, they had a destiny together. "I promise. You wait here."

He joined Heinrich, who was examining the rock face below the edge of the break.

After a few moments Heinrich pointed out a horizontal gouge in the cliff about three meters down at one end of the bite mark. Then pointed to a similar gouge another meter below that. When Laurent looked carefully, he detected more gouges on the rock face at the other end of the bite mark.

Heinrich shook his head. "It's ingenious. A professional job. If I'm not mistaken, those are drill marks, though the stone is so crumbly you'd need to know what you were looking for to spot them. He probably lowered himself over the cliff with a rope attached to one of the trees in the garden and used a drill to start cracks along the section he wanted to fall off, then let gravity do the rest. The combination of her mother's weight and the vibrating motion of the swing probably set it off.''

''What do you mean 'a professional job'?'' Rory said from behind them. Despite the intense heat, she was shivering.

Heinrich deferred to Laurent.

Laurent had never felt so angry. So without power. First he had lost Marielle. He was not going to lose his princess. ''It is what you would call a hit man, madame. Someone was hired to do this.''

LAURENT STUDIED THE KNOBS on the gas range. He had never used a stove before, but Rory was huddled with her cat on the windowseat with a glazed look in her eyes. She needed a cup of tea. And he'd much prefer the bodyguards attend to their duties and keep his princess well protected.

He selected a knob. With a clicking sound, a flame appeared in the front left burner. He moved the kettle to that burner. Then he opened kitchen cupboards searching for a teacup and saucer. There were none. But he found some large mugs with ghastly surfboards and seagulls on them.

It was easier to locate a teaspoon, although the drawer in which it resided was in need of tidying. The kettle was whistling by the time he unearthed the tea bags in a canister on the counter. The princess most definitely needed a household staff, as well as a dresser and a lady's maid. Except that Laurent had no intention of allowing her to remain here. It was too dangerous.

He'd already notified Prince Olivier that the princess would be taking up residence in the hotel.

He poured water into the mug and added the tea bag. The scent of strawberries steamed from the mug. He had no idea what to do with the tea bag once he deemed the tea properly brewed. For lack of a better solution, he set it on the rim of the sink beside a bottle of vitamins. He had not seen any trays in the cupboards so he carried the tea to her on a sandwich plate.

"Drink this," he ordered.

Rory pulled herself out of her fog of grief and saw the mug of tea on the plate and the concern on Sebastian's darkly handsome face and felt less alone. She was still wrestling with shock and guilt that her mother had died in her place. She was shaking too much to drink the tea so she set it on the cushion beside her. "Thanks." Her hand sought the comforting sleek softness of Brontë's flank. "So, how do we go about finding out who killed my mother?"

Sebastian frowned at her disapprovingly. "*We* leave the matter in Heinrich's capable hands, because that is his job, and *we* begin the business of teaching you your duties, which is our job. Heinrich will make inquiries through the proper government channels and get a copy of the police report and request that experts examine the drill marks. There may be some evidence that he can connect to intelligence gathered by Estaire's or Ducharme's police agencies. In the meantime, our priority is to keep you safe. Your brother is making arrangements for you at the hotel. It's not safe for you here."

Rory dug in her heels. In the past thirty-six hours she'd experienced enough upheaval. Even though she was scared, she was not going to be chased out of her home. The hit man had worked his booby trap with the light fixture and was probably long gone by now. And if he decided to come back he'd be caught by Heinrich and his band of bodyguards, which suited Rory just fine.

"Well, you should have consulted me first. Brontë has a cracked rib and a broken leg. The vet told me she needs a tranquil environment to recuperate in. It would be too stressful to move her to an unfamiliar environment."

She'd annoyed him. Even though his face was carefully composed, she knew by the pulse that throbbed just above his starched collar that he expected her to do whatever he said. Too bad. She had a mind of her own.

"May I point out that the assassin may have rigged other booby traps."

"You think I haven't thought of that? I'm sure Heinrich is itching to search the house to find them—if he hasn't already. I'm *not* leaving."

Two indentations dug into the corners of his mouth. Rory sighed inwardly, wondering what it would be like to kiss the firmness of Sebastian's lips. Would he be as controlled as he appeared? Or was there a dark untamed passion lurking beneath the surface?

"Then you will consult with Heinrich to secure your residence and your person with suitable protection?"

"Just because I don't want to be run out of my home, it doesn't mean I'm stupid. It feels like I'm consigning myself to jail, but yes, I'll consent to some security. However, I'm not going to walk around in public surrounded by Heinrich's merry men. If I have to have bodyguards, I don't want them to look like undertakers." She reached for her mug of tea. "It would be nice if one of them was a woman."

Amusement—or it might have been respect—flickered warmly in his inky eyes. "Now that that is settled, I should like to discuss your schedule. With your permission, we will start our lessons first thing in the morning.''

She inhaled the soothing scent of strawberries from her mug. "I'm sorry, you'll have to schedule the lessons for the afternoons. I work at the Book Nook weekday mornings.''

"Of course. You haven't had time to hand in your notice.''

Rory jerked her head up. Tea splashed over the rim of her mug and spotted her skirt. She rubbed at it. Fortunately, the multicolored Hawaiian print would hide the stain. "Who said I was quitting?''

Sebastian bowed his dark head. "My apologies. Given the circumstances, I assumed you would be handing in your notice. You have a great deal to learn and very little time. Your brother was hoping for a formal announcement of your engagement in the beginning of September, with the ceremony to be held in February. It's impossible to plan a royal wedding in under six months.''

September! Rory gulped. In six weeks she was going to be officially engaged to a stranger. Panic threaded through her. She thought she was going to hyperventilate. As if sensing her distress, Brontë lifted her head and meowed, What's up? as her yellow-green gaze met Rory's.

Rory put the mug out of spilling range and huddled over her cat, shutting Sebastian out. She'd never been in love. But she wanted love in her marriage. The kind of deep, lasting love that she'd read about in books. A love that was respectful, nourishing and passionate. Could she really give herself to Prince Laurent without that? She didn't even know what he looked like. Would she respect him?

"Rory?" Sebastian gently touched her hair.

Rory shivered as her scalp prickled with warmth. She resisted the urge to lean into his touch, to depend on his strength. He wanted her to marry his prince. "You can schedule the lesson for one-thirty. I...I'll let you know if I change my mind about quitting my job. Now, please, just leave me alone. Tell my brother I'll call him later." She wasn't quite ready to admit to herself—or to anyone else—that her life had unalterably changed.

HE LOUNGED BY THE POOL, the sun baking his skin and glinting off the gold medallion circling his throat, as if granting a benediction for a job well done. There had been no word yet on the news, but therein lay the brilliance of his work. The fatal accident could occur at any time. Science told him that the nuts he'd loosened on the chandelier wouldn't hold for long. The vibrations caused by the simple opening and closing of the door should be enough to jar them loose. Then, bye-bye princess.

The first few bugle notes of "Taps" on his cell phone broke into his soliloquy. He reached for the phone on the poolside table beside the piña colada he'd been sipping.

The caller's tone was icy. "I was under the impression I'd hired the best. I could forgive the first error. But once again the princess has escaped the tragic accident you'd planned for her. Need I remind you that you will not receive the remainder of your fee until the job is done."

"Chill. I *am* the best, which is why you have nothing to worry about. Do you think I only planted one booby trap? I always have a plan B. Even if she escaped being sliced to ribbons, it's only a matter of time until the princess closes her pretty blue eyes and never wakes up. You can bank on that."

Chapter Six

Rory felt a rush of homecoming as she slid the key into the lock of the Book Nook fifteen minutes before the store's opening. She glanced back anxiously over her shoulder.

Heinrich hadn't been able to supply her with a female bodyguard on such short notice, but the men assigned to her were wearing golf shirts and dress slacks. Franz, the hawk-nosed bodyguard, was feeding coins into the *USA TODAY* distribution box on the corner. The other bodyguard was parked in her red convertible across the street.

They had told her they would keep the bookstore under surveillance from different locations, occasionally entering the store to browse. If she left the store, they would discreetly appear. Heinrich had equipped her with a container of pepper spray that looked like a pen and a pretty little bracelet that had a panic button. All she had to do was press the button and they would come running.

It was a compromise she could live with. At least she wouldn't have them constantly hovering over her shoulder while she was waiting on customers.

The shop bell tinkled cheerily as she pushed the door

open and was instantly enveloped in the scent of books. Rory loved everything about the shop, from the cozy reading nook in the shop's front window to the white-painted custom-built shelves that lined the walls.

Rory locked the door behind her, flipped on the lights and went into the back office to plug the kettle in for a cup of pineapple Waikiki tea and to remove the cash for the till from the locked bottom drawer of the filing cabinet.

She hadn't slept well last night. She'd been too worried about Brontë and the announcement of her engagement in September. She hadn't felt hungry this morning so she'd taken a vitamin and brought a yogurt cup with her to work.

Monday mornings in the shop were traditionally quiet after the weekend rush. Her first task, once she'd hung the Open sign, was to tidy the shelves and stock any books that had arrived Friday afternoon, but Rory went to the travel section instead.

She selected the European travel guides and carried them to the front desk where she booted up the computer.

Time to do a little research on Estaire and Ducharme.

She looked up Estaire first.

It gave a brief account of the wealthy Austrian Prince Valcourt, who purchased the land from a bankrupt Falkenberg count in the 1700s and created the principality. The Falkenbergs had attempted to take back the land by force twice, but failed. It also described Estaire as a fairy-tale land of medieval castles, lush Rhine meadows and quaint villages. The capital city was Val des Monts. There was nothing about her father. They only mentioned that her brother Olivier was the ruling prince.

The books told her that Ducharme had a population

that was sixty percent German-speaking and forty percent French-speaking. The German population affectionately called it Liebenfels, meaning charming rock. The small kingdom had once been part of the Roman Empire and its history had been molded by the armies that had marched across it and by the treaties and alliances the powerful Falkenberg family had made with France, Spain, Prussia, Bohemia and the Netherlands in the seven hundred years of their rule.

Rory winced, wondering how many of those treaties had been marriage treaties. She rubbed her temple, feeling the beginning of a headache.

She snacked on the yogurt she'd brought for breakfast as she looked up Ducharme's official Web site on the Internet and clicked on an English version of the Web page. Pictures of cobbled streets, gracious fountains and mansions built by wealthy Renaissance burghers lined the top of the screen. She clicked on an inset picture of the royal palace Schloss Hohenheim, a magnificent blend of medieval and neo-Gothic architecture. The breath whooshed from her body.

Not in a million years could she imagine herself living there, much less sharing a bed with Prince Laurent.

She clicked on an inset picture of King Wilhelm—an imposing elderly man with iron-gray hair, black brows and a stern mustache. There were no pictures of Prince Laurent or other members of the royal family.

Next she tried an image search through Google. Over a dozen postage-stamp-size pictures appeared on the screen. Rory peered at the tiny pictures of the slender, dark-haired prince. Some were taken when he was a child, some were family groupings—the royal family of Ducharme she imagined—and some appeared to have been taken in his teen and adult years. She clicked on what she hoped was a recent photo to enlarge it. But the link took her to a page of German text and no picture. She tried the other images. The same thing happened. Frustrated, but determined not to be outsmarted by technology, Rory saved several of the pictures on the hard drive, then enlarged them on her own. Unfortunately, the photos were too grainy to tell whether her prince was totally hot or a total toad.

On a whim, she did a search on "Lorelei." A chill brushed her skin when she realized what Sebastian had been reciting while she'd picked slivers of glass from his back. He'd been reciting a German poem written by Heinrich Heine of the legendary Rhine mermaid Lorelei, who sat combing her hair on a high rock overlooking the Rhine near St. Goarshausen. Her beautiful song lured boats to their doom.

Did Sebastian think she was a mermaid who would lure his prince to his doom?

The bell on the door tinkled. Rory hit the close button and summoned a smile as a sunburned man in his twenties wearing board shorts and a navy tank top stepped into the shop. His streaked blond hair was parted in a ragged line, and the blunt ends swept his jaw. He wasn't one of her regular customers. She'd have remembered him.

"Hi, can I help you?"

His English was laced with a strong French accent. *"Allo, mademoiselle."* He leaned comfortably against the counter. "I need some books to read at the beach. Can you recommend something?"

"Fiction or nonfiction?" she asked.

His golden-brown eyes skimmed her with blatant interest, then grazed the travel books she'd spread out over the counter. "Fiction is more entertaining, *non?*"

"Okay, fiction. Do you like thrillers, mysteries, science fiction?"

"Something set in California."

"We have a shelf with works by local authors. There's a mystery set in a vineyard in the Napa Valley. And a thriller set in Los Angeles."

She showed him to the section displayed on a table near the door. "Are you a tourist?"

"Yes. A lonely tourist."

Rory flushed. Was he hitting on her? Maybe he meant bored. "You're never lonely when you have a book to read."

He selected several hardcovers off the shelf at random and handed them to her. "I'll take these."

"That was easy."

His lips twitched in a cocky grin. "I am that kind of guy. Easy."

Now Rory knew he was hitting on her. She scurried back to the cash desk to ring up the purchase, feeling flustered. He handed her a gold credit card. She quickly rang in the purchase and checked the name on the card: Claude Dupont.

La Jolla was a wealthy enclave. While many of the Book Nook's customers were well heeled and well traveled and of varying international backgrounds, the fact that Claude Dupont had a French accent put her mildly on edge. Was he from Estaire? Was he involved in a plot to kill her?

She felt the blood drain from her face. She practically thrust the bag of books at him, reddening when one of the books tumbled out onto the counter.

"I'm sorry." She clumsily jammed the book back into the bag, watching him closely. If he even looked at her suspiciously, she was pressing the panic button.

His fingers brushed hers as he took the bag from her. A ripple of uneasiness washed through her stomach.

"Are you free, *mademoiselle,* for dinner? I would very much like to get to know you better. In my country, we dream of California girls during the long winter."

Long winter? He must be French Canadian. Still, she wasn't interested in Claude's dreams. She just wanted him gone. "Sorry, I don't date strangers."

Claude propped an elbow on a travel book and gave her a cunning, pearly toothed smile. "Then it is very simple. I will make a point of becoming your friend."

She looked over in relief as the door signaled the arrival of another customer. It was Franz, checking on her. Good ol' Franz. Excellent timing.

Okay, maybe she was jumpier than she'd thought. Even though Sebastian had left a message on her answering machine that an electrician had found no evidence that her chandelier had been tampered with, she was grateful that he'd silkily maneuvered her into agreeing to the bodyguards.

Claude took one look at Franz's don't-mess-with-me expression and tapped two fingers to his forehead, saluting Rory. *"À bientôt, mademoiselle."*

Rory managed a tepid smile. *Don't count on it.*

"Are you all right, Your Serene Highness?" Franz inquired politely after Claude had gone.

"I'm fine," Rory lied, hugging herself. She turned back to her research. She didn't like this fear that Sebastian and Olivier had instilled in her. Was she destined to spend the rest of her life being afraid?

BETWEEN CUSTOMERS she printed off the information she'd found on the Internet about Estaire and Ducharme, including the lineage of the Valcourts back to the first prince of Estaire. She'd also found an article on the Falkenberg royal family, although it was in German. With the help of a German dictionary, she was attempting to translate it.

She wasn't making much progress.

She was happy to put it aside when one of her favorite customers dropped into the store at eleven-thirty. Stoop-shouldered, his skin freckled and weathered from the sun, Otto Gascon made a regular habit of dropping into the Book Nook to browse on Mondays and Thursdays before joining his cronies for lunch and an afternoon of chess.

Rory didn't know much about him except that he was in his seventies, retired and a widower. He lived in her neighborhood and she occasionally saw him walking on the beach or sitting on a bench with a plaid blanket covering his lap, reading a book.

His watery-gray eyes met hers warmly. His brow was damp with perspiration as he doffed his straw hat with a gnarled, blue-veined hand. "Good morning, young lady. You are looking hale and hearty. I've come about a book."

Rory laughed as he handed her a newspaper clipping from his wallet. Every week without fail, Otto brought in a review clipped from the book review section of the paper and requested a book. "I hope we have it."

She wasn't surprised to see he wanted a biography of a famous news anchor. Otto's reading tastes leaned toward biographies, travel, books about the world wars and the occasional political thriller. "We don't have it in stock yet, but it should be any day. I'll set one aside for you."

"Wonderful. I'll just browse in case something tempts me." He glanced down at the counter at the travel books and the German dictionary. "Are you planning a trip?"

"Actually, I'm trying to translate an article."

"Do you speak German?"

Rory grimaced. "No, that's what makes it hard."

"Perhaps I could help. I'm a little rusty, but I should be able to manage. My wife was from Germany."

"You never told me that." Rory slid the article toward him. "Would you?"

Otto nodded. "Ah, I see. It's an interesting choice in articles, although it's three years old. It's about King Wilhelm of Ducharme. He was asked when his son Prince Laurent, then twenty-seven, would succeed him to the throne. The king responded that he doesn't believe in making his son wait until his death, but that he would like to see his son married and settled with children before he assumes the responsibility."

Ice encased Rory's heart. Sebastian had told her about the feud, but he hadn't mentioned this.

Was Prince Laurent determined to marry her for altruistic reasons and the good of his country, or because his father was holding the treaty over his head and it was the only way he could get the crown?

Did it matter?

Otto peered at her. "May I ask what spurs your interest in Ducharme and King Wilhelm? Ducharme is a beautiful country. Excellent wines. Castles. The Rhine. Everything a young girl finds romantic."

"It's a long story, Otto."

"I'm retired, my dear. I have nothing but time."

Rory hesitated, tempted to confide in someone. She'd known Otto for years—well, for the two years she'd been working in the bookstore, anyway. But he wasn't a stranger. He was a neighbor, and the fact that he knew

German might prove helpful in figuring out what she was going to do about this marriage treaty. But her brother's warning about telling anyone of her new status made her hold back.

"I appreciate the offer, but I don't feel like talking about it today. Do you know anything else about the royal family of Ducharme?"

Otto frowned. "Well, the queen died years ago. Tragic. Some sort of illness. King Wilhelm never remarried. Prince Laurent has a reputation as a playboy. Lots of women. There's a younger brother, Prince Leopold, I think. He's a top-ranked soccer player."

So Prince Laurent was a playboy. Her brother thought she was going to marry a playboy?

Rory had heard enough. It was about time she asked Sebastian some serious questions about Prince Laurent.

FIVE MINUTES BEFORE her shift at the Book Nook ended, Rory received a call from Sebastian.

"Come out the rear exit when you're finished. The limo will be waiting."

More cloak-and-dagger stuff. Rory didn't bother asking about her car. She figured the bodyguards would take care of it. She'd planned to go to the bank after work with the check from her trust fund, but it would have to wait until tomorrow. "Will you be there, too?" she asked.

His voice was firm, reassuring. "Of course."

Hearing his voice, Rory realized how quickly she'd come to depend on him, and how disappointed she was that he'd only given her one side of the story about his prince. Still, what had she expected? He did work for Prince Laurent. "Good, because I have a bone to pick with you."

She hung up on him before he could respond.

Her knees trembling slightly and her fingers clutching the research she'd gathered, Rory walked out to the limo ten minutes later. Thank God nobody shot at her or pelted her with tomatoes.

She gave the bodyguard a nervous smile and slid into the limo's icy interior.

Rory took a deep breath. For the rest of her life, every time she smelled sandalwood or linen, she would think of Sebastian. His inky eyes compelled her to look at him as if he suspected the hurt she carried. He was so incredibly handsome. So incredibly what she wanted, so completely not what she was allowed to have. The ache in her heart grew.

Okay, be smart, she told herself. Keep it business.

He bowed his head, his tone perfectly composed. "Your Serene Highness."

"Sebastian." She plopped the stack of papers onto the perfectly creased oatmeal-colored linen stretched taut over his sleekly muscled thighs. He was wearing a snowy, crisp cotton shirt and a yellow silk tie that brought out the blackness of his eyes.

Laurent was instantly on guard. In her white gauzy sundress, Rory resembled a goddess on the warpath. Her skin glowed with a dewy sheen, and her blue eyes sparked with lightning. The discomfort of the stitches in his back was superseded by the taut reaction of his body to her beauty.

Holding himself in check, he examined the pile of documents. "Is this the bone you wanted to break?"

"Not break. Pick. You pick a bone. And yes, this is it," she snapped. "You neglected to tell me a few crucial pieces of information about Prince Laurent."

Laurent could think of only one crucial piece of information he'd left out. His real identity.

He read the top document. It was in German. Something she'd downloaded from the Internet. "You read this?"

"Well, duh! I used a dictionary. You didn't mention that King Wilhelm was holding this treaty over Prince Laurent's head. It says right there that the prince won't become king until he's married and has a family."

"You figured all that out with a dictionary? Impressive." He thumbed through the other documents, admiring her initiative and her thoroughness. She hadn't accepted anything that he and Prince Olivier had told her at face value. She'd researched Estaire and Ducharme. And him. At least there were no pictures of him, thanks to the foresight of the palace press office, which had posted notices that the sites were under maintenance.

"You didn't mention that Prince Laurent is a playboy, either. Do I strike you as the type of girl who would be happy married to a playboy?"

Laurent's conscience stirred, rumbled like a fabled beast with dark grasping tentacles. He could give her everything she had told him she wanted out of a marriage: a family, children, a partnership. Even the dog and the cat. "Is that what you think marriage is about—happiness?"

"No, I think marriage is about love. Commitment. What does a playboy know about love?"

Enough, Laurent thought. Love had destroyed his mother. It had destroyed Marielle. And it had nearly destroyed him.

"You shouldn't believe everything you read. The press wants to sell papers. People would rather read about the 'playboy prince' out on the town than the 'hardworking prince' who carries out his duties."

"You didn't answer my question."

Laurent's gaze was drawn to the haunting blueness of her eyes. To the hunger and vulnerability that lurked there. His jaw clenched. Rory was so naive. He didn't think he could bear it if their marriage destroyed her. He sought the right words. This was the lesson that would define their marriage and forge their relationship. "I think the prince will commit every day of his life to this marriage. To your future together. To your children. He will be your partner in every sense of the word."

"You didn't say anything about love."

He didn't hesitate. "No, I didn't. So very few royal marriages founded on love are successful. A royal marriage is a business partnership founded on mutual respect."

"So, no hot sex?"

The question stunned him and fed an image of making love to her on the beach, her body soft and golden beneath him, her hair fanned over the wet sand, her enchanting white gauzy dress unbuttoned to her waist and the surf foaming at their joined hips. Laurent had never entertained such an uninhibited assignation, not when he knew the paparazzi could be lurking anywhere, hoping to make his private life next week's paycheck.

For the second time since he had met Rory, Laurent wished he wasn't a prince. He was enjoying the anonymity of reacting to her like an ordinary man. He was tempted to run a testing finger along the plump curve of her bottom lip and ask her what she meant by hot. But he knew she was goading him. Testing him.

He hid a smile at her cleverness. "This would be one

aspect of your American upbringing that needs toning down.''

She folded her arms across her chest, the movement stretching the gauze fabric tight across her breasts. ''I'm not allowed to talk about sex? Or to have sex?''

Laurent felt uncomfortably hot under the collar—and under his briefs. She wasn't wearing a proper bra for the dress. The pert tips of her nipples and the shadows of her areolae were apparent. And distracting. The afternoon's lessons weren't beginning quite the way he'd planned.

''I believe I have made my point.''

She clapped her hands, twice. ''Very smooth, teacher. You appeared to answer the question and refrained from answering at the same time.''

He minutely adjusted the cuffs of his jacket. He easily commanded large audiences, and yet his control waffled precariously in her presence. ''Glad you were paying attention.''

''Oh, I'm paying attention. I'll be having sex with the prince, but only for procreating. And, by the way, my American ideals don't need toning down. Your medieval ideas need updating. No wonder my mother left my father.

''Oh, God, I can't believe I said that.'' Rory's throat swelled with tears. Her mother. Her quirky, vivacious mother, who could confidently choose the newest trends and yet never spoke about her personal feelings.

''Did your mother never talk to you about her marriage?''

She shook her head. ''Once when I really pushed the subject, she said they hadn't known each other well enough before they got married.'' And yet, her mother had never uttered a desire to marry again. She'd socialized, but rarely dated the same man more than a few times.

Was it an inborn reticence or had her mother's love for her husband never died? Had she held it all inside her, hoping that Prince August might see the error of his actions and return to her? Was that why her mother had told her she wanted Rory to marry for love? It occurred to her that her father had never remarried, either.

Rory sighed. She wondered if she would ever find any answers that would bring her peace. "I always thought my mother was my best friend. I thought I knew her better than anyone." Resentment crept from her heart to her voice. "Now I feel as if I didn't know her. How could she keep such a big secret from me? Everything I loved about her is colored by the lies she told me." It hurt.

Sebastian cupped her chin firmly, his intense inky gaze studying her. "What if the answer is very simple, and how do you Americans say…staring you in the face?"

"What do you mean?"

"What if she was trying to protect you?"

"FYI, I can take care of myself."

"FYI? What does that mean?" Sebastian asked her in a husky tone. A warm liquid rush, intoxicating as a fine liqueur, tingled through her body and spilled down to her belly, dangerous and exciting and inappropriate.

She had to remind herself that Sebastian was here on Prince Laurent's behalf, to convince her to go through with the marriage treaty.

Rory crossed her legs, the warmth gathering in her belly pulsed with awareness of Sebastian's closeness. Of the hard muscle beneath the armor of his exquisite suits. Of his scent. She thought it would be immensely satisfying to wrinkle his clothes while she had hot sex with him. Here in the back of the limo…just for the fun of it. She had to smile in irony. Yeah. When pigs could fly.

She cleared her throat. "FYI means 'for your information.'"

"I see." He quirked a brow. "Would you like to hear your schedule for the afternoon, FYI?"

He was teasing her, his German-accented English sexy in the extreme. Rory wondered whose brilliant idea it had been to send him to be her teacher. "Enlighten me. I hope you arranged for some of the lessons to be done at my house so I can keep an eye on Brontë."

"I have taken that into account. First, you will have lunch with your brother, followed by a palace protocol lesson. At two-thirty, you will meet with Prince Laurent's press secretary, your brother's personal secretary and a Hollywood stylist to consult on your image."

"My image?"

"Yes, how you are going to present yourself to the world—clothes, hair, comportment."

Rory squirmed. She knew exactly how she presented herself to the world. Bookish, klutzy and sincere. Obviously Sebastian and her brother didn't think she was up to snuff. But submitting to the lessons was her ticket to understanding her father and the world he'd inhabited. She might even meet people who had known her mother when she was Princess Sophia.

"Now, at 5:00 p.m.," Sebastian continued, "you will begin language studies. One hour of French, followed by one hour of German."

She hoped it wouldn't be too hard to learn how to order chicken from a menu in German.

"Then a brief course in table manners before you dress for dinner. Prince Olivier will join you."

Rory stared at Sebastian as if he'd asked her to fly to the moon. "I'm afraid takeout and an ocean view are all the hospitality I can provide at this late notice."

"Do not concern yourself with the meal, madame. The prince's staff will see to everything. You need only concentrate on your lessons."

"Well, we can skip the table manners. FYI, my mother showed me which fork and glass to use."

Sebastian shot her an unreadable look. "In Europe, the continental style is preferred. And you will need protocol instructions for state dinners."

"Believe it or not, I know the continental style is preferred." She performed a fair imitation of his accent. "My mother taught it to me on one of our trips to France." Rory had been thirteen. They'd made a game of it. Had her mother been preparing her for her future?

Rory sighed. She gazed out the window at the mustard, cream and salmon-colored stucco homes and the palm trees lining the streets. A young woman on in-line skates zipped down the sidewalk with the wind tousling her hair as if she didn't have a care in the world.

This was the only home she'd ever known. Sure, she and her mother had traveled, but Southern California was home.

Rory imagined sleeping in the castle where her father had been raised—and his ancestors before him.

Sebastian tapped her on the thigh. "A princess crosses her legs at the ankle only."

Rory suppressed a quiver at the touch of his fingers on her bare skin. She quickly uncrossed her legs. "You sound like my mother."

"A photographer likely earned a year's salary over a

scandalous photo of your mother's legs while she was married to your father. The paparazzi are infamous for climbing over walls, under tables, through windows to get a headline-grabbing photo.''

Rory's brain fed her an image of a famous photo taken of Lady Diana Spencer's legs. A photographer had coaxed her into posing for a photo. The sun was to her back, revealing her legs through her thin cotton skirt.

"Point taken." Rory had no desire whatsoever to make headlines doing anything stupid. "How does Prince Laurent stand it? Photographers and journalists hovering around like vultures 24/7, waiting for the smallest mistake, the tiniest bit of scandal?''

An odd, sad look crossed Sebastian's face. "Even after a lifetime, one never really gets used to it. And don't forget the political detractors, and—''

"And what? The assassins?" A shiver flayed her spine. The world Sebastian painted of royal life was the extreme opposite of her common life. Marrying Prince Laurent seemed destined to make her unhappy and deny her the unconditional love of a husband.

Her heart clenched.

Was that a sacrifice she was truly willing to make?

CLAUDE DUPONT CURSED as he wove through traffic, trying to keep Princess Charlotte Aurora's limousine in sight.

He'd slammed the bag of books he'd purchased onto the hood of a parked car and hopped onto his motorcycle when he'd spotted the princess exit the back door of the book shop and climb into a waiting limousine.

He had missed his opportunity with her earlier. He

wouldn't miss another. Time was running out. Prince Laurent would press for a quick engagement, and Claude owed it to Marielle to stop the wedding from taking place.

Chapter Seven

Despite her doubts and uncertainties, Rory was delighted to have a brother. As Prince Olivier greeted her with a kiss on both cheeks, she gave him an impulsive hug.

When his arms slipped around her and hugged her back, Rory held on tight for a moment, regret filling her for the years they'd been strangers.

"*Ça va?*" her brother inquired. He studied her, his eyes reminding her of the pensive blue of the ocean at dusk. He was wearing slacks and a polo shirt and looked more like an ordinary big brother, caring and protective. She didn't even mind when he called her Charlotte Aurora. It gave her a sense of shared history.

He touched her chin. "You are frightened, *ma petite soeur.* I am very sorry about your mother. We will not allow whoever killed her to go unpunished. You have my word on that. But you must not let fear govern you.

"Just before I left for university *notre père* told me that I would encounter many people who, for one reason or another, might resent me for my birth. He warned me that if people who would be your enemy smell fear, it gives them power over you."

Rory swallowed the lump in her throat. "Are you afraid sometimes, Olivier?"

"Yes. My greatest fear is that I will not live up to my responsibilities." His face took on an ashen tinge. "Penelope is taking my inability to get her pregnant very hard. There is a fertility clinic she wants us to visit next week, to get another opinion."

"Will you go?"

"Of course."

"What is Penelope like? I looked up Estaire's Web site and saw pictures of you both. And of Estaire. Your wife is very beautiful."

"Beautiful and smart." Olivier guided her to a sofa. "She's British, the daughter of an earl. I met her at Oxford. She's a lawyer, an expert in international business. She is exceedingly good at winning a point."

Rory knew her brother considered Penelope's business experience a plus for Estaire. Had her father married her mother for similar reasons? "Are you in love with her?"

Her brother smiled wryly. "I assume this has something to do with the marriage treaty. When you are a royal, your first inclination is to be wary of anyone's intentions toward you. Penelope and I were honest about what we hoped to accomplish together. Since our marriage, she has devoted herself to Estaire, which makes me love her more every day. She is the best partner I could ever hope to find." Olivier met her gaze, his expression frank. "I think if you and Prince Laurent are honest with each other, you can come to an arrangement that will satisfy you both. He's a good man. I have a great deal of respect for him. And I have a great deal of respect for our father's judgment."

Unfortunately, Rory didn't share Olivier's opinion of

their father's judgment. "What was my father like?" she asked.

"Very disciplined. Very private. He didn't like to show weakness of any kind. He worked very hard to give his people a high standard of living, employment, good medical care, education. When he died, there was hardly a man, woman or child in Estaire who didn't attend his funeral."

"Except for me," Rory said, unable to keep the bitterness from creeping into her voice. "His own child."

Olivier tilted her chin up, apology in his tone. "He thought of you often. I found pictures of you in his wallet after he was gone."

Grief mixed with the bitterness that gnawed at her soul. Her father had carried her picture everywhere, and she hadn't even been allowed to know him. "Pictures?"

Olivier nodded. "Your mother sent them with annual reports of your progress, telling him about your birthday trips. Renald Dartois, my father's secretary, gave me the letters after my father died. I brought them with me because I thought you might like to have them. The trips were his gifts to you."

"They were?" Rory gave up any pretense of trying to hide the tears blurring her eyes.

"*Mais, oui.* You will meet Renald after lunch. He is my secretary now. We will ask him for the letters."

Rory sniffled and wiped the flood of tears from her cheeks. Why did she never have a tissue when she needed one? Olivier offered her a snowy handkerchief from his pocket. She took it gratefully.

"Did my mother know when he died?"

"Yes, but she chose not to attend the funeral. After that, she stopped sending the yearly updates."

Probably hoping Olivier would forget all about the

marriage treaty. Rory angrily wiped her tears. *You guessed wrong, Mom.*

RORY DIDN'T HAVE much appetite for the grilled mahi-mahi salad. She sipped a glass of iced tea and asked Olivier questions about his life. Her brother loved speed and the outdoors. He loved to ski, race power boats and mountain bike. She promised to teach him how to surf and to in-line skate.

After their lunch, Olivier introduced her to Renald Dartois, his private secretary. Rory judged Renald to be a few years older than her brother. He had a sharp, pointed face, his jaw outlined by a thin, meticulously trimmed beard and a haughty expression that made Rory feel as if she had dirt on her nose.

Her spine stiffened.

He was judging her on her mother's choices, not hers. But she wondered what her reception would be like from the rest of Prince Olivier's staff. Sebastian had told her she would need to win their hearts, and their loyalty. She could see that he was right.

"Renald, do you have the letters for the princess?"

Rory's fingers trembled as her brother's personal secretary offered her a portfolio from his briefcase.

"They are organized by date," he explained.

"Thank you. These letters mean a great deal to me."

"Renald will be escorting you home and giving you a lesson in palace protocol."

Rory felt alarmed by the prospect, then remembered what her brother had told her about not showing fear to her enemies. "Will Sebastian be coming?"

Sebastian had discreetly disappeared when they'd arrived back at the hotel. Somehow she felt safer when he was with her.

Her brother's personal secretary gave her a cold, polite smile as if he could read her thoughts. "He is already at your residence with the others. There were several tasks requiring his attention."

"Enjoy your lessons. I'll look forward to our dinner and tour of your home," Olivier said. "I have a golf game with representatives from the motion picture industry to discuss incentives to encourage their continued filming in Estaire."

Rory wished him good luck and allowed Renald Dartois and several bodyguards to escort her to the limousine. She bore Renald's continued disapproving silence until they reached the privacy of the limo. Then she decided she was going to take matters into her own hands and make conversation. She was not going to allow her brother's secretary to intimidate her. Besides, Renald had worked for her father, as well. And she ached to know whatever he could tell her.

She gripped the portfolio of letters in her lap, wishing she were alone so she could read them. "Prince Olivier told me that you were my father's personal secretary."

"I was privileged to serve him for the last three years before his death."

"You must have known him well."

"I'm afraid I cannot say, Your Serene Highness."

Can't? Or won't? Rory wondered. "Did my father and mother ever talk—or ever meet—after their divorce?"

Renald flushed from his angular cheeks to his thin pointy beard. "My apologies, madame, but I am not at liberty to divulge any details of my years of service with Prince August. As a member of the palace staff, I was required to sign a confidentiality agreement. The penalties are quite severe."

Rory found her face turning warm, as well. "But you gave my brother the letters after my father's death."

"As the new sovereign it was his decision whether Prince August's private letters should be preserved or destroyed."

And Olivier had chosen to give them to her. But she wondered uneasily if Renald's attitude was a reflection of her father's attitude toward her. "Well, I would like to learn more about my father and Estaire. May I have a biography of his life and a résumé of important dates in Estaire's history? I want to brush up on my facts."

His hazy blue eyes considered her thoughtfully. Something about his expression reminded her fleetingly of her brother, Olivier. "I have already provided this information to Odette Schoenfeldt, Prince Laurent's press secretary. You will meet her this afternoon."

Rory listened as Renald explained that when she returned to Estaire she would be assigned a suite of rooms in the palace and her own staff consisting of a personal secretary, a press secretary, a bodyguard, a butler, a dresser and a lady's maid.

Under consultation with Prince Olivier and Princess Penelope she would select a small number of public duties to ease her into her role as princess and introduce her to the people of Estaire. "Once the engagement is officially announced, we anticipate that your office will receive a large number of invitations and requests for appearances. Your personal secretary is to submit them to me for approval prior to accepting. I will coordinate any joint appearances with Prince Laurent through Sebastian Guimond."

Rory realized that Renald wielded a great deal of power in the palace with his weighty rubber stamp. By the time the limo finally squeezed into her driveway beside several vehicles, she was anxious to escape Renald's protocol instructions and his condescending reminders that she was not to embarrass the royal family under any circumstances.

Rory got the message. Renald considered her an embarrassment—a byproduct of her father's imprudent marriage to an American.

"Let me make myself very clear," she said as she waited for the bodyguard to open her door. "I may not fit your ideal of a proper Estairian princess, but I have no intention of embarrassing my brother or his wife—or embarrassing Estaire, as you so evidently appear to think I will. I had no input into the choices my parents made—I'm just trying to deal with the impact of them."

Renald's mouth thinned at her outburst. If he wasn't her enemy before, he definitely was now. He'd probably only send her to tea parties in nursing homes where she couldn't possibly say anything inappropriate. "With all due respect, madame, I am providing you with the necessary tools to smooth your reception in Estaire. Your mother disgraced Estaire and your father when she asked for a divorce and took you back to America. There are many who will remember…who thought her unworthy. Naturally, they will view your return with skepticism."

"Did the people of Estaire know about the marriage treaty?"

"Certainly not. A sovereign prince does not need to explain his decisions to his people or to anyone else."

Especially not to his wife or daughter, Rory thought bitterly. "So they judged her without knowing all the facts." As she said the words, Rory realized she was judging her mother's decision to keep her from her father without knowing all the facts, too. Maybe the letters her mother had sent to her father would help her understand what had motivated Sophia's actions.

The bodyguard opened her car door. "Thank you for the lesson, Renald. It's been enlightening."

Fuming, Rory wished she could be alone to decompress and read her mother's letters. But if the house was as crowded as the driveway, she wouldn't be given an opportunity to be alone. Not with Sebastian's lesson schedule.

And Brontë couldn't possibly be getting the rest and quiet she needed.

Rory shoved her house key into the lock. Or tried to, anyway. It didn't appear to fit anymore. Giving up in frustration, she rang the doorbell.

A butler opened the door. Her door.

There was a butler in her house. A proper English butler with a bald pate, papery skin and craggy salt-and-pepper eyebrows. Rory's temper shot up another notch. She'd given Sebastian permission to arrange her lessons and order dinner, not change her locks and hire a butler.

The butler bowed. "Welcome home, Your Serene Highness. My name is Pierce."

"Hi." Rory gaped at him, conscious that Renald was watching her every movement. Waiting for her to do something embarrassing. She was not going to give him the satisfaction. "Pleased to meet you, Pierce." She extended her hand.

Pierce looked at her hand as if he didn't know what to do with it, then shook it gallantly. Rory realized too late that she probably shouldn't have shaken hands with the hired help. However, this was America, and she'd shake hands with whomever she pleased.

"You are expected in the living room."

''Please show Mr. Dartois to the living room. I need a few moments to freshen up.''

Ignoring whoever was in the great room, Rory went directly to the kitchen to check on Brontë. Three strangers had taken over her kitchen. One was chopping vegetables, one was making fresh pasta and the third was operating a food processor.

Brontë was not in her favorite spot on the windowseat. Rory seriously considered strangling Sebastian with her bare hands. She hadn't given him permission to invite all these people into her home. No doubt the noise and the strangers had sent Brontë into hiding—most likely in Rory's room.

Rory hurried down the hallway to her room and encountered another invasion into her personal space. Her closet doors were wide-open and three-quarters of her wardrobe had been thrown into two garbage cans. Someone had gone through her dresser drawers, as well.

Rory felt steam escape her ears. Sebastian was dead meat.

But she'd deal with him after she found her cat. She hid the portfolio containing her mother's letters under her pillow, then checked under the bed. ''Are you under there, girl?''

There was no answer. Rory searched her bathroom next. She finally found Brontë curled up on the foot of the vibrant yellow silk throw that covered her mother's bed.

''There you are, kitty. Did you come in here to hide?''

Thank God nothing in this room appeared to have been disturbed. Before she'd left for work this morning she'd hidden her mother's evening bag, which contained her birthday necklace, between the folds of a blanket in her mother's closet. She scooped Brontë into her arms for a cuddle, then opened the closet to ensure the purse was still there.

She slipped her hand between the folds of a woven Mexican blanket. The purse was right where she'd left it. After work tomorrow she would put the necklace in a safe deposit box at the bank.

As she closed the closet door, she turned around to find Sebastian hovering in the doorway, a guilty expression making him look almost boyish. Less severe.

He should look guilty. Her house was overrun by strangers!

"My apologies. I didn't mean to disturb you," he said. "I wanted to ensure you found Brontë safe and sound. I carried her in here—away from distractions."

"Distractions?" Hysteria crept into her voice. "There are strangers inhabiting my kitchen and tossing out my clothes. And a butler answering my door!"

"They've all signed confidentiality agreements."

Rory rolled her eyes. "Oh, that makes it all better. Where did the butler come from?"

"He's part of your new household staff. We are still working on finding you a lady's maid."

"My household staff? I don't need a household staff. I'm only one person."

"You need to become accustomed to having a cook, a butler and a lady's maid. Consider it practical experience for your return to Estaire."

"Where are they supposed to sleep? Your bodyguards are already occupying the guest room."

"At their residences. They are day staff."

"And just when am I allowed to be alone with all these people around?"

His gaze grew troubled. "I am afraid, Your Serene

Highness, that you will find yourself far too alone in the days ahead.''

''What's that supposed to mean?'' Rory snuggled Brontë close to her, unsettled by Sebastian's troubled gaze. Was there something he wasn't telling her? Had they found another booby trap in the house? Or had Prince Laurent asked him to return to Ducharme?

''The most difficult aspect of accepting your title will be coping with the isolation from the public and from those within the intimate royal circle. Your position will forever define and change the way you are treated— even by your closest friends and family. I would be remiss in my duty if I did not adequately prepare you for that.''

Rory swallowed the lump in her throat that went down like a pinecone. Okay, that bit of insight was just as alarming as finding another booby trap. ''How does Prince Laurent deal with the isolation?''

Sebastian's rich voice gentled. ''He remembers how privileged he is. And he reads. Poetry, mostly. Goethe. Hugo. Longfellow. Byron.''

''Thoreau.''

He nodded, his dark eyes studying her intimately, unlocking the door to the private world inside her that was nourished by words. The world she'd never been able to share with anyone—until maybe now. ''Yes, Thoreau.''

A frisson of awareness danced through Rory, a kinetic connection with this man as if they were both plugged into the same channel. Both experiencing the push and pull of a growing attraction that swept her off her feet like an ocean swell. She didn't want the connection to be severed.

But Sebastian was the one man she could never have.

Falling in love with him would cause an even greater rift between Estaire and Ducharme. She could imagine the tabloid headlines: Princess Dumps Prince for His Secretary!

No she couldn't fall in love with Sebastian. Renald would surely consider a scandal of that magnitude embarrassing to the royal family.

Still, Rory took in the mouth-drying breadth of Sebastian's shoulders clad in charcoal-gray wool and the sensual firmness of his lips. She ached to feel his bare chest against hers and the strong sureness of his fingers around her waist. With a bittersweet smile she wondered if Sebastian was as indispensable to his prince as he was becoming to her.

"They are waiting for you, madame. I am curious to see you find yourself."

She flashed him a less-than-confident grin. "You and me both." Rory kissed Brontë. "You'd better stay here, girl. This could get ugly."

RORY TOOK ONE LOOK at the two women sifting through a rack of clothes with Renald in the great room and wanted to hurry back to her bedroom to change. Except, someone had thrown out her clothes.

One of the women was blond and reminded Rory of champagne in a slender crystal flute—refined, delicate. The other was ebony-haired, with vibrant velvet-brown eyes and tiny hands that moved expressively when she talked.

They turned curious eyes on Rory as Sebastian made introductions. The white-blonde was Prince Laurent's press secretary, Odette Schoenfeldt. Her English was flawless, her Continental accent charming and gracious. Rory had a sinking feeling she'd never live up to the press secretary's expectations. The brunette was Chandale Allard, a Hollywood stylist to the stars.

"You'll have to forgive me for raiding your closet," Chandale said, her tone cheerful and businesslike. "It's the only way I can research a new client, and there's a rush on this job. But you'll thank me in the end." She clapped her hands together, then made a circle in the air with her index finger. "Turn around for me."

Rory reluctantly followed orders, aware that Sebastian had taken a seat in a leather armchair to watch, keeping himself rigid so his wounded back didn't rest against the cushions. She could feel his eyes on her. Somehow it gave her courage. The truth was, when she finally met Prince Laurent she did want to look her best.

"Uh-huh. Show me your hands."

Rory held out her hands for inspection. She'd never been a girlie-girl or into doing her nails.

"Have you ever had a professional manicure or a pedicure?"

Rory flushed, feeling unfeminine. Unprincessish. "No."

"Do you use nail polish?"

"It's too much maintenance. The sea and the sand chip it right off."

"What about makeup?"

"Lip gloss and sunscreen—unless it's a special occasion."

Chandale nodded. "Walk across the room now. These are the type of clothes you would normally wear to work. Clothes you feel comfortable in?"

Rory studied the white sundress she'd worn to work. She'd bought it because she felt Bohemian in it. "Yes. The Book Nook is a casual environment." She walked toward the wall of windows that framed the ever-

changing vista of the ocean. It was a beautiful afternoon—perfect southern California sunshine. Not a cloud
in the sky. She paused in front of the picture window,
caught up in the warmth of the sun cascading into the
great room. The sand on the shoreline glistened like
white lace against the indigo ruffled water.

She felt an urge to be out there in the surf, diving
under the waves. She turned around, tripping on the
edge of the zebra-striped area rug.

"Obviously a few lessons in deportment are in order," Renald said critically.

Odette bestowed Rory with an encouraging smile.
"She is understandably nervous. A swan evolves from
a cygnet with careful nurturing. With the proper clothes,
the right makeup and some coaching, she is going to be
gorgeous. The question is defining her image. Prince
Laurent is one of the most eligible bachelors in the
world. She will be a future queen. She must be seen as
his equal in every way."

"She is a princess of Estaire first and foremost,"
Renald reminded her curtly.

"Naturally," Odette allowed. "I did not intend to
suggest otherwise. The challenge lies in downplaying
her Americanism and emphasizing her Estairian heritage. Prince Olivier and Princess Penelope are a modern
couple—young, outgoing, professional, hardworking.
She must complement that image, Chandale. The polished long-lost daughter, returning to her country. It's
such a shame she isn't more gainfully employed. There
must be some sort of positive spin we can put on the
book clerk job—"

Anger burst in a hot flash in Rory's chest. She wondered if her mother been told to downplay her Americanism. "Hey, people, I'm in the room. And I hope

you're not suggesting there's anything wrong with working in a bookstore. Books educate minds. Where would society be without a record of its history? Or without new ideas, new experiences, new stories to entertain and teach us?''

Sebastian steepled his fingers together, his elbows braced on the chair arms. His firm lips twitched. ''I believe the princess has just given you your spin, Odette.''

Color stained Odette's pale cheeks. ''So it seems. Renald, perhaps we could involve her in literacy causes. Do you read French or German, Your Serene Highness?''

''A small amount of French,'' Rory admitted.

Odette shrugged. ''No matter. You will learn. In European schools, children learn two or three languages as a matter of course. Americans always seem to think the rest of the world should learn English to accommodate them.''

Rory bit the inside of her cheek and told herself that Odette was only trying to help her.

Odette's gaze traveled from the coffee table with the bronze dolphin sculpture leaping from its center to the clear acrylic shelves floating on the sunset-red walls that showcased the objets d'art her mother had collected. ''Your home suggests you have an interest in art.''

''That's my mother's doing. We traveled a great deal and she collected things wherever we went.''

''So you enjoy travel?''

Rory thought nostalgically of the trips she and her mother had shared. ''Yes.'' She wondered how her mother would have introduced this birthday adventure—happy birthday, Rory, you're going to princess boot camp! Even though she was still angry with her mother, she would give anything right now for one of her mom's hugs and an explanation. She hoped this image consulting would wind up shortly so she could read her mother's letters.

"Well, that is something at least," Renald said. "Her duties will require travel. Do you have other interests or hobbies that we can optimize?"

"I like to surf and in-line skate."

Rory could tell that answer went over big.

"Volunteer work?"

"I donate blood regularly."

Perspiration dotted Rory's upper lip even though the air-conditioning in the house was functioning. She felt as if she were being interviewed for a job and failing miserably. Odette and Renald continued to pepper her with questions until Sebastian turned to Chandale, who had been listening intently to the interrogation with her chin propped on a balled fist.

"What do you think?" he asked.

Chandale waved a hand as if she were a witch casting a magic spell. "I've heard and seen enough. It's time to try on some clothes and find her look."

Odette cleared her throat delicately. "What about her hair? Will it be a problem?"

Chandale sent Odette a patient look that made Rory feel she wasn't the only one sensing the press secretary's mild antagonism. "Not in the right hands. It will become her trademark."

A bubble of hysterical laughter formed in Rory's diaphragm. This, she had to see.

CLAUDE CRUISED PAST Princess Charlotte Aurora's house on his motorcycle, hoping to learn if the princess was still residing in her home. The number of vehicles jammed in the driveway gave him his answer. He also saw a bodyguard watching him.

Claude's lips thinned. Did Prince Laurent see the need to protect his princess?

Too little, too late, Laurent.

Was Laurent with the princess now? In the three years since his sister's death, Claude had been unable to get close enough to Laurent to perform the duty of a brother.

Claude revved the engine, the power of the motorcycle humming through his thighs and into the rest of his body. A smile warmed the emptiness inside him when he discovered a public beach access down the street. This could be the opportunity he had been waiting for.

He parked his bike beside a classic blue VW bug and removed his helmet. The princess's home was only four houses down. Claude could watch the princess's driveway from here if it weren't for the presence of an elderly man in a straw hat who was seated on one of two benches near the wooden staircase that led down to the beach.

The old man had a book in his lap and a thermos on the bench beside him. A pair of binoculars hung around his neck. He looked as if he planned to stay the afternoon.

Claude swore under his breath and removed a backpack from the saddlebag on his motorcycle. The backpack contained the handgun he'd purchased in a bar after his arrival in California a few days ago.

He concealed his eyes with a pair of sunglasses and gave the man a curt nod as he strode past him to the stairs.

Maybe he could find a way up to the princess's property from the beach. He had a score to settle with Laurent.

Chapter Eight

Laurent observed Rory's rebelliousness grow—a quiet storm that raged in her eyes and compressed her lips as each successive outfit was tried on, critiqued and accepted or rejected by Odette and Renald.

Laurent knew his princess would require up to four changes of clothing on her busiest days. Unfortunately, far too few outfits were making it onto the accepted list. Those that did were elegantly tailored suits with simple lines in understated colors that no one could possibly find fault with. A professional princess's wardrobe. Yet with each critical comment Rory seemed to shrink farther behind the clothes like a turtle withdrawing into its shell.

When a coral silk gown that displayed Rory's entrancing figure and brought out the first real smile of pleasure to her lips was rejected as being too showy, Laurent firmly put his foot down. "That gown is exquisite. Definitely that one for the engagement announcement."

"But, sir," Odette protested. "Don't you think a shade of blue that brings out her eyes would be more suitable for the official photograph?"

Laurent could tell exactly what Rory thought about that suggestion from the expressive tilt of her eyebrows.

"I agree with Mr. Guimond," Chandale said. "This one is stunning. The woman underneath is wearing the clothes, not the other way around."

Laurent felt a thrum of passion stir in his veins at Chandale's words. *The woman underneath.*

"She will have that one," he declared, admiring the lustrous coral tinge the vibrant dress coaxed into Rory's cheeks. He could imagine his sexy princess's golden skin shimmering with the heat of passion as this dress slid down her bare body. He would ensure she had delicate underwear that matched the dress. "A gift from her fiancé."

From me, he wanted to add as her hyacinth-blue eyes lifted to his, wide and wary, and her lips spread into a tremulous smile.

Laurent impatiently awaited the day when there would be no more secrets between them and he could claim those lips.

THE OLD MAN didn't leave his position on the bench until after the sun had set. Claude reached the summit of the wooden steps, relieved the way was clear at last. The cliffs had been too steep to climb up to the princess's property from the beach.

He had an alternate plan.

Checking that no one was watching in the darkness, he pulled himself over the vine-covered stucco wall that bordered the property nearest the beach access. He dropped down onto a low-growing succulent that made a peculiar popping sound as it crunched beneath his weight.

He froze, listening. His stomach growled. The granola bars he'd eaten on the beach hadn't been enough.

There were lights on inside the house. He took another step, wincing as the thick spears of iceplant popped beneath his feet. He swore silently, praying the sound could not be detected over the relentless pounding of the surf. His parents had endured enough pain over Marielle's death. He did not want them to see their last child in jail.

Cautiously Claude moved through the shrubbery toward the opposite fence. A climbing rose scratched his legs as he scaled the fence. This time he landed beside a swimming pool. He crept around the pool and into the next yard undetected, though he ripped his shorts on the metal pickets of a wrought-iron fence.

Princess Charlotte Aurora's house was next door. He could hear music playing in the backyard. Chopin, he thought. He concealed himself in the shrubbery and peered over the wall. A table was set for two in the courtyard beside a fountain. The gossamer tablecloth stirred in the faint breeze. Garlands of the same gossamer fabric and lights shaped like blue flowers were strung in the trees.

A bodyguard patrolled the courtyard. A second bodyguard stood on the side of the house near a rack that held two surfboards.

Claude's breath burned with a charge of adrenaline as he waited to be sure the guards hadn't seen him. He counted five people inside a room with bloodred walls. He recognized Marielle's friend, Odette Schoenfeldt, who had been at the yacht party the night Marielle died. Claude had heard she was working in the palace press office—some people had no loyalty.

The princess was speaking to Prince Laurent. She gazed up at the prince the same way Marielle had once looked at him. With love in her eyes.

Bitterness coated Claude's stomach like vinegar. Prince Laurent had deprived Marielle of her dreams.

He had deprived the Dupont family of a sister and a daughter.

He inched open the zipper of the backpack. The weight of the semiautomatic was heavy as he curled his palm around the handle and found the trigger.

He braced his shooting arm on the top of the stone wall and waited for Prince Laurent and Princess Charlotte Aurora to venture into the courtyard and into his line of sight.

The time of final reckoning had come.

"WE'LL TAKE OUR LEAVE NOW," Laurent told Rory, sending a nod in Heinrich's direction. "Heinrich just advised me your brother should be arriving any minute. How were the language lessons?"

"Bien. Recht Gutt." She rubbed her neck. "Exhausting, actually. I hope you aren't expecting great advances."

He arched a brow. "I am expecting your best."

A worried frown etched her forehead, and she glanced back toward Renald and Odette who were deep in conversation with Chandale.

"Will you think less of me if I confess that I hate the clothes? Well, most of them, anyway. I love the coral dress—and this one isn't bad."

Laurent felt a smile building inside him. The sultry copper and blue cocktail dress with the short hip-hugging skirt was much more than not bad. It made Rory look sexy and flirtatious and beautiful.

Acting on impulse, he took her hand. "Come outside a moment. I'm going to tell you a secret."

"What…?"

She giggled as he opened the patio doors and dragged her out into the courtyard. Laurent thought it the most entrancing sound he'd heard in ages. It made his chest hurt with the yearning to laugh with her. When was the last time he had truly laughed?

His princess was doing the most peculiar things to him. Like the mermaid Lorelei, she was entrancing him with her song and her beautiful hair. Luring him into danger.

But he told himself that he was wise enough to resist her allures and stay on solid ground.

He pulled her close, breathing deeply of the alluring tropical scent of her and wishing the candles and the music and the meal were for the two of them to share. There was still so much he wanted to learn about his princess if they were to be husband and wife. But she needed to bond with her brother first.

"I hate the clothes, too," he murmured in her ear.

Her eyes widened. "You do?"

"Unequivocally yes."

She laughed again. "Oh, Sebastian. I wish—" She paused, blushing furiously. "Do I have to wear them?"

Laurent couldn't resist touching her pink-tinged cheek. He traced the heated golden softness with his finger and tilted her face up to his. He had to fight to remind himself that he was her tutor, her mentor, not her lover. He took a deep breath.

"Renald and Odette have the best of intentions, but you will have to take some initiative and make their advice work for you. Choose things that make you feel like a princess and you'll always be appropriately attired."

"Are you sure I won't cause an international incident?"

He chuckled. "Perhaps a minor one. But it will be worth it to see you looking radiant."

She moistened her lips, and Laurent felt her pulse

quicken in the sensitive underside of her jaw. The music beckoned him to touch her, hold her. Make her his.

He reacted to the music. "Dance with me, Princess," he commanded.

She moved toward him shyly, her toes clumsily stepping on his. Her eyes implored Laurent's forgiveness, and embarrassment blossomed in her cheeks like a profusion of roses. If he lived forever he would never tire of watching the changing colors in her petal-soft cheeks.

He squeezed her fingers reassuringly. "It's a waltz. Very simple. Imagine we are skating on ice. That's what my mother taught me when I was twelve and taking my first lessons. Step, glide."

Rory stepped on his toe again. "I'm so sorry."

"You should be," he scolded her with mock severity. "Despite the fact that you are a princess, you must always allow your partner to lead. Relax. It's a beautiful evening. Pretend you are in-line skating."

Relax? He had to be kidding. Rory couldn't possibly relax. Sebastian was holding her, looking at her as if he thought she was beautiful. Special. Every nerve in her body recorded the overwhelming effects of his nearness: determining the precise degree of his heat; gauging the potent hardness of his body; and identifying the components of his sensual scent.

Her body melted into the steady warmth of his embrace. She had never felt so safe. So happy to be alive. She didn't want to ever meet Prince Laurent.

Sebastian's breath caressed her cheek, his lips precariously close to her own. For a tiny exhilarating second she let herself believe that he intended to kiss her. Instead, he twirled her away from him.

A sharp retort like the backfiring of a car split the night—followed by several others in rapid succession.

At first Rory thought it was fireworks.

Sebastian snatched her hand. He jerked her across his body and threw her toward the pool. He didn't let go. He fell into the water with her. Out of the corner of her eye she saw one of the bodyguards drawing his gun.

Then the water swallowed her up.

PANIC POUNDED in Rory's ears as she clung to Sebastian. The sky was as black as the lid of a coffin above them.

His face swam before her eyes, calm, resolute. His hands squeezed her shoulders, reassuring her that everything would be okay. But everything wasn't okay. Someone had shot at them! At her!

He kicked, pulling her with him. She came up gasping for air. Sebastian shielded her with his body near the edge of the pool.

"Are you hurt?" he whispered breathlessly.

"Sebastian, are you all right?" she demanded at the same time, running her fingers over his chest to ensure there were no bullet wounds. She checked the water for trickles of blood. She couldn't stand the thought of him taking a bullet for her.

Dying for her.

He cupped her nape with his hand. His lips brushed the damp hair from her temple and touched her skin in a fiercely tender kiss that chased the fear from her heart with an emotion so powerful that she trembled with the truth of it. She flattened her palm to his chest, seeking the solid hammering of his heartbeat through his damp shirt. Sebastian made her feel safe. Secure.

"Stay quiet, *mein Lorelei*. I am unharmed," he murmured in her ear.

She nodded dumbly in pure relief, her fingers latching on to his tie. She was not letting go of him.

His lips formed a wry smile. "When we are most afraid is when we must remain calm and think clearly. We must stay here and wait for instructions from the guards." His words belied the rapid beat of his heart and the dark fire in his eyes.

Rory started as the lights in the courtyard, the pool and inside the house were abruptly extinguished. Two bodyguards appeared at the pool's edge with their guns drawn and formed a human shield for them. Rory heard them speaking in low urgent tones into their headsets. Had they caught the shooter? Had anyone been hit?

"Hurry, now," Sebastian urged her. "Into the house." The five-hundred-dollar shoes that were so appropriate for dancing were treacherously slippery as she climbed out of the pool. Sebastian kept a protective arm around her as they raced the few yards to the patio doors.

He moved her briskly past the racks of clothes to the hallway where the catering staff and the others waited in the dark.

"What's happened, Sebastian?" Odette demanded in an imperious tone infused with fear. "We heard shots."

Rory was shivering. Her sopping-wet dress molded like a cold glove to her body as her eyes slowly adjusted to the darkness. But her trembling wasn't just from chill. Someone had tried to kill her—again.

Sebastian spoke calmly, soothingly. "We are safe, that is all that matters. Odette, I trust you will ensure that everything is under control. One of the neighbors may have called the police. The princess is soaked and needs to change out of her wet clothes."

Odette's shoulders snapped taut, her face pale, but her tone was brisk and businesslike again. "Understood, sir."

Renald stepped beside Odette. "I will assist Odette, sir. Prince Olivier has been diverted to the Hotel Del."

"Very good." Sebastian steered Rory past them to her bedroom. "This way, Your Serene Highness."

Serene, ha! Maybe once, when her life had been normal, back before she'd found out she was a princess. Except for some sullen door-slamming in her teens, Rory had never thrown a tantrum in her life. Much like her mother, whenever she was upset, Rory retreated to think until she'd regained her equilibrium.

But her life had disintegrated to a nightmare, and Rory was on the verge of a drama queen rant.

Too much had happened in the past few days.

Her mother—the person she'd trusted most in the world—had *lied* to her about her birth. A brother she'd just met expected her to marry a man she'd *never* met. And for the second time in three days, someone had tried to kill her.

Rory's stomach pitched. Oh, God, it was probably the same person who'd murdered her mother!

As if all that weren't enough to send her screaming into therapy, the most incredible man she'd ever known had just kissed her and was calmly leading her down the pitch-black hallway toward her bedroom so she could remove her wet clothes. She stamped her Manolo Blahnik-clad foot on the floor. Pain jarred through her ankle. "I am nowhere near being serene. Someone just tried to—"

He pressed a warning finger to her lips. "Hush!"

Rory did *not* want to hush. She felt an insane urge to nip at his finger. Or suckle it…just a little bit to see if any of this was real. What the heck, maybe she'd go for broke and plaster herself to his chest and kiss him. *Really* kiss him.

He pushed her into her room, his hand firmly at the base of her spine. "Don't turn on the light. We'll be visible to anyone lurking outside. Where's the bathroom? I'll get you some towels."

"Sebastian?" Her courage wavered. What if she kissed him and he didn't kiss her back?

Never in her life had Rory so desperately needed to hold on to someone. She reached for him in the dark, her fingers encountering soaked cotton and tiny wooden buttons. Her fingers found skin between the buttons. The scorching heat of his body seared her right down to the soles of her feet like hot sand on a ninety-degree afternoon.

Her voice trembled. "Thank you for saving me!"

Her lips tickled the stubble riding the edge of his jaw, her mouth feeling cold against the hardness of bone as her thumbs tried to ease his jacket off his shoulders. She rose onto her tiptoes, so she could find his mouth. She needed him. Needed his kiss.

He smelled so good, even with a dose of pool chlorine.

Her lips found the corner of his mouth. Found the firm warmth of a welcome.

Groaning, Sebastian gripped her shoulders. "I'm supposed to be helping you get your clothes off, madame."

Rory whimpered with need at the thought of him peeling this skimpy little dress from her breasts, from her hips. Her breasts ached, puckered with an overwhelming need for his touch. For hot, healing sex. She didn't care that the house was filled with people or that a hunt for a killer was going on outside. This moment and the way she felt about Sebastian were the only things that mattered.

Proving to herself that she hadn't imagined Sebastian's attraction to her was the only way she could stay sane.

"So, do it. Take my clothes off," she urged, inching his jacket off his shoulders. It fell to the floor with a wet plop. She reached for his tie. The muscles in his throat constricted.

He was going to argue with her. His fingers closed around hers, stopping her as she yanked the knot loose. "Princess... It is hardly appropriate—"

"Not Princess. Rory, or better yet, Lorelei." It was highly erotic knowing that he thought of her as his mermaid.

His enchantress.

Rory felt enchanted. Enchanted by the iron-hard feel of Sebastian's body, by the sexy spikes of damp black hair that curled toward his aristocratic forehead, and by the fierce smoldering heat in his inky eyes that suggested he wasn't nearly as composed as he pretended.

She pressed her pliant breasts into his chest, let him feel the sensitive nubs that craved his touch. His kiss.

He hitched in a breath. "Do you realize what you're saying? I work for—"

She yanked his head down with a sharp tug on his tie and closed her eyes. A sigh of pent-up satisfaction swelled in her throat as her mouth made bold, hungry contact with his. Desire tumbled through her in a kaleidoscope of colors. Red for passion. Black for intrigue. Yellow for the golden prisms that sparkled behind her eyelids like droplets of sun-kissed water. Dazzling blue for the depths of things to be explored. Green for the sense of coming home. And purple, purple for royalty.

His kiss was incredibly masculine, sensual and far too restrained. His hands hovered inches from her waist, his fingers splayed as if he desired to touch her but an invisible barrier prohibited it. She sensed him holding back, warring an ethical battle with his conscience even while his arousal pressed against her belly.

Though she was sopping wet, Rory felt moist heat slicken the most intimate part of her. She felt more powerful than she'd ever felt in her life. Unlike the men she'd dated in college, Sebastian wasn't a premed student or an accounting major looking for an easy score. He was a principled, well-educated man. And so incredibly sexy she wanted to rip the buttons off his exquisitely tailored shirt and shock his socks off.

She held on to his muscled shoulders for dear life, catapulted through the kiss as if she was surfing through the barrel of a wave, waiting to see if she'd emerge exhilarated and still standing, or be crushed.

Inexpertly she nibbled at the crease of his lips, imploring him to deepen the kiss, open the gate to the depths of Sebastian that she yearned to explore.

"Nein," he groaned, ruthlessly prying her from his body as if she were a barnacle glued to a ship's hull. "That did *not* just happen." His breath feathered hotly on her cheek, proving him a liar. She wanted to point out that he was breathing as raggedly as she.

His gaze avoided hers as he adjusted the cuffs of his shirt, an action that bordered on the ridiculous because she could hear the dripping of their clothes onto her red oak floors. She wished she'd torn his silly, officious buttons off. She'd like to hear him explain how that didn't happen!

The darkness cloaking the room like black chiffon veiled his expression. "You are distraught, madame."

His rejection crushed her. Wounded her in the same way that her mother's death had. Rory stood there in the shadows, hugging herself, wishing she was a Lorelei and a wave would come and sweep her away.

With heart-wrenching clarity she realized that it didn't matter if Sebastian cared about her, desired her. He was just like her father and her brother. He would always put his duty to his country above his personal feelings.

She'd embarrassed him and humiliated herself by acting upon what should never have been acknowledged. She hadn't taken into account his unwavering loyalty to his prince. Or the fact that he only cared about her because she would be his country's future queen.

Now she'd placed them both in an uncomfortable situation and proved herself unworthy of Prince Laurent in his eyes.

She struggled to find words to repair what couldn't be undone. To retain a strand of her dignity. "You're right, Sebastian. Someone just tried to kill me, and I don't know what I'm saying or doing."

Whirling away from him, she marched into the bathroom and slammed the door, locking it behind her. She leaned against the door, her heart aching with love and loss.

"Rory?" Sebastian knocked on the door, his voice impatient. "Please, let me in."

"No." Rory squeezed her eyes tight to hold back tears she was not going to let fall. She couldn't ever let Sebastian in, not where she wanted him to be.

"Go away. No more lessons, no more people." *No more kisses.* "I order you to go away."

Her teeth were chattering. She stepped inside the glass shower enclosure and turned the hot water on full blast. Then she peeled the wet dress from her body and kicked it from her. She'd never wear it again.

The hot water pummeled her chilled flesh, but even the driving heat couldn't erase the yearning for the forbidden touch of her prince's deputy secretary.

WHEN SHE EMERGED from the bathroom over an hour later, Rory was wrapped in a sky-blue fleece robe with cloud-shaped pockets. Her room was dark, and Sebastian was gone.

She tiptoed to her bedroom door and locked it. Then she quietly slid a chair beneath the knob for good measure. One of Heinrich's merry men could probably break the chair into matchsticks with one kick at the door, but it was the principle of the thing. She wanted a barricade from the chaos that had erupted in her life.

Since she didn't know if it was safe to turn on the lights, Rory collected pillows from her bed, a thick blue candle studded with seashells, a lighter and the portfolio containing her mother's letters and carried them into her closet. She made a cozy nest on the floor with pillows and set the candle in a safe spot where she couldn't possibly knock it over. Then she lit the candle and curled up with the letters. Brontë snuggled beside her, lending moral support.

The warm smell of candle wax and the coziness of the closet was comforting, intimate. Rory trembled as she started to read the first letter. Would her mother's letters give her a clue to her parents' relationship?

Cher August,
I have grown tired of living in hotels. I have bought a beach house with the vast Pacific Ocean at our back door. The ever-changing song of the surf drowns out the grief in my heart. But I am resolute in my decision. As intractable as you are in yours.

Charlotte Aurora—I call her Rory now—loves the beach. She took her first steps in the sand. She is fascinated by the shells and the kelp that wash up along the shore. And she squeals with joy when the waves tickle her toes. She is growing so fast—without her father.

Is this really what you want?

Sophia

Rory studied three photographs that were paper clipped to the letter. In one she was toddling across the sand in a ruffled pink bathing suit, a yellow plastic sand pail clutched in her fingers. In the second her mother stood ankle deep in water, lifting Rory by the hands as a wave washed over her toes.

The third photograph hit Rory straight in her heart. It was a close-up of her and her mother taken beside the magenta blooms of a bougainvillea. Rory's head was nestled beneath her mother's chin. Sunlight highlighted Sophia's short cap of curls with red fire as she stared directly into the camera as if staring into her ex-husband's eyes, her somber eyes silently asking why.

Tears traced Rory's cheek and splashed onto the sheet of blue stationery. She saw the strength in the sorrowful, stubborn tilt to her mother's chin. In the resolute firmness in her gaze. Yes, her mother had lied to her. But she'd also taken a position based on her belief in what was best for her child, and she was not going to back down.

Rory read the next letter. It included a description of her second birthday and a picture of her taken on Santa's lap at Christmas. At the bottom of the letter her mother had added a postscript:

It has been two years now—two irreplaceable
years. How do you think your daughter will feel
when she learns the truth? Will you expect her to
love you? Will your people appreciate the sacrifice
you have made?

The sacrifice. Was that how her father had viewed the
treaty—as a personal sacrifice for the good of his country?

"I am keeping to the terms of the agreement," her
mother added. "But I warn you, I am teaching your
daughter to think for herself."

Rory discovered in the next letter that her father's
response to her mother's last letter had been to initiate
the birthday adventures. Her mother had included a photograph of Rory eating pancakes shaped like mouse ears
and had thanked him for the birthday trip to Disney-
world.

After that, there were no further references to the bar-
gain her parents had made. Rory sensed that her mother
had given up hope of her father ever changing his mind
about the treaty. The rest of Sophia's letters were no
more than a curt account of Rory's activities.

There were sixteen letters in all. Just as her brother
Olivier had told her, Sophia had stopped sending the
yearly updates after her father's death.

Rory thumbed back through the letters and reread the
postscript added to the second letter:

It has been two years now—two irreplaceable
years. How do you think your daughter will feel
when she learns the truth? Will you expect her to
love you? Will your people appreciate the sacrifice
you have made?

I am keeping to the terms of the agreement. But I warn you, I am teaching your daughter to think for herself.

Rory felt the tightly packed wad of emotions in her chest loosen. She was still angry with her parents. Still hurt and troubled that her mother had left her in the vulnerable position of learning of her father and the treaty from a lawyer rather than from her mother's lips.

But Rory saw from her mother's own hand how much she had loved her. Her mother had protected her to the best of her ability against the inevitable. That message was clear in her mother's words. "I am keeping to the terms of the agreement. But I warn you, I am teaching your daughter to think for herself."

"You sure did, Mom," she whispered softly. Odd…she realized that Sebastian—in his own way— had told her the same thing when he'd coached her about her wardrobe.

Sebastian. Pain pierced her heart as if pricked by a needle.

Rory blew out the candle and hugged the letters to her chest in the dark. She knew what she had to do.

Chapter Nine

Prince Olivier barged past Odette into Prince Laurent's suite as the hotel's doctor was departing.

"Prince Laurent is indispos—" Odette objected, trailing at Olivier's heels as if she were a Corgi sniffing an intruder.

She had summoned the hotel's doctor to ensure that Prince Laurent's unexpected plunge into the pool tonight had not caused further damage or harmed his stitches. The doctor had cleaned and rebandaged his wounds and cautioned him to be on the lookout for any signs of infection.

Prince Olivier dismissed Odette with a flick of his wrist. "He will see me. Leave us."

Odette curtsied in acquiescence, but her gray-green eyes met Laurent's gaze through her darkened lashes. "You will call me if you require anything further?"

Laurent found her uncharacteristic fussing touching, if unnecessary. *"Ja."* He eased a white terry bathrobe up over his shoulders and turned to face Prince Olivier, who was pacing in front of the drawn curtains, his hands clasped tightly behind his back. Prince Olivier was still dressed for dinner in a black tuxedo with a white silk scarf draped around his neck. His blond hair was ruffled and portended his mood.

"I just spoke to Heinrich. He informs me the assassin managed to escape. He's contacted the authorities to report the incident—discreetly, of course."

Laurent closed his eyes, hearing once again the popping sounds of the shots and the whine of bullets skimming past his ear. He saw the horror and awareness that had exploded in Rory's eyes as he'd pulled her into the pool. "It's a miracle she wasn't hit."

It was his duty to respect her, care for her and keep her safe. And he'd nearly failed. Not only that, but he realized, to his shame, that keeping his feelings for his bride-to-be in the proper perspective was proving more difficult than he had first imagined.

His heart still thundered in his chest like the deep resonant chimes of the grandfather clock in the Schloss. Rory had begged him to remove her dress and had savaged his mouth with fervent inexpert kisses.

He'd wanted to strip the damp knit from her body and fill his palms with the soft full warmth of her breasts.

He'd wanted to whisper poetic words to her as he slid inside her. He wanted to hear her scream his name when she shattered and found her fulfillment at his touch. He wanted to hear her beg him for it again.

She had been promised to a prince, and yet she desired *him,* Sebastian, the deputy secretary. The wonder of her innocent passion rattled every disciplined bone in his body and warned him that the box in which he caged his emotions had glass sides.

But he could not dishonor Rory by making love to her without first revealing his identity. There would be many nights after they were married when they could delight in hot consuming sex. His primary responsibility now was to prepare her for the role that awaited her. She had no idea of the pressure that would descend upon her sun-kissed shoulders once the paparazzi learned of her existence.

Laurent viewed the hours they were allowed to spend together without being hounded by flashbulbs and tele-photo lenses as a precious gift.

Prince Olivier halted in midstride. "Heinrich wants a police forensics team to search the grounds for evidence. I asked him to hold off until Charlotte Aurora has left for work. I don't wish to frighten her further." He lifted his head, his blue eyes stark. "There have been three attempts on her life including the unfortunate tragedy that killed her mother. My sister is clearly not safe here. We should return to Estaire immediately. She'll be safer in the palace. We have more guards. More resources to ensure her security."

Laurent hesitated. "Did you discuss that with her?"

"No. I'm told she has retired for the night."

Laurent thought of Rory battened down in her bathroom, keeping him and the world at bay. She had thrown him out after his rejection. Guilt festered in his stomach.

She was so vulnerable. All the more reason these lessons in protocol were so vital to her happiness and her survival.

"I agree she would be safer under your immediate protection," Laurent said. "But do you feel she is prepared for that step? It has only been a few days. If she is caged like a thrush her only focus will be to seek freedom. Far better to prop the door open and allow her to come and go and feather her nest of her own free will. Then she will sing."

Laurent told himself that was how he envisioned their marriage. Each of them able to come and go at their choosing, finding their strengths, rearing a family.

Prince Olivier resumed his pacing, the tails of his silk scarf fluttering. "What do you propose, then? The assassin has changed his tactics. This time he came within gunshot range."

"Perhaps. Or it was a different assailant." Laurent thought of the deranged woman who had stabbed his date in the ladies' room. He had no way of knowing if that incident was related to Marielle's overdose. "And how does that differ from what we face every day, *mon ami?* Weren't you assaulted by a pensioner's cane last year? And didn't Princess Penelope have a frightening encounter in a palace corridor with a footman who was armed with a knife?

"We place our trust in the experience of the good people who risk their lives for our safety. Charlotte Aurora needs to view that level of protection as something to be desired, not resented."

Prince Olivier pursed his lips thoughtfully. "You possess an annoying ability to be right."

Prince Laurent winced. He only hoped Rory would agree that he had made the right decision tonight when he'd prevented her kisses from getting out of hand.

AN ELECTRONIC RENDITION of "Taps" woke the hit man. He had been out on the job conducting surveillance. Gaining access into the princess's house again would be a challenge, considering all the firepower staked out on her property.

A challenge but not impossible. He was still confident his backup plan would succeed, but if not, he was already considering several new options. He wanted the second half of the hundred Gs. He fumbled around on the bedside table for his cell phone and hit the talk button. "Yeah?"

"What do you think you're doing? You nearly shot Prince Laurent last night!"

He sat up in bed, shaking the cobwebs from his sleep-fogged brain. "Shot? What are you talking about?"

"It's supposed to look like an accident, not an assassination!"

He was wide awake now. "What happened?"

He listened to the details of the shooting. That explained the firepower crawling around the shrubbery like ants swarming a picnic. "It wasn't me. I don't do guns. They leave too much evidence that can get you locked up. But I don't like the idea of another party invading my turf."

"If you had completed the job as contracted, we would not be having this conversation," his client reminded him.

"You wanted an accident. No evidence. Sometimes you have to be patient. It should be any day now."

"I don't care how she dies. I just want her buried."

"I'm on it." He turned the phone off and glanced at the clock. It was barely 5:00 a.m.

What the hell. Time for plan C. He climbed out of bed. The princess loved to surf. That had to be an accident waiting to happen.

THE COAST WAS CLEAR.

Sebastian would be furious, but Rory didn't care. Dressed in a purple rash guard and matching board shorts, she eased her teal, orchid-painted surfboard from the rack along the side of the house just before 6:00 a.m. and walked swiftly down the drive in her bare feet, stifling a cry of pain as a sharp stone bit into her tender insole.

She reached the end of the driveway and ducked down behind the stone wall bordering her yard when she heard one of the bodyguards exit her front door. He carried a stainless steel coffee mug.

She waited several long minutes until he continued his patrol of the grounds, then she ran down the sand-swept sidewalk toward the Windansea beach access. Cars jammed the tiny parking area.

After the search that had ensued last night for the shooter, she doubted anyone would be hanging out in her shrubbery, waiting for another opportunity to kill her. If the shooter had been caught, she hadn't been told. But then, she'd made it clear to Sebastian last night that she didn't want to be disturbed.

It was a small miracle that the police hadn't shown up asking questions. Any neighbors who'd heard the shots had probably erroneously assumed, like her, that the gunshots were test fireworks for the nightly show in Mission Bay.

The morning was overcast, the sun hiding behind opaque low clouds blanketing the coast. A perfect morning for burrowing under the covers and catching twenty minutes more sleep. But it was high tide and the waves were rolling in with glassy five- to six-feet faces on the sets. More than a dozen surfers were bobbing in the water. Windansea was one of La Jolla's favorite spots for surfers.

Rory trod down the stairs to the beach, the breeze tugging playfully at her ponytail. Huge sandstone boulders hunched over the white sand like beached whales providing private crannies for sunbathing. A hut roofed with palm fronds stood like a sentinel, waiting for the afternoon crowds. Rory filled her lungs with the damp briny air tainted with the tang of seaweed and board wax and felt perfectly safe. Free.

She needed to take back control of her life. She needed her worries to be lifted from her shoulders by the soothing swell of the ocean's currents. No one was going to attack her in broad daylight on a beach full of witnesses.

Rory reached the water's edge and paused a moment to attach the rainbow-striped surf leash around her right ankle. It prevented her from losing her board when she wiped out. Then she plunged into the chilly sixty-degree water, catching her breath as she was immediately submerged up to her thighs. The beach was steep at Windansea, creating a dangerous shorebreak surf that crashed hard at the shoreline—capable of causing serious injury to unsuspecting surfers and bathers. Sliding onto her board, she quickly reconnoitered her way past the shorebreak surf. Another glassy wave came at her, cresting with a white foamy lip. She took a deep breath and ducked under it. The wave pummeled over her like a steamroller.

Rory surfaced, laughter bubbling inside her. For the first time since her mother's lawyer had arrived on her doorstep, she felt like herself again. Dreamy, bookish Rory Kenilworth, a surf diva who loved the ocean. If only Renald and Odette could see her now.

She paddled hard toward the takeoff zone, riding the swells and judging the waves. The surfers who'd arrived before her were cued, defending their positions. There were rigid rules among surfers for taking off. She got into the lineup, her thoughts drifting to last night and what had happened between her and Sebastian.

Or what they'd both agreed had *not* happened. Her

cheeks burned with embarrassment. After reading her mother's letters, she'd made some decisions.

Sebastian had been right to prevent that kiss from going any further. She had been distraught—being shot at was a terrifying experience. She was grappling with too many changes forced upon her at once, and she had reached out to the one person who was offering advice and encouragement and a strong protective shoulder.

Sebastian was an incredibly handsome man. Intelligent and articulate. She'd have to be blind and deaf not to be attracted to him.

But no matter how tempted she was by his dark sexiness, she needed to keep an open mind about becoming a princess of Estaire and about this marriage treaty to Prince Laurent. Maybe, just maybe, she would want to rip the buttons off Prince Laurent's shirt. After all, she hadn't seen him yet.

No matter what happened, she was *not* going to continue to be bullied into living up to someone else's concept of who she should be. She needed to think for herself, like her mother and Sebastian had both said. Otherwise she could be in danger of losing herself.

Rory's turn at the takeoff zone arrived. She eyed the perfect wave coming in and started paddling hard. This was hers. And it was a beaut. She popped up on the board, leaning forward and maintaining her balance as the board shot along the curl. She felt powerful again. First thing after breakfast she was going to call Chandale and cancel the outfits that made her feel like a paper doll.

And she was going to be the soul of propriety in Sebastian's presence.

In her peripheral vision, Rory detected a blur of movement. A rogue surfer in a black wet suit cut across her path on a black short board with a row of shark's teeth painted across its curved tip.

Rory arced desperately, trying to avoid a collision and failed. Her board struck the black board and she wiped out, tumbling roughly into the water.

What did that idiot think he was doing horning in on *her* wave?

The wave crushed her. She tumbled around like a sock in a wash cycle, trying to determine which way was up. Something slammed her hard in the back, the impact forcing the air from her lungs. Her board? A rock? The other surfer? She wasn't sure. She needed a breath soon.

She started to swim toward the surface, but was stopped short by her leash. There were coral reefs in the water. The leash must have gotten caught on a reef.

She kicked hard, but the leash held her fast. Rory didn't waste time. She couldn't hold her breath much longer. She reached down to undo the leash around her ankle, when something smacked her broadside at her waist.

What the hell? God, she hoped it wasn't a shark!

She twisted around, relief sweeping through her as she saw the dark silhouette of a surfboard rocketing up toward the surface. The glimmer of gleaming white teeth told her it was the rogue surfer's board.

Had he gotten caught in the reef, too? What a jerk! This beach wasn't for novice surfers. The lifeguards weren't on duty until 9:00 a.m.

Rory quickly unfastened her leash. Kicking hard, she swam toward the surface. She'd check on the other surfer after she'd gotten some air. But she'd barely broken through and opened her mouth to suck in oxygen when another wave pounded her.

Silently swearing, Rory had to forget about the other surfer and worry about her own safety. Her chest burned from lack of oxygen.

She fought her way back to the surface, this time managing to catch a sufficient breath before ducking under another oncoming wave.

When her head poked free again beside a slimy patch of kelp, she scanned the water and the beach, looking for the other surfer and her board. Fortunately the rogue surfer was being helped out of the shorebreak by two of the Windansea rats. One of the local surfer rats gave the rogue a shove, ousting him from the beach. The rogue scrambled to his feet, his fists clenched, his blond hair hanging around his face like a string mop. Rory hoped there wasn't going to be a fight. The rats could be pretty territorial against aggressive outsiders.

A swell lifted her and she saw her board bobbing solo in the water thirty feet from her. She swam toward it. By the time she'd reached it, the other surfer had his board tucked under his arm and was swaggering off the beach.

Rory suppressed a shudder as she gazed at his stiff back and the hair stringing over his shoulders. Something about him seemed familiar. She didn't think she'd seen him at Windansea before, but she couldn't place him. She turned her board around and paddled back toward the takeoff zone. She wasn't coming in until she'd macked one good ride.

RORY CURLED UP on the windowseat beside Brontë, eating a breakfast of blueberry yogurt sprinkled with granola and slices of papaya and strawberries prepared by Alice, her new cook. The tiny Philippino woman had arrived with her own cooking pans and potted herbs, along with Pierce, the butler, while Rory had been surfing.

Sneaking back into the house this morning had not been as easy as sneaking out. One of Heinrich's merry men had caught her tiptoeing up the driveway. Remembering that she was taking control of her life, she'd wished him a good morning and told him the waves had been great.

He'd nodded politely, but she'd had the feeling that she'd never be able to sneak past him again. No problem. She'd realized last night when she'd asked Sebastian to leave that she could draw boundaries and establish rules.

She'd tried the same tactic on Pierce and Alice when she encountered them getting acquainted in the kitchen. She'd told them what she wanted for breakfast and where she usually took it, then went off to shower.

And here she was, dressed in a misty-blue sleeveless silk dress she'd found hanging on the clothes rack in the great room. It was more sophisticated than the clothes she normally wore to work, but she liked the shell-shaped lace overlays that added pizzazz to the skirt. And while she'd eyed the matching flirty square-heeled shoes with distrust, she'd tried them on and found them surprisingly comfortable.

Which reminded her that she still needed to call the Hollywood stylist at her hotel. Rory quickly finished her breakfast and did without her daily vitamin because the bottle wasn't on the counter where she normally kept it, then she asked Pierce to bring her the phone.

The stylist answered on the first ring.

Rory chased away the twinges of anxiety that hovered just below her breastbone. Her mother had never hesitated to be individualistic and to express her personality through her clothes, her home and her belongings. As a trendsetter, Sophia had sought out furniture and home accessories that would help other people define themselves.

Rory's voice wavered. "Chandale, this is Rory Kenilworth."

"Just the person I was thinking of!" Rory could picture Chandale's hands waving enthusiastically. "I've been on the phone all night talking with designers. I'm going to have some drawings and sample outfits for our meeting this afternoon. I think you're going to love them!"

Rory swallowed hard. She imagined a whole wardrobe of pastel suits and dresses with matching shoes and handbags. Maybe matching hats. She had to nip this in the bud! She told Chandale how she felt about the majority of yesterday's outfits. "I just don't think they're a reflection of me—although, I love the dress Sebastian Guimond picked out."

Heat flooded her belly at the thought of how Sebastian had looked at her when she'd modeled that dress. But it cooled when she realized that he had no doubt been seeing her with the idolatry of a subject fawning over the future queen of his country. He'd warned her that people would treat her differently because of her position. It hurt to discover that he was one of those people.

"Then we're on the same page!" Chandale said with a trill in her voice.

"We are?" Rory was confused.

"My thoughts were exactly the same, which is why I was on the phone all night. I see you in warmer, more vibrant colors. A modern princess who can surf the Internet and the ocean. We'll play up your natural beauty, your love for the outdoors and your love for the written word. No pretensions of grandeur—just an intelligent American girl discovering her roots. How does that sound?''

"Like you're a miracle worker and my new best friend."

The stylist laughed. "I'll see you this afternoon."

Rory put down the phone and ran a hand down the curve of Brontë's sleek back. "It's going to be an interesting day, girl," she whispered so Alice and Pierce wouldn't hear. "Let's just hope it doesn't involve bullets."

Brontë's purr sounded like a chuckle. Rory kissed her beloved pet behind the ears and checked her watch. She'd be late for work if she didn't hustle. She had no idea how Alice and Pierce were going to keep themselves occupied all day, much less who was paying them and how much, but she didn't have time to bog herself down with the details.

Rory brushed her teeth, then stopped in her mother's room to pick up the birthday necklace commissioned for her by her father. Sebastian hadn't yet told her if he'd found out anything about the necklace's making. Maybe it had slipped his mind with everything that had happened.

To her dismay, her mother's evening bag felt suspiciously light when she tugged it from the folds of the blanket. Had it felt that light when she'd hidden it?

Her heart knocking rapidly against her chest, she plucked out the velvet case and opened it.

The jewelry box was empty.

Rory sank onto her mother's bed. Someone had stolen her precious gift from her father.

How could she have been so careless? The necklace was the only gift from him.

No, that wasn't true, she told herself, pressing her fingers to her temples. She had the birthday adventures her father had picked out for her. That showed caring and thoughtfulness. And she had wonderful memories of those adventures, which could never be stolen.

She tried to think logically. Figure out who had taken the necklace. It was obviously valuable, but thanks to Sebastian's tutelage, she suspected its theft was purely political—a ploy to cast her in a poor light and create an atmosphere of distrust between the two countries when the theft was reported.

Although the necklace was a birthday gift, it was a signature piece that she would be expected to wear while performing certain official duties. The people of Estaire and her brother would be insulted by her carelessness. She could imagine the finger pointing that might take place between her brother's staff and Prince Laurent's staff if she brought up the theft.

She went back to her bedroom and checked her jewelry box to see if any other valuables were missing. Her mother's Rolex and her diamond pear-cut earrings were still nestled in their silk-lined compartments.

Rory did a head count of the people who'd been in her home yesterday. It was tempting to suspect Renald and Odette because they obviously didn't approve of her. But the fact that they held high positions of trust made their guilt unlikely. Her best guess was that one of the bodyguards had been bought. It was difficult to imagine Chandale, Pierce or one of the caterers taking the necklace. Sebastian, of course, had been in her home yesterday. But he was the only one she didn't suspect.

Her heart flinched with humiliation as she relived his

rejection of her last night. But not for a minute did she
think he would betray her or act against the best interests of his country. He'd proven that when he'd refused
her advances. His prince wanted this marriage. Ducharme had so much to gain.

Rory's skin grew clammy as she considered that the
necklace might have been stolen on Sunday. She hadn't
checked that it was in its box after she'd arrived back
from the vet's and discovered Sebastian inside her
home. He'd told her he'd found her door unlocked. Had
the person who had rigged her chandelier returned?
She'd left her evening bag within plain sight on the
foyer table.

But now that she knew the necklace was gone, what
was she going to do about it? Inform her brother? Inform Sebastian? Or keep quiet and hope the thief would
give him or herself away?

Pierce tapped on her door and told her that the car
was ready to take her to work.

"Coming." She returned the royal blue velvet case
to its hiding place in her mother's closet, then grabbed
her purse and double-checked that the check from her
new trust fund was still safely inside. She knew exactly
what to do with the money. But she'd have to ask Otto
for a favor.

PRINCESS PENELOPE RECEIVED an update from her faith-
ful spy as she lay in her silk dressing gown on the bed,
resting before dressing for dinner. She'd had an ex-
hausting day touring the children's hospital and hosting
a luncheon to raise funds for new equipment.

Olivier had informed her that an assassin had fired at
Charlotte Aurora minutes before he'd arrived at his sis-

ter's home for dinner. No one had been hurt, but the assassin had escaped.

Penelope's limbs turned to ice at the thought of what might have happened if Olivier had been present. Meeting the children today had been painful. All of them so beautiful and so vibrantly alive in the face of the terrible illnesses they were struggling to overcome. It had made her long for a Valcourt heir growing in her womb. A boy.

"Did the guards manage to get a description of the shooter?" she demanded. Olivier had not told her.

Renald sniffed disdainfully. "It was too dark."

Princess Penelope silently cursed the bodyguards' incompetence.

She rubbed her flat abdomen. She missed Olivier. Missed his smile and the adoration in his eyes when he tenderly made love to her. They had made so many plans together...she couldn't bear to think of Olivier placing Estaire's future in the hands of an *Americaine*— a Beach Boys' "California Girl," as Renald had described her.

Princess Penelope shuddered. At least Princess Charlotte Aurora was not illiterate—and an alliance with Ducharme would benefit Estaire.

But Charlotte Aurora was not taking away everything Princess Penelope had worked for. She and Olivier had tried hormonal therapies and artificial insemination. In vitro fertilization was their last hope to conceive a child. Renald had helped her research several clinics and their success rates. She'd finally chosen this clinic in France.

Princess Penelope pursed her mouth. "Prince Olivier's security must be your top priority, Renald. With this assassin roaming free, the prince could still be in danger. Our appointment at the clinic is next week." By autumn, she hoped the palace would be issuing an official announcement that Their Serene Highnesses were expecting a child.

"I understand."

"I know that you do, Renald." She thought of the stories Olivier had told her about Renald's parents. Dark and elegant with a body like a swan, Emilie Dartois had been a lady-in-waiting to Olivier's mother. She had dutifully nursed the princess during her last difficult pregnancy, which had ended sadly in the princess's—and the baby's—deaths. Emilie's husband had held a high position in the treasury. Renald was making that awkward transition from boy to man when his father died in a train accident on his way to Geneva. Prince August had taken a special interest in Renald after that. The prince had encouraged him in his studies and handpicked him for service in the palace.

Gratitude touched her voice. "Your loyalty is a gift I cherish." Just as she would cherish a Valcourt heir.

STILL FRETTING about the theft of the necklace, Rory worked her shift at the Book Nook anxiously keeping one eye on the clock. She had her pepper spray and her panic button. And her bodyguards frequently checked on her.

With the exception of two phone calls, wrong numbers where the caller listened to her greeting then hung up, the morning passed uneventfully. Rory was relieved when Tom, the owner, arrived to take the afternoon shift. Tanned and fit in navy slacks and a yacht club shirt, Tom was lugging a bag of books in a Book Nook bag and had a fistful of mail.

"You look great today," her boss said, eyeing her new outfit. "Got a date for lunch?"

Rory blushed. "No."

Tom winked at her. "Keep wearing that dress and you will." He set the bag of books on the counter.

"Are you returning some purchases?" she asked.

"No, the mail carrier found these this morning when he was making his rounds." Tom emptied the bag.

Rory paused, staring at the titles, recalling the blond man with the French accent who'd bought them yesterday.

Unease shifted within her. He'd seemed more interested in hitting on her than buying books. It occurred to her that the rogue surfer on the beach this morning had been blond. Was it the same man? She shook herself. She was becoming paranoid. They had tourists in the store every day from all parts of the globe. But still. Maybe it wouldn't hurt to take note of his name. Run it by Heinrich.

"I remember the customer. He paid by credit card. I could look through yesterday's receipts if you like."

"That would be great," Tom said. "We'll leave the books here with his name on them, and if he doesn't claim them in a week, I'll credit his account."

Rory went into the office at the back and found the receipt with Claude Dupont's signature on it. She made a copy of it and tucked it inside her purse. Maybe Claude Dupont was an ordinary tourist and would come back to collect his books. But after the frightening attacks she'd experienced, she couldn't be too careful.

She wrote Dupont's name on a sticky note and left it with Tom. She slipped her sunglasses on as she stepped out into midday sunshine that was blindingly bright. Her bank was just on the corner.

Franz, her hawk-nosed bodyguard, escorted her into the bank while she made her transaction. When they exited, the other bodyguard was waiting for them at the curb behind the wheel of Rory's red Mercedes. The top of the convertible was up.

She hoped Sebastian would be meeting her at her home to continue her lessons. She wanted to ask him about the necklace and talk to Heinrich. But instead of heading toward Neptune Place, the bodyguard drove into La Jolla Shores past lushly landscaped Spanish-Craftsmen- and Mediterranean-style homes that sprawled luxuriously across the hill. He zipped up and down quiet residential streets at a speed more suitable to a freeway.

"Where are we going?" she asked Franz, who was routinely checking the side mirror to see if they were being followed.

"La Belleza. You have an appointment."

Rory knew the exclusive spa. Being pampered for the afternoon sounded less intimidating than trying on clothes or reciting German phrases. She caught her breath as the Mercedes pulled into a palm-lined, gated drive. An oval looking-glass was intricately worked into the massive brass-plated gates.

The bodyguard punched a code into a keypad and the gates automatically swung open. They drove into a slate courtyard. The spa was a majestic Italian-style villa, a graceful cream stucco building with arched windows and a double staircase that parted in a heart shape around a Venus de Milo fountain.

The interior of the spa possessed a timeless air with travertine floors and trompe l'oeil designs embellishing walls that were the faded, golden hue of late-afternoon sunshine. Cello music played in the background, and potted palms and stone urns massed with exotic flowers made Rory feel as if she'd entered a peaceful courtyard.

Odette rose from a tasseled chaise, where she'd been taking coffee in a porcelain cup with a palmetto design, to greet Rory. She looked elegant and princess perfect in a classic Chanel black-and-white silk dress. The publicist's gray-green eyes assessed Rory's misty-blue dress critically. She finally nodded approvingly. "Much better. I hope you're in the spirit to focus on details today. A princess needs to be impeccably groomed—hair, makeup, nails, legs." Odette paused a beat. "Eyebrows."

Rory's stomach churned. She'd rather be riding a wall of water or indulging herself in the latest hot read than be tortured with smelly color rinses, facials and tweezers. "I'm in," she said, defeated.

"Excellent." Odette gave Rory a reassuring smile that seemed forced. "By the end of the day you're going to walk out of here a new woman."

Rory thought of hot wax and shuddered.

ODETTE HADN'T EXAGGERATED.

Four hours later Rory stared at the miracle of her hair, dazed beyond words. Her amber curls had been hacked at, layered and conditioned into submission. Her hair now framed her face in striking silky ringlets that made her feel beautiful. Unique—just as Chandale had predicted.

She'd worried that the makeup artist would slather layers of color on her face and eyes, but the result was sparing and gave her skin a polished glow. Oh, this was much better than reading the latest antics of Janet Evanovich's female bounty hunter! Although, she was convinced the impeccable French manicure would be ruined the moment she hit the beach.

She met Odette's gaze in the mirror, awaiting her

verdict. Odette had sat in a chair all afternoon with her hands folded delicately in her lap and her legs crossed at the ankles, observing the transformation with a critical eye. Rory had taken advantage of the opportunity to ask the publicist questions about her life in the hopes of becoming more comfortable with her. Although Odette had chosen her words carefully because their conversation was being overheard, she had revealed that she was a career woman, single and still hoping to meet the right man, and that she'd known her employer most of her life. Their families had taken Mediterranean cruises and enjoyed ski holidays together.

Though Odette provided slim details, Rory realized from the affection that laced the publicist's voice why Prince Laurent had appointed her to the task force of transforming Rory into a princess. Odette was a trusted member of the royal family's inner circle. She understood what was fully at stake for the marriage and she was determined to ensure that Rory meet her high level of expectations.

Which made it seem all the more unlikely that Odette had stolen the necklace. It was more logical that opposition to the marriage would come from within Estaire.

Odette still hadn't said one word.

Rory nervously fingered one of her silky ringlets and wished she were sharing this moment with her mother. "What do you think?"

Odette rose gracefully from her chair, an enigmatic smile tracing her lips. To Rory's surprise, the blonde squeezed her shoulder in a sisterly overture. "I think your fiancé will find you irresistible."

"Thank you." A bubble of relief popped inside Rory at the high praise. She wiggled her newly polished toes and couldn't help wondering if Sebastian would approve of the dramatic change in her appearance, then told herself to stop. It wasn't Sebastian who needed to approve.

She would give Prince Laurent a fair chance—if it killed her. But it would be much easier if she at least had a mental image to connect to the sparse personal information she was learning about him.

"Do you have a picture of *him?*" she asked Odette, hoping she would be more sympathetic to her request than Sebastian had been. She understood why Sebastian wanted her to focus on her lessons, but then, he also seemed to think there was nothing wrong with expecting her to marry a perfect stranger out of a sense of duty to a father she'd never met. She hoped Odette, who was waiting for the right man to come along, would understand her curiosity.

Odette blanched and turned away to retrieve her purse from a marble-topped console. "The car is waiting. You have a fitting with the stylist next on your schedule. Then a deportment lesson."

Rory grabbed her own purse and thanked the makeup artist, who presented her with a goodie bag containing the cosmetics she'd purchased. Clutching the bag, Rory raced to catch up with Odette in the galleria outside their private salon. She laid a hand on her arm. "Please."

Odette paused, her gray-green eyes indicating she was mulling over Rory's request. "I'll see what I can do."

Chapter Ten

"Follow me, sir. The princess is in the midst of a deportment lesson."

Laurent followed Pierce to the great room at a clipped pace, anxious to reassure himself that his princess was okay. He and Prince Olivier had thought of little else but the princess's safety all day. The police had retrieved five bullets from tree trunks and the wall of Rory's home, as well as five bullet casings. And they had tracked the shooter's path through the neighboring yards where some fingerprints had been found on a wrought-iron fence. The police had obtained fingerprint samples from the bodyguards to eliminate the possibility that a guard had left the prints while pursuing the shooter.

Under Heinrich's recommendation they had moved up the defensive-driving course and self-defense lessons in the princess's schedule. Laurent also thought she should be instructed in how to fire a gun in the event she ever needed to pick one up to defend herself.

The butler announced his arrival. Laurent barely heard the butler's voice. The corners of the vibrant-red room blurred as if he were viewing them through the flicker of a gas flame as he laid eyes on the stunning

young woman in the gossamer gold organza dress. She
would grace his side for the rest of his life. She teetered
across the room under Odette's coaching in a pair of
spike heels like a gosling learning to walk.

Her hair. It had always entranced him, but now a
surge of sexual need drove an impulse to catch a fistful
of those curls as he brought his mouth down on her lush
glossy lips. He had thought Rory beautiful before but
now he found her—

Without conscious volition, he drew back a step as if
some inner part of him instinctively recognized danger
and urged him to retreat. But the draw of the sexual
surge was as magnetic as the song of a siren to a
doomed vessel.

His abdomen tensed as Rory met his gaze with wide,
hyacinth eyes. Everything that had passed between them
last night flashed in his heart as she hobbled unsteadily
toward him. Laurent sensed disaster impending as her
spike heels wobbled, but finally her delicate ankles
straightened and she beamed at him.

Then she blushed.

Laurent remembered in vivid detail the feel of her
wet, pliant body and the hungry softness of her mouth.
She'd wanted him.

He trembled inside, unable to restrain the rampant
erotic images filling his mind.

Stiffly he bowed to her, struggling to keep the distance and formality he'd been trained to maintain at all
times. "Your Serene Highness. You are a sight to be-
hold." He failed miserably at shutting out the images.
He imagined peeling the filmy gold fabric from her
beautiful breasts. He imagined the taste of her in his
mouth.

"I'm flattered."

Laurent wanted the room cleared. He was iron hard with a need that demanded release.

Odette checked her diamond wristwatch. "We've nearly finished, Sebastian. Perhaps one more time across the room, madame? Imagine you are a ballet dancer and you are tapping your toes in front of you with each step. It's not a heel-toe motion as if you are wearing a sandal."

Rory shrugged. "Duty calls." She turned, wobbling precariously as she attempted to tap her toes as instructed.

Laurent feared for her ankles, but the sway of her sexy bottom as she strained to balance increased his desire.

"Perhaps we should consider a shoe with a lower heel," Odette murmured to Chandale. "She doesn't need the extra height."

Laurent discreetly shielded the front of his trousers with his hands as he observed Rory's progress. She was metamorphosing into a dazzling swan. "It will come," he assured both women confidently, even though he was sure his princess would always tread charmingly on his toes.

He glanced down at *her* toes, transfixed by the polished glow on her nails and by the tiny gold starfish that dangled from a chain circling her ankle.

His fingers craved to be as intimately close to her skin. "How is her wardrobe coming along?" he inquired in a passably neutral tone.

He sensed tension pass between Odette and Chandale.

Rory finished her walk without incident and propped her hands on her hips. A glow of pride illuminated her face. "It's in the works. I've made some choices that

I'm comfortable with, and Chandale has asked some designers to submit designs.''

Odette smoothed a finger along her brow as if smoothing away an imperfection in her makeup. Laurent knew that gesture well. His press secretary excelled at smoothing out problems before they snowballed into media crises. ''But of course they must meet with Sebastian's final approval for color and suitability,'' she said diplomatically, smiling at him for confirmation.

Laurent took the hint. Odette obviously perceived a problem with Rory's choices.

Rory pursed her glossy lips, and Laurent felt perspiration dampen his temples. ''I hardly think Sebastian's approval is required. The guidelines you and Renald provided me with were very clear. And you did say I would have an experienced lady's maid to help me make appropriate decisions.''

Odette smoothed her finger over her brow again.

While Laurent understood Odette's concerns, he was pleased to see his princess grasping the reins of her new role. ''As you wish, madame. If today's dress is any indication of your preferences, I'm confident you're on the right path. Now, if you ladies will excuse us, I am to escort Her Serene Highness to dinner with her brother.''

Even with Sebastian's praise washing over her, Rory knew she was going to break her neck in these shoes. Sebastian was looking at her as if she were a princess. And even though she worried she'd offended Odette, his display of confidence in her was worth the price.

Rory floated unsteadily in her shoes as Chandale handed her a gold-fringed silk shawl from a hanger and a gold dragonfly evening bag. She excused herself to powder her nose and rotate in front of a full-length mirror to ensure that all the details of her appearance were perfect and no embarrassing labels or price tags were showing as Odette had taught her in her deportment lesson. Odette had said that little trick would make her feel confident.

Looking at the stranger in the mirror, Rory did feel confident. Although she firmly told herself that she was going to give the marriage treaty due consideration, her heart was spinning around like a carnival ride at the prospect of being alone with Sebastian for a few minutes.

Take a deep breath. You're just nervous because you're going to ask him about the necklace, she told herself.

Liar, her reflection replied.

A balmy breeze tugged at her shawl and rippled through the trees, rattling palm fronds as Sebastian slowly escorted her out to the limo. Rory found it almost impossible to concentrate on tapping her toes when Sebastian's strong fingers were creating a disturbance on her elbow.

Determined to stay true to her mission, she broached the subject of the necklace as soon as they were settled in the buttery soft backseat of the limo. "So much has happened in the last few days, I haven't had a chance to ask you if you'd found out any information about my father's necklace."

"Forgive me, madame. I made some inquiries yesterday and received a fax at the hotel this afternoon. Apparently, your father commissioned the necklace from a Swiss jeweler ten years ago. Then the necklace was kept in storage with the crown jewels of Estaire."

"What's the jeweler's name?" she asked.

"I have it here." He passed her the fax. "I hope this

settles any doubts you may have about your brother's sincerity.''

Rory took the paper and wondered if she was making a mistake in not telling him what she intended to do with the information. But before she pointed an accusing finger and created a rift of suspicion between two already feuding countries, she needed substantial proof. ''Thank you.''

However, she saw no reason why she couldn't share her suspicions with him about the customer at the bookstore.

Haltingly, she told him about her encounter with the blond man with the French accent and how the bag of books he'd bought had been found in the street. ''I'm probably being paranoid, but I went surfing this morning and a blond man sideswiped me and knocked me off my board.'' She hesitated, not certain how much to tell Sebastian. A fierce glower was rising in his inky eyes. ''I can't be sure because I didn't get a good enough look at him, but he might be the same man.''

''Where were your bodyguards when this occurred?'' Sebastian asked in a low, dangerous tone that suggested heads were about to roll.

Rory gulped. No one was going to get fired because she'd chosen to ditch them. ''I didn't take them with me or tell them I was leaving. I wanted—I needed to be alone. This is all so overwhelming. I just needed some space. And when I'm on the water, I feel like I'm in control.''

Sebastian's eyes studied her face. Rory felt a chill, unable to guess what he was thinking. ''And were you in control when this man sideswiped you?'' he asked brusquely.

"Yes and no," she admitted. "I had trouble with my leash."

At his puzzled expression, she explained. "It's a cord that you attach to your ankle to keep you from losing your board. It got caught on something. When I was trying to release it, something bumped into me. The man—or his board—I'm not sure." Her voice trembled. "But I was scared and I was running out of air. By the time I was free, he was already being helped off the beach by the Windansea rats."

"Rats?"

"Local surfers. They're protective about people who horn in on their breaks without following proper etiquette."

"So someone else saw this man? Other witnesses?"

Rory knew he was thinking the man could be her assassin and that she was lucky she had survived without harm. "Yes. But I can do you one better than that." She whipped the copy of the sales receipt from her purse. "I know his name and I even have his credit card number."

"What is his name?"

"Claude Dupont."

To Rory's astonishment, Sebastian lifted a telephone and spoke to the driver. "Stop the car. Now!"

CLAUDE DUPONT. Marielle's brother. Laurent felt ill as the name wormed through him like a fatal poison.

Claude had been on the yacht the night Marielle had overdosed. Had he taken it upon himself to avenge his sister's suicide by attacking the women Laurent showed an interest in? Or was someone trying to pin Rory's murder on Dupont?

Laurent took the sales receipt from Rory's hand and

squeezed her chilled fingers. *Gott sei Dank!* Thank God she had escaped harm this morning at the beach. He would never forgive himself if he lost her. His princess was becoming far more precious to him than he knew was wise.

The rear door opened and Heinrich joined them on the facing seat. *"Ja?"* he asked Laurent.

Laurent explained what had happened and showed Heinrich the sales receipt with Dupont's signature on it. If Heinrich immediately recognized the name, he was too professional to give any indication of that in front of Princess Charlotte Aurora.

"These books you mention. This Dupont touched them?"

"Yes," Rory said. "We put them aside in case he returns to the store for them."

Heinrich nodded. *"Gut.* His fingerprints will be on these books. We can ask the police to compare them to the fingerprints they found on the fence after the incident last night."

"The police?" Rory rounded on Laurent. Her voice rose. "You called the police and they found fingerprints? And you didn't tell me?"

"It was not your concern. You have more important matters requiring your attention."

"Someone is trying to kill me and you don't think I want to know that some evidence was found? I'm not a Barbie doll who can't think for herself. Granted, leaving the house this morning without protection was not the smartest decision I've ever made, but I'm the one who brought you this receipt. I want to be kept informed."

"You are not a Barbie doll, madame. I apologize if I led you to believe that I considered your position ornamental in nature. I'm afraid that threats to a member of a royal family are commonplace. Heinrich is working with the police to handle the matter as expediently as possible and to see that the perpetrator is identified and apprehended. Prince Olivier was informed immediately.''

"Well, that makes it all better—you told my brother! How patriarchal!'' Her blue eyes narrowed dangerously. "I think I need to have a talk with my brother, but I'm not finished with you.''

Laurent's lips thinned. He did not need to defend his decisions to anyone except his father, the king.

Rory waggled a slender finger in front of his nose. "What happens on my property, to me, is *my* concern. This man killed my mother. I want to help.''

He stared down his nose at her finger. His mother, in all her life, had never dared raise a finger or speak in such a manner to his father. "Your mother would wish to see you protected.'' He captured her finger. "As do I.''

She gasped, her eyes widening as a frisson of awareness spontaneously combusted between them at his touch. She jerked her finger away, her eyes glittering with the brilliant fire of sapphires. "I'm not a child. I can protect myself.''

Laurent dropped his hand to his thigh, his fingers clenched. She was not being reasonable. "You are made of flesh and blood. You could die and I would never be able to live with myself,'' he said far more harshly than he meant, his patience at an end. He was reminded that her mother with her romantic ideals of equality and love had not lasted more than two years in the Estairian court.

Even though his own mother had foolishly loved his

father and had suffered from his unfaithfulness, she'd at least fulfilled her duty.

But because he feared Rory might do something ill-advised like go off again without her bodyguards, he added, "I will refrain from going into specific details, but there have been two other incidents involving women whom Prince Laurent has seen socially."

Rory paled. "What? This has happened before?"

"It is difficult to determine if these events are related or coincidence. But one woman died under suspicious circumstances. Her last name was Dupont."

"Oh, my God!"

"We are not leaping to conclusions," Laurent reminded her. "We are going to let the experts handle the matter."

Heinrich nodded vigorously. "If I may, sir. If this credit card is legitimate, it may tell us a great deal about this Claude Dupont and where we can find him."

Rory frowned. "What do you mean *if* it's legitimate?"

"It could be a fake or a stolen identity," Heinrich explained. "Someone could be setting up Dupont.

"If I could obtain a picture of Claude Dupont, Your Serene Highness, could you assist me in showing it to the surfers who were at the beach this morning?"

"Of course."

"*Gut.* With your permission, then, I will accompany you to your place of work tomorrow to pick up these books and request the police run any prints they find through Interpol." Heinrich carefully removed a glass from the minibar and instructed Rory to grip it with her right hand so the police would be able to identify any fingerprints that might be hers. He preserved the glass in a motion-sickness bag, then repeated the procedure with Rory's left hand.

They were almost at the hotel. As the limo pulled up at the rear entrance, Laurent met Rory's defiant gaze and realized worriedly that his princess would not bow to his every command. He found her independent nature both a source of consternation and admiration. "Heinrich has suggested that you receive some immediate instruction in self-defense training. Are you amenable to that?"

"Of course," she said indignantly.

"Then you will begin tomorrow."

Laurent's chest tightened as he waited for the all-clear signal that it was safe to depart the vehicle. His fingers protectively circled Rory's elbow as he hustled her out of the limo and into the hotel. He saw the concentration in his princess's beautiful face as she struggled to walk with dignity in those shoes. Somehow he felt events were moving far beyond his control.

ODETTE DISCREETLY ENTERED the salon of Prince Laurent's suite and found him standing at the window, gazing out at the bay, his back to her. Only one lamp illuminated the salon, casting a puddle of light on the desk where he rigorously attended to his royal duties.

She hesitated to disturb him when he was seeking a moment of solitude from his work. He was stripped to the waist, a snifter of brandy clasped in his elegant fingers.

She trembled, her heart tightening with suppressed fury at the pale bandages gleaming against his bronzed skin. Twice in one week they had almost lost him—all because of this American princess.

She wondered if he was thinking of her now. Odette

knew her prince well. Knew that even though he fought it, he desired Princess Charlotte Aurora. Perhaps was even falling in love with her. Tonight, when he'd arrived to escort her to dinner, he'd looked at her as if she were the only woman in the room. Odette had only once before seen Laurent behave like this—with Marielle.

And he'd been oblivious then, too, to the ways that women schemed. His precious Marielle had plotted behind his back. Just as Princess Charlotte Aurora schemed now.

Odette knew where *her* loyalty lay. With Laurent. "Am I intruding, *Königliche Hoheit,* Your Royal Highness?"

She saw the fatigue and the worry etched in his handsome features as he faced her. He took his duties so seriously. She knew sometimes that he could not sleep and spent lonely hours deep in thought or with his books.

"Not at all," he said. "I assume this concerns Princess Charlotte Aurora's wardrobe?" He held up a hand. "She will learn best from her own mistakes."

Odette smiled softly. He possessed all the qualities of a great king: wisdom, compassion, strength. "*Nein,* that is not what brings me here. But I will hold your philosophy in mind." She stepped farther into the richly furnished room. Prince Laurent set down his snifter of brandy and reached for his black silk dressing robe, draped over the back of the desk chair.

"*Bitte,* don't trouble yourself," she bade him. "I know the stitches in your back pain you. We are alone."

"*Danke.*" He left the robe on the back of the chair.

"The Princess asked me today if I could give her a picture of you. I was not sure how to respond."

His noble brow furrowed. "How did you reply?"

"I told her that I would see what I could do."

"She is curious. If her curiosity is satisfied she will concentrate more on her lessons. Give her a photo of my brother Leopold."

"You're sure? If I may speak freely, she does not strike me as a woman who appreciates dishonesty."

She felt a prick of alarm when his shoulders stiffened. Had she gone too far in questioning his judgment? The lines furrowed deeper in the corners of his mouth, and his jaw set with false conviction. "She will understand my reasons. She is not ready to meet her fiancé face-to-face."

"As you wish." Odette wished him good-night and left him to his solitude. Men were such fools.

RENALD JERKED AWAKE at the sound of Odette Schoenfeldt's voice on the sensitive listening device. He checked his watch. What was she doing in Prince Laurent's private rooms at one o'clock in the morning? Was the playboy prince sleeping with his press secretary?

Renald thought that little suspicion might well come in handy. He noted the date and the hour. Leaked to the right tabloids, this information could fuel a rat's nest of allegations that might make Princess Charlotte Aurora and Prince Olivier reconsider the wisdom of this marriage.

CLAUDE DUPONT was a desperate man on a mission. It was 3:00 a.m., and the shops of La Jolla Cove were darkened, the streets deserted beneath a crescent moon dangling high in the star-studded sky.

The ocean, obscured by the shops, rumbled and sighed as his deck shoes slapped on the pavement.

He had tried to make contact with Princess Charlotte

Aurora three times now. Tried to save her from Prince Laurent. But there had been no mention in the media of a man being shot or fatally wounded on Neptune Place.

He'd missed his opportunity and nearly got caught. He'd failed Marielle again. Just as he'd failed to listen to his sister that night on the yacht. He'd been too preoccupied with finding a girl to share his bed, and he'd seen Marielle go off with a girlfriend. She'd had a shoulder to cry on. He'd thought she would be okay.

Remorse weighed on his chest and shoulders. For three years he'd wished he could relive that night.

He reached the door to the Book Nook and slid an envelope into the brass mail slot.

This had to work. He couldn't allow the marriage to take place.

RORY WENT TO BED angry and couldn't sleep. Her dinner with her brother was strained. Like Sebastian, her brother, Olivier, seemed to be living in the Dark Ages and actually thought he had a right to make decisions for her. He'd given her a brotherly kiss and suggested they learn to understand each other's ways.

"One is not right and the other wrong, *ma petite soeur*. They are just different." Then he'd explained that according to the laws of Estaire, she must seek his permission in writing to take on public duties, to marry, to divorce and to resign all rights to the succession of the throne.

Rory tossed and turned over the injustice of it until Brontë mewled with concern and hobbled over the sheets to nest herself against Rory's stomach. She buried her fingers into her pet's silken fur. "Sorry to bother you, girl."

Brontë grumbled throatily as if saying, ''Pet me and I'll forgive you.''

Rory debated finding a pen and paper and resigning her claim to succession of the throne of Estaire right now. Her mother had been murdered and someone was trying to kill her. Sebastian had as much as told her that even if the police caught her mother's killer, there would always be other threats. What kind of life was that?

It was the life she would have known if her parents hadn't separated, she thought miserably. She'd have been raised with the responsibility of knowing she might one day rule Estaire. Or be expected to make a sacrifice for her country by making a politically strategic marriage.

Rory hugged Brontë, feeling more pressure than she'd ever known.

RORY HAD EXPECTED Heinrich to accompany her to work in the morning, but not Sebastian. Funny, how she could be annoyed as hell with him and still find him drop-dead gorgeous. He wore a perfectly tailored black suit that fit him like a delectable coating of dark chocolate. His shirt was a dazzling white and his burgundy-and-black silk tie was a power statement.

He looked hot. Hard and composed, not a care evident in his aristocratic features as he greeted her cordially. She wanted to pull him into the shower, suit and all.

After her sleepless night, she wasn't in the mood to be reminded that her feelings for Sebastian were inappropriate. He was Prince Laurent's deputy secretary. She groaned inwardly as the rich timbre of his voice bewitched every hormone in her body with a desire to run her fingers through his thick dark hair.

She'd done her best to apply her makeup as she'd been instructed yesterday, but her eyes looked puffy and she wasn't satisfied with the results. At least Pierce and Alice had reorganized the kitchen cupboards yesterday and found her vitamins. She'd dutifully eaten the breakfast Alice had prepared, even though she wasn't hungry, and swallowed a vitamin.

How could Sebastian behave as if nothing was wrong? She felt as if she had just lost her new best friend. At least Heinrich had encouraging news to share, though his expression was guarded. Rory assumed there was a rule against smiling on duty.

"Dupont's credit card seems to be legitimate, and the police are checking with hotels in the area. I have been promised a copy of his passport photo today or tomorrow at the latest."

As the bodyguard preceded them to the limo, Rory whispered pointedly to Sebastian, "I'm glad someone around here is respecting my desire to be treated like an equal."

Sebastian speared her with a harsh look that jolted her to her soul. He opened his mouth to say something, then snapped it shut, a muscle flexing visibly in his jaw.

She wanted to apologize. Deep in her heart she knew he was being a gentleman and pretending that nothing awkward had happened between them. But she was hurt and confused and she'd wanted to rumple him. She'd never met a man who'd affected her this way.

A strained silence stretched between them in the car. She wanted to tell him about her mother's letters to her father and somehow regain that same level of intimacy they'd shared last night before he'd kissed her and called her his Lorelei, but she knew it wouldn't be wise.

She would follow his example and maintain a cordial distance between them. Maybe if she could convince him to show her a picture of Prince Laurent, she could replace Sebastian's face and body with the image of the man she was destined to marry.

When the limo pulled up outside the Book Nook, Rory hoped that Sebastian would stay in the car, but he stepped out onto the curb as if the world were at his command.

She sighed and dug her keys out of her purse.

She unlocked the door. The bell jingled merrily as she shoved the door open. She bent down to pick up a large manila envelope on the floor.

Rory flipped the envelope over, expecting to see a postage stamp. Someone had printed with a black marker: ''For Your Info.'' That was odd. Rory hit the light switch, flooding the shop with light.

''Where are the books?'' Heinrich asked.

''There, right behind the counter.''

Sebastian followed Heinrich, his hands clasped behind him as he paused to peer more closely at a book display.

Rory smiled. You could always tell a book lover. She slid a finger underneath the gummed flap and tore open the envelope. It contained newspaper clippings. For a moment she thought of Otto Gascon. He was always bringing in book reviews.

But these weren't book reviews. Rory's heart froze as she looked at the top clipping and saw the photograph. Sebastian's handsome face was captured in profile—each aristocratic line edged with light, his gaze hooded as he lifted the hand of a beautiful brunette to his lips. The brunette smiled demurely up at him as if she had a secret, her almond-shaped eyes clearly adoring.

The headline read: Crown Prince Implicated in Lover's Death.

Rory forced her gaze to the caption beneath the photograph. Her frozen heart thunked to her toes and broke. The couple in the photograph were identified as Prince Laurent of Ducharme and Marielle Dupont.

Her fingers crumpled the clippings as she swallowed the bitter truth. Sebastian wasn't the deputy secretary. He was her prince.

And he'd lied to her.

Chapter Eleven

Rory trembled with shock.

Discovering that Sebastian was the prince she was destined to marry should have been wonderful news. She was halfway in love with him and she knew that he desired her.

But he had deliberately misrepresented himself and not told her who he was. And he had been in love with Marielle Dupont.

Rory ignored the shard of pain that had lodged in her breast at the first sight of the headline. Maybe there was a reasonable explanation for Sebastian/Laurent's actions.

She scanned the opening paragraphs of the article:

Weeks after shipping heiress Marielle Dupont, 25, was found dead on her family's yacht after consuming an overdose of the drug popularly known as Ecstasy, authorities are still closemouthed about what role Crown Prince Laurent of Ducharme may have played in his lover's death.

The couple had been dating three years, leading gossip rags to speculate that a royal marriage might be in the offing for Ducharme's playboy prince.

Rumors abound that Prince Laurent supplied Ms. Dupont with the drugs. Witnesses attending the party on the yacht the night Marielle Dupont died claim that the couple had been involved in a lover's spat earlier in the evening and Prince Laurent left suddenly. One witness, who requested her name be withheld, suggested Marielle Dupont had committed suicide because she'd learned the prince was seeing another woman.

Rory peeked at the headlines of the other articles. They speculated on whether Marielle Dupont's death was an accident, a suicide or manslaughter.

She'd read enough. Her fingers were devoid of feeling. "Heinrich, could you please wait outside? I need a moment alone with *Prince Laurent.* Several moments, in fact. You have time to go for coffee."

Sebastian's, or rather, Laurent's head snapped up as he swiveled around and pegged her with a steely gaze. He swore under his breath in German. "Rory—"

She held up a hand, stopping him. "Please."

Rory followed Heinrich to the door on rubbery sea legs and locked it after him, checking to make sure the closed sign was facing out. Not that it mattered. Heinrich stood sentinel in front of the door, blocking the sign with his massive body. She glanced back at Laurent and her stomach lurched.

Oh, God, she wasn't sure she wanted to have this conversation. He looked so intimidating. She wasn't sure she wanted answers to the wariness that streaked his inky eyes like jagged flashes of lightning.

Then she remembered that although he was a prince, he was still a man.

He ran his thumb along his jaw. "How did you know?"

"These." She fanned out the articles. "They were in the envelope at the door. They're articles about Marielle Dupont's death. There's a picture of the two of you together. Someone obviously believed they contained information I needed to know." She laughed uneasily. "They were right."

"Claude, no doubt." Laurent blinked. Rory recognized it for a wince of pain—an attempt to maintain rigid control of his emotions. "We had words at Marielle's funeral, but he was grieving. I didn't take them seriously."

Rory rattled the articles warningly. "I'm waiting for an explanation as to why you lied to me."

He took a step toward her.

"I would really prefer you stay where you are," Rory said, her voice shaking. "Now, enlighten me."

He sighed and Rory felt a deep penetrating chill as if the California sun would never warm her again. "Much of it you already know. Your brother and I were concerned about your safety in light of the treaty. Marielle's death was very odd. She did not abuse her body with drugs."

"The article says you'd had an argument that night."

He nodded, his eyes stark with grief. "I severed our relationship. She was beginning to have expectations that I knew I could never fulfill. It wasn't fair to let her hope that I would propose. I told her I was already betrothed. I felt she deserved to know the truth."

Rory stared at him in disbelief. "You loved her and you ended your relationship, anyway?"

"Yes."

"But you loved her," she protested.

He swallowed, his posture as inflexible as a bronze statue. "Love has little to do with a royal marriage."

Ah, yes. Duty. Rory finally understood. He'd severed his relationship with Marielle out of duty. And he intended to go through with the marriage treaty with her out of the same sense of duty.

She felt sick. "The article suggests she may have committed suicide."

"Newspaper and magazine articles suggest many things. Marielle was understandably upset, but I don't believe she would take drugs—or deliberately commit suicide."

"What do you think happened that night?"

"I think someone put the Ecstasy in her drink without her knowledge."

Rory hugged herself. "Why?"

"Either one of my own countrymen viewed her as a threat to my commitment to the treaty or an Estairian wished to discredit me in your brother's eyes and hoped that he would call off our marriage. I had no proof— only suspicions. But my suspicions grew last year when a fashion designer whom I was dating was assaulted by a woman with a knife in the ladies' room of a club we were visiting. Fortunately Nathalie did not suffer serious injury, but her attacker was never caught."

"Oh, my God!"

His eyes bored into her, fiercely determined. Primal. "You could see why I was concerned for your safety. Olivier and I thought it would be safer if I traveled to meet you as part of his staff. We kept our plans as secret as possible, but obviously there is a leak in our security."

Rory decided now was not the time to mention the theft of the necklace. She wanted to know the whole truth first. "That still doesn't explain why you passed yourself off as your deputy secretary."

"I should think that would be obvious."

"Humor me. Spell it out."

He inclined his proud head. "You'd just discovered that you had a brother and a family history of which you were unaware. I thought it more important for you to establish a relationship with him and gain confidence in your status as a princess. You were under enough pressure without the added stress of being courted by a fiancé." He moved toward her, his eyes softening. "And while I had not anticipated this benefit, meeting you as Sebastian has allowed us to know each other as individuals. That is the basis of any partnership."

Rory held her ground. "I would think honesty is the foundation of any partnership," she said flatly.

"I had every intention of telling you when I felt you were ready." His tone gentled with the intimacy that she'd longed for this morning when he'd greeted her. "And I assure you that I have answered the questions you have posed to me about Prince Laurent with the utmost honesty. You know me as no one else ever has."

"But I said things... I did things—" She halted abruptly, blushing, as she remembered the way she'd begged him to take off her clothes and make love to her.

Huskiness seeped into his European accent. "I found nothing you said or did in any way offensive, Lorelei."

Lorelei. Goose bumps rasped over her arms. Laurent's gaze swept to her mouth as if he intended to kiss her.

She stepped back. He was two yards from her, but that was two yards too close. It was hard to think rationally when her heart was fluttering as if it wanted to escape her rib cage. She wet her lips, hungry for the taste of his mouth and the feel of his arms around her.

But no, she couldn't forget that he'd given up the woman he'd loved because of his obligation to marry her. Did she really want to give her heart to a man who didn't believe love had a place in their marriage?

"Somehow I'm not comforted being compared to a siren who lures men to their doom."

He chuckled.

It was the most dangerous sound Rory had ever heard.

"Ah, but you do lure me with your mind—and your body—and I am helpless to resist."

Her scalp prickled. A bonfire of warmth ignited in her belly, threatening her resolve. But misgivings crowded her heart. He was attracted to her. But he would never allow himself to love her, just as he'd never allowed himself a future with Marielle. She knew his duty to his crown would always guide his actions.

Could she really spend the rest of her life with a man who would never love her?

For three days, Rory felt the tension crackle between her and Laurent. Now that his secret was out, she addressed him formally in front of the staff, though he had asked her to continue calling him Sebastian, which was his second name, in the few moments when they were alone. Just as she had asked him to call her Rory to remember who she was, he'd told her that he felt the same need to be called Sebastian.

She suspected it was a trick to court her. He needed this marriage. His father had been quoted as saying that he would not allow his son to take over the monarchy until he was married and settled with children.

But as angry as Rory was at Laurent for lying to her,

for arrogantly making decisions on her behalf, a part of her craved to know him more intimately. Craved to share his pain and the inner workings of his mind. Craved to call him by a name that no one else had the privilege to use—especially not Marielle.

It ate at her that Laurent had loved the shipping heiress. She'd read the articles in the envelope many times over. Heinrich had wanted to check them for fingerprints, but Rory only gave him the envelope.

Heinrich had a passport photo of Claude Dupont. His hair was cut short, but Rory was sure it was the same man who'd entered her store. She'd gone down to the beach with Heinrich on Thursday morning and showed the photo to the two Windansea rats who'd ousted the rogue surfer from the beach. The rats thought it could be the same man, but weren't one hundred percent certain.

Rory hoped the police would find where Claude Dupont was staying and arrest him soon. Even when she'd been down at the beach with Heinrich, she'd felt as if someone was watching her.

Working at the Book Nook on Thursday had been so nerve-racking that she'd handed in her notice, effective immediately, at the end of her shift. She'd told Tom that she'd learned she had a brother in Europe and she was going to meet him. But the truth was, she felt like a sitting duck in the store and she was terrified an innocent customer might get hurt in the crossfire.

She still hadn't told her brother or Laurent about the necklace. She'd hoped to enlist Otto's assistance in purchasing an exact replica on Thursday when he came into the bookstore, but Franz was in the store when Otto arrived and she couldn't talk privately. She'd have to figure out another way to talk to Otto.

So instead of working on Friday, Rory took self-defense lessons in the morning, learning how to evade grabs and block blows with her arms until her bones throbbed and her skin bore bruises. She spent the afternoon at a firing range learning how to fire an assortment of loaded guns. She learned how to hold her body in the Weaver stance and verify if a firearm had a safety before she pulled the trigger. But she couldn't even hit the target. The noise and the smell of gunpowder made her sick. She hoped she would never have to shoot someone.

That night Heinrich informed her that the police had lifted fingerprints from the envelope that matched the fingerprints they had found on her neighbor's fence after the shooting. Unfortunately, Interpol didn't have Claude Dupont's fingerprints on file. But the police had issued a warrant for Claude's arrest.

Saturday morning she was given a break from her lessons. She took Olivier and their entourage of body-guards skating at Mission Beach. It was fun. She bought her new sister-in-law a California bikini with a matching sarong, board shorts and a T-shirt for Olivier, and muscle shirts for the bodyguards. Spending the morning laughing with Olivier made her realize how much they'd missed out on over the years. She was reluctant to see him go on Wednesday, but she didn't want him to miss his appointment at the fertility clinic.

Once her brother left, she'd be alone with Laurent. Would he court her? Or would he continue to maintain his distance? He'd held himself aloof the past three days.

Rory endured more self-defense lessons on Saturday afternoon. Her arms were black-and-blue, and she tripped herself more frequently than she tripped her at-

tacker, but Heinrich was relentless. With enough prac-
tice, he assured her the movements would become in-
stinctive and she would feel more sure of herself.

That night Rory had a nightmare. Someone grabbed
her by the shoulder during a walkabout. Without thinking, she gripped her attacker's arm and slammed them
onto the hard sidewalk, only to realize she'd assaulted
an arthritic elderly woman wanting an autograph.

By 5:30 a.m. Sunday, she was wide awake and dread-
ing the defensive-driving lessons on her schedule for
this morning. She had images of crashing the car. She
wished she could go surfing, but with Claude Dupont
still at large, she settled for fifty laps in the pool. She
was taking her vitamin with a glass of orange juice
when Pierce announced that Prince Laurent had arrived.

Rory told herself to breathe and went into the great
room. She hadn't seen Laurent yesterday.

She greedily took in his appearance. For the first time
since they'd met, Prince Laurent was dressed casually
in jeans and a navy-blue polo shirt. But even beneath
the casual clothes she sensed his rigid control.

Her heart jolted with uncertainty as she met his inky
gaze. "I wasn't expecting you this morning."

"Since I'll be staying with you for a few weeks, I
thought I might benefit from the instruction, too."

"A few weeks?" This was the first she'd heard of it.

"You still have much to learn. And I had hoped that
we could spend more time together. I would like to see
more of your home through your eyes. Just as I hope to
show you more of my home."

Rory wondered how his words could melt her de-
fenses as if she were made of wax. He was offering her
a partnership built on mutual understanding and respect.
It was the most irresistible offer she'd ever been made.

Without realizing it, Laurent was giving her glimpses into his mind, into his heart, into his soul. It wasn't nearly enough. She wanted so much more from him. But she foolishly let herself hope this might be a beginning.

THIS WAS INSANE. Rory sat behind the wheel of the Beemer and waited for the next simulation to begin. The driving school had a test area that was similar to a movie set. Building facades lined a Main Street that was several blocks long. There were signal intersections and four-way stops, parking lots, even a highway and something called a skid pad.

Rory felt strangely shaky. They'd begun the lesson with how to get into her vehicle. The most vulnerable time for a carjacking was upon entering or leaving a car. When she'd climbed into her assigned car, a man had risen out of the back seat and pressed a phony gun to her head.

And some people thought being a princess was all about wearing a tiara.

In the second lesson, a car bumped her rear bumper when she was driving down a side street. Her heart jumped at the unexpected impact. Instead of stopping, she drove to the phony town's police department and earned high praise for avoiding being the victim of a bump and rob.

In the last simulation a car had come up close behind her, weaving dangerously. She'd pulled over to let the car pass, but the instructor told her via the headset she wore that she should have made a right turn as soon as possible to get out of harm's way.

Rory closed her eyes, overwhelmed by fatigue. Having cars come at her from all directions and attackers popping out of the back seat was unnerving and ex-hausting.

A peculiar pressure built in her chest as the instructor told her to turn onto the test highway and accelerate to forty miles per hour.

God, what next?

Rory soon discovered what came next.

A car approached her on the highway test strip from the opposite direction. To her dismay, the car crossed the center line and barreled toward her.

Rory jerked the wheel to the right to avoid a collision, but her fingers weren't functioning properly.

"That's it," she heard the instructor coach her in her ear. "Pull off the road steadily without losing con-trol—"

"I can't—" Rory experienced sheer horror as her body quit obeying her brain. She couldn't brake. Her mind went black as the BMW swerved out of control and started to roll.

"RORY!" LAURENT'S HEART pitched in horror as her car went off the pavement and flipped over in slow mo-tion, raising a cloud of dust. Once. Twice.

He heard the ominous crunch of steel and crackling glass and saw smoke billow from the engine.

"Call an ambulance!" He ran toward the car, praying it wouldn't explode. It came to a groaning stop on its roof, its wheels spinning crazily in the air. They had to get her out of there.

The track's techs beat him to the car with a stretcher. They had the door open. Rory hung like a rag doll from her seat belt, pinned in place by the airbag. Her eyes were closed. Blood trickled down her left arm and dripped from her fingers.

The techs eased her out of the car and laid her on the stretcher. Laurent helped them carry her a safe distance from the vehicle.

A tech leaned over her. "She's not breathing."

Laurent squeezed her lifeless hand as one of the techs began artificial respiration. "Breathe, Lorelei. We are not finished yet."

The techs exchanged worried looks. Tears slid onto Laurent's cheeks. "Stay with me, Lorelei. I can't lose you, too." He pressed her hand to his mouth and kissed it, tasting her blood on his lips.

He saw Marielle's body in a satin-lined coffin.

Not again. Please, not again.

Chapter Twelve

Laurent rode in the ambulance with Rory to the hospital, the sirens clamoring in his ears. He reluctantly surrendered her into the care of the emergency room personnel, demanding that she receive the best care available. The top specialists. Whatever was required. Cost was no object. And he insisted that Heinrich remain with her for protection.

A nurse gave him forms to fill out. He did his best, but he didn't know her medical history or whether she was on any medications. He'd clenched the pen so tightly it snapped in his grip.

He and Olivier had pushed her too hard, expected too much. They should have waited to tell her about the marriage treaty until after she'd grown accustomed to the shock of learning she was a princess. It was too much pressure. Although how else would they have explained the threats to her life?

When Olivier rushed into the waiting room accompanied by Renald and two bodyguards half an hour later, there was still no news from the doctors. Olivier was pale beneath his tan. "*Qu'est-ce qui se passe?* What's happening? I want to see her."

Laurent massaged the tight muscles in his neck. "I haven't been told anything."

"She is breathing on her own, *non?*"

Laurent shared the stark fear he saw in Olivier's eyes. "I don't know."

Olivier frowned and wiped his face with his hand in an impatient gesture. "You said she lost control of the car? I should never have allowed her to take such a course. It was too dangerous—"

"Sebastian Guimond?"

"Yes?" Laurent, Olivier and Renald turned simultaneously. A doctor, finally!

The doctor eyed the three men. "Are you family?"

Laurent took charge. "I am Ms. Kenilworth's fiancé and this is her brother. Mr. Dartois is a family retainer."

"She's very lucky to be alive. She's alert and breathing on her own."

Relief sapped the strength from Laurent's body.

Rory was alive!

"She says she blacked out while she was driving," the doctor continued. "We're running some tests. We suspect she may have overdosed on narcotics as her pupils were very small when she arrived. Other than the scalp laceration, there are no other internal injuries to cause her to be unconscious. Has she taken any medications this morning? Or eaten anything?"

Laurent was stunned. Drugs again? He instructed Renald to call the house and ask the servants what Rory had eaten.

Renald discreetly stepped away to make the call.

"We're running some tests," the doctor continued. "We've stitched up the head wound. The stitches will need to be removed in about a week."

"May we take her home soon?" Olivier asked.

The doctor hesitated. "We'd prefer to observe her overnight to make sure she has no other injuries."

Renald returned. "Ms. Kenilworth had a glass of orange juice, two slices of whole wheat toast and a vitamin this morning. She takes a vitamin every morning. Pierce didn't know if it was important, but he felt he should mention that Ms. Kenilworth noticed the bottle was missing after the dinner party the other night. He found it in a kitchen cupboard after a thorough search."

Laurent knew Olivier was thinking the same thing he was. The vitamins had been tampered with. It wasn't safe for Rory to remain in her home.

The doctor frowned. "I'd like to see this bottle of vitamins."

Renald nodded. "I'll have it delivered immediately."

"May we see her?" Laurent demanded, unable to control his anxiety.

"Of course. Only two of you, for a few minutes."

They followed the doctor into an exam room. Heinrich stood guard at the foot of Rory's bed.

"Tu m'as fait peur, ma petite soeur," Olivier scolded gently, approaching Rory's hospital gurney. He kissed her affectionately. "You gave us a scare. But Laurent assures me the car looks worse."

Rory laughed, the sound of her laughter immediately lifting Laurent's spirits. "Is he here?"

"Where else would I be?" Chaotic emotion stirred in his chest at his first sight of her.

Her blue eyes were enormous in her pale face. She looked frail, her body tucked beneath a yellow blanket. Her amber curls fanned over the white pillow and a bandage was taped to her left temple. The nurse had not done a proper job of cleaning the blood from her face.

Laurent threaded his fingers through hers as he tenderly kissed her brow.

Rory caught her lower lip between her teeth. Tears swam in her eyes. "I was so scared I was going to die! The doctor said I'd been drugged. But how?"

Laurent gathered her in his arms and inhaled the sweet scent of her hair. She was shaking. "We think it was your vitamins."

His throat ached. Despite all the security precautions and the bodyguards, he'd failed to keep her safe. Cold dread surfaced in his thoughts like scum on a pond. The killer wouldn't stop until Rory was dead. If he didn't call off the marriage treaty, his princess might die.

But Laurent couldn't bring himself to say the words that would sever their relationship, and his reasons had nothing to do with politics or the feud. His father had not raised him to be a servant to fear. Even though he knew that Prince Olivier would ensure that Rory received the highest level of protection, Laurent couldn't walk away from his sense of personal obligation to her. "We're relocating you and Brontë to other quarters until this person is caught. And we're not accepting any objections. You are outvoted two to one. Is that clear?"

Rory recognized a command when she heard one. She withdrew from the comforting strength of Laurent's shoulder. The shaking stopped when he held her. He gave her a strength she'd never known she possessed. "Absolutely clear," she stated quietly. "But my vote is the only one that counts."

She looked from Laurent to her brother and set her chin mulishly. Her head hurt, her body throbbed and she felt nauseous, but she was determined. Someone close to her brother or to Laurent had stolen her necklace and was probably in league with her assassin. Rory preferred to catch the mole on her own turf. ''I'm not going to be chased out of my home.''

Her gaze shifted to Heinrich. ''Throw out everything consumable in the house—medicines, food, even the cleaning supplies and paper products. And search every square inch of the place for more booby traps. I want everything in the house cleaned—from the doorknobs down to the last spoon. Whoever is trying to kill me is obviously very clever.''

As soon as she was released, Rory was going to see Otto. He was fluent in French and German. He could help her purchase a copy of the necklace from the Swiss jeweller. Then she would set her own trap.

RORY HAD TO WAIT until Tuesday morning to execute her plan. She'd been released from the hospital Monday morning and had spent the day resting and supervising Pierce and Alice as they carried out her orders to thoroughly cleanse her home, room by room.

Her blood tests had shown traces of opiates. The hospital lab had examined her vitamins for the presence of opiates but came up empty. Heinrich wasn't surprised. He didn't think a professional hit man would leave evidence behind. The doctor had told him that a large dose of morphine hidden in a gel capsule would be strong enough to make her lose consciousness.

Rory was glad for another reprieve from her lessons—even if only for a day. Her temple was swollen and her stitches still throbbed. Laurent and Olivier had hovered over her protectively, the two of them making a tour of the house and grounds with Heinrich. Rory felt guilty for plotting to deceive them. But she didn't change her mind.

When Laurent arrived Tuesday morning to review her

schedule for the day, she told him that she would like to skip her French lesson to go and buy her brother a painting of La Jolla as a parting gift, since he was leaving the next day.

Laurent was hesitant. "I'll grant your request and advise Heinrich of the change in plans. In future, you might wish to give your staff more advance notice. The French tutor will be compensated for the inconvenience."

"I'm sorry," Rory said, uncomfortably meeting his gaze. "I only thought of it this morning."

His inky eyes narrowed on her, warm and appraising. "I'm glad you're forming ties to your brother. Would you mind if I accompanied you? I would like to select something that will remind you of home when you visit me at Schloss Hohenheim." His palm cupped her cheek, and Rory's world tilted off centre as he claimed a whisper-soft kiss from her lips. "I want you to know there is a place for you there."

Goose bumps tingled over her suddenly hot skin like the sparks from a brushfire. How could one gentle kiss from this man who had deceived her be so incredibly erotic?

Even though a cautious voice inside her warned against letting herself be seduced, Rory touched her fingers to his firm mouth, delighting in being able to touch him like this. "Are you courting me, Sebastian?" she asked warily.

He smiled down at her, a confident male smile that made her heart race. "That was most assuredly not courting." He touched his tongue to her fingertips and nibbled gently. "Nor was that courting," he murmured against her fingers.

His strong hands slid around her waist and tugged her

toward him until her pelvis was cradled against the hardness of his body and the ridge of his arousal. His eyes twinkled with virile amusement. "When I am courting you, my princess, you will have no doubt as to my intentions."

To her shock, he kissed her again. This time coaxing her mouth open with a mastery that had her sighing in surrender. His kiss took her in the most sensual way Rory had ever known. His tongue seduced her, teased her, gratified her. She clung to his shoulders as his hands cupped her bottom and fitted her more closely, more exquisitely against his arousal.

Rory gasped, gripped by a need so strong she forgot they were in her great room and anyone could walk in.

Until someone did walk in. Odette.

"My apologies. Excuse me," Odette murmured.

Rory nearly slid to the floor in a lump of rampaging hormones as Laurent reluctantly broke the kiss and released her. Odette looked as mortified as Rory felt.

While Prince Laurent explained the schedule change to Odette, Rory informed Heinrich that she and Prince Laurent were going into the cove on an errand.

There's no turning back now, she told herself, suppressing guilt as they got into the limo. Heinrich took the front passenger seat beside the driver.

Still dazed and sexually charged from Laurent's unexpected kiss, Rory jumped when Laurent took her hand and stroked the pulse point in her wrist with his thumb.

He frowned. "You're nervous of me, yes?"

Rory shook her head. "No. I mean, yes. Maybe."

He tucked a curl behind her ear, making her shiver in reaction. "I'm sorry we were interrupted. I look forward to the time when there will be no interruptions. I find you very beautiful, *mein* Lorelei."

Heat rushed up Rory's neck to her face. He'd used that name for her again. She imagined what it would be like to have him naked, inside her. Her pulse throbbed against his thumb. She had no doubt that he would be an experienced lover. But would he be restrained with her in bed?

Rory was a mass of unsettled nerves by the time they arrived at the gallery on Prospect Street.

She gave herself a pep talk. She could do this. She pasted on a smile as they entered the swank interior. "I'm sure we'll both find something here," she told Laurent confidently. "This was my mother's favorite gallery."

Joffre Wells, the gallery's owner, greeted them with a gentlemanly Southern accent that made Rory think of antebellum mansions and private country clubs. Rory explained what they were looking for, and Joffre immediately guided them toward a collection of oil seascapes.

Rory picked out an oil painting of Windansea Beach for her brother while Laurent chose a large seascape of the ocean at dawn. "Someday I will make love to you at dawn," he whispered silkily in her ear as they proceeded to the cash register.

Stunned by his promise, Rory dropped her purse on the floor, then bumped heads with Laurent as they both bent to retrieve it.

Knowing she had to act now, Rory paid for her purchase and excused herself to use the ladies' room while Laurent paid for his painting. As she had expected, Heinrich shadowed her to the rear of the gallery. Her heart thundering rapidly, Rory entered the bathroom and spent a few moments examining the double-hung window with its Cubist-inspired stained-glass panes over the toilet. It unlocked easily. She anxiously waited another minute, then flushed the toilet and opened the door.

She gestured furtively at Heinrich, feeling her face heat with embarrassment. "I'm having a female problem. I need tampons." She handed him twenty dollars. "There's a drugstore down the street, would you mind?"

Heinrich reluctantly took the money. His thick neck reddened. "I will send Franz."

She smiled in genuine relief. "Thank you!"

Rory didn't have a second to lose. She turned the tap on to mask sounds and opened the window. Then she contorted herself like a pretzel and dropped to the ground behind a Dumpster.

Now came the tricky part. Prospect Street curved into Prospect Place, which was crowded with little boutiques, international shops, restaurants and retail outlets. There were plenty of nooks and crannies and arcades where she could hide. Rory figured that as soon as Heinrich realized she was gone, he'd concentrate his search for her in that area.

Resisting the urge to look over her shoulder, she walked to the Cave Store on Cave Street where tourists paid a fee to climb down 145 steps to the famous Sunny Jim Cave. She'd call a taxi from the store.

The place had a laid-back atmosphere and tempted tourists to comb the shelves for starfish, sand dollars, pink murex, tiger cowries and other shells after viewing the cave. Rory ducked behind a postcard rack and studied the street through the window to make sure she wasn't being followed. She breathed a sigh of relief. There was no sign of the limo or her bodyguards. She was alone.

HE HAD HER. Claude couldn't believe his good fortune. Because of the heightened security around the princess, he had not ventured onto her street in the past few days. Instead he had noted that the cross streets that led to her neighborhood intersected with La Jolla Boulevard, a main arterial route. He'd taken to sitting outside a little pizza shop on La Jolla Boulevard, reading the newspaper and keeping an eye out for her limo or her car.

He had finally spotted the limo this morning and had jumped onto his motorcycle to follow it. He was disappointed when Prince Laurent exited the limo with Princess Charlotte Aurora outside the gallery. He had hoped that the newspaper clippings would have been enough for the princess to send Prince Laurent packing.

Apparently not.

But Claude still had the gun.

He'd taken up a position in the shade of a magnolia tree and was debating the risks of shooting Prince Laurent on a public street when he'd glanced into his side mirror and saw the princess crossing the street behind him. Opportunity had knocked again and Claude was driving through full throttle.

He parked outside the Cave Store and bided his time.

THREE MINUTES AFTER he had dispatched Franz to the drugstore, Heinrich noticed that the sound of the water running in the bathroom was too constant. He knocked on the door. No man felt at ease dealing with a woman's monthly female problems. "Franz will return shortly, madame," he said.

There was no reply.

Heinrich tried the door. It was locked, but he defeated it with a tool from the pick set he carried.

As he feared, the bathroom was empty. The princess

had run away. For the first time since his appointment as Prince Laurent's royal protection officer, Heinrich feared his position was in jeopardy.

OTTO'S HOUSE was a board-and-batten bungalow painted a soft, silvery sage. The shrubs and grass had the well-tended look of being painstakingly trimmed by hand. A car was in the driveway, giving Rory hope that Otto was at home. She walked up the cement driveway and smiled at Otto's next-door neighbour, an elderly woman in a peacock-blue muumuu, who was carrying a poodle to her car.

"Don't bother ringing the bell," the woman said, depositing her poodle and her handbag on the passenger seat. "Otto's showing his nephew the garden around back. He never hears the doorbell. Just go through the gate."

Rory thanked the woman, but she hesitated as she reached the gate. Otto had company and she didn't want to intrude. Maybe they could arrange to meet later in the day.

She opened the cedar gate and walked down a flagstone path edged with variegated hostas and pink-plumed astilbe. She could hear low voices speaking in French.

As she rounded the corner of the house, Rory spotted Otto and his nephew. Their backs were to her as they stood examining a waterfall feature in the small garden. Otto's nephew wore a flint-gray suit.

Rory was about to call a greeting when the nephew turned his head toward Otto and she saw him in profile.

Her heart jolted in instant recognition of the thin beard that framed his angular jaw. Instinctively she dropped to her knees behind the arching branches of a plumbago. She'd been wrong to come here. The world of political intrigue was small and very treacherous. Otto's nephew was her brother's secretary: Renald Dartois.

Chapter Thirteen

Rory had run away.

Laurent's despair and guilt increased as the minutes ticked by and Heinrich and Franz failed to find her. She'd been under so much pressure. He'd seen the fear in her eyes when she'd lain in that hospital bed after the accident. He understood her need to escape. Laurent had often felt the same.

But Rory was out there alone, unprotected, and there was a killer after her. Laurent had to find her.

He turned to the owner of the art gallery. "Ms. Kenilworth has experienced emotional episodes since her mother's tragic death. I'm afraid our visit here today may have triggered one. She told me that this gallery was her mother's favorite. I'm not sure where she has gone—perhaps to a place where she feels close to her mother. I wonder if I might trouble you to call the taxicab company and inquire if anyone matching her description has been picked up in this area in the last hour."

"Of course, sir," Joffre replied. Laurent had no doubt that the gallery owner would be able to get the information out of the taxi company. Laurent had just purchased a thirty-five-thousand-dollar painting. "You might wish to tell the taxi company that there will be a substantial reward for the information,'' he added. "It is very important that I find her before she hurts herself."

After fifteen minutes of phone negotiations, Joffre gave Laurent an address on Playa del Norte Street and directions. "The driver remembered that his fare had a bandage."

Laurent tipped Joffre one thousand dollars in cash and raced to the limo. He didn't know why Rory would go to this address. He just hoped his Lorelei was safe.

"I CANNOT ALLOW ESTAIRE to fall into Ducharme's hands, *mon oncle,*" Rory heard Renald tell Otto as she was trying to extricate herself from the plumbago branches. She froze in her movements. Was Renald about to confess he'd hired the assassin? Was Otto involved, as well?

"You have met Princess Charlotte Aurora," Renald continued dismissively. "She is not our future."

Otto folded his arms over his chest, his head bent over a flower bed. "I see. And you believe that you have the right to change history? How is it that you are so confident that only you know what is best for Estaire? What of Prince Olivier? It is his decision is it not?"

"*Pfft!* Olivier is weak. He does not consider all his options. You have been in America twenty years. You do not know the full situation, *mon oncle.*"

"But I do know the princess. Perhaps you need to take the time to know her. You have the same father."

The same father? Nausea swirled in Rory's stomach. *She had another brother!* She thought of all the years that she'd seen Otto nearby in the neighborhood. Had he been spying on her and her mother all these years?

"You are not listening, old man. If Olivier cannot father an heir, then your great-nephew—with our flesh and blood—will one day rule Estaire!"

"How do you propose to achieve that?"

"I'll be accompanying Olivier tomorrow. He and Princess Penelope have an appointment at an in vitro fertilization clinic Thursday morning. I am hopeful that this clinic will aid them in their desire to have an heir. If not, I intend to assist the process. The one advantage of being my older brother's secretary is that I am often entrusted to handle errands of the most delicate nature."

Rory was frozen in place, her legs falling asleep. She couldn't believe what she was hearing. She was afraid to leave.

Otto slowly toured the perennial border, stopping before a Victorian gazing ball. Rory hoped he couldn't see her hunched behind the shrub in the ball's reflective surface. "Prince August was very good to you. And this is the way you repay him? By scheming to lay claim to the throne and hiding your identity from your own brother?"

Renald shrugged, his face stony with resentment. "Prince August had no compunctions about luring my mother into his bed. She was married. The end justifies the means."

"That's what Émilie thought when she embarked on an affair with Prince August after his wife died. She wanted to give her husband the one thing he desired most—a child. Émilie did not tell Prince August the truth until after her husband's death—she thought you needed a father's guidance. Prince August never should have told you the truth."

Rory had heard more than enough. Renald hadn't said that he'd hired the assassin, but she was willing to bet

he had stolen her necklace because he believed her unworthy of it. She willed feeling back into her legs as
she inched backward along the walkway on her
haunches. Pins and needles stabbed her numb feet. She
bumped into an iron shepherd's hook that suspended
ceramic wind chimes.

"What was that?" she heard Renald say. "Are you
expecting someone?"

Otto's answer was lost to her.

Rory grasped the shepherd's hook and tried to stand.
Pain shot up her legs as her blood rushed back to
cramped limbs.

Fear scattered through her like a deck of cards tossed
to the ground. She'd managed to stumble to the gate
when she heard Renald cry out, "Princess!"

Rory ran down the driveway toward the street. She
needed help.

The man came out of nowhere. His arm circled her
throat, choking off her breath. She smelled the sweat of
his body and his mouthwash-tainted breath as he jabbed
the gun roughly into her bruised temple and whispered
into her ear, "It's time we had a talk, Princess."

RORY GRABBED THE ARM choking her, but it felt as inflexible as a steel bar. What was she going to do now?

"Don't scream. I just want to talk."

"Let go of me!" she gasped, twisting her neck an
inch so she could see him. She saw long, blond hair and
a sunburned nose. Claude Dupont. He dragged her into
the deep shadows beneath the umbrella of a catalpa tree.

Had Renald seen Claude grab her? Even if he had,
he was more likely rubbing his hands together with glee
than rushing to her aid.

She was on her own. Rory forced herself to relax.

Struggling would only enrage Claude further. She tried to assess her surroundings. Maybe a neighbor would notice she was being held against her will. "You're Marielle's brother. I'm so sorry about your sister."

She cried out as the barrel of the gun thrust against her bandaged temple.

Anger reverberated from his hard-muscled body. "She died because of you—because of him. She didn't want to live without him." His voice choked with grief. "She told me that Laurent dumped her, and I let her cry on her girlfriend's shoulder instead of mine! I should have stayed with her!"

Even though she was terrified, Rory felt enormous sympathy for his pain. She'd give anything if she could turn back the clock and prevent her mother from sitting in the swing that day. "Is that why you left me the clippings? You hoped that I would think he had caused her to kill herself and I would refuse to marry him?"

"I couldn't let you marry him. He was Marielle's."

Tears choked her at the truth of Claude's statement. Laurent *was* Marielle's. She'd seen the sadness in his eyes and heard the deep regret when he spoke of her.

"He still loves her. Misses her," she admitted painfully. "You shot at us the other night."

"I wanted to kill him. He doesn't deserve to live."

Rory swallowed hard. "You stabbed Laurent's date in the bathroom, didn't you?" Claude wouldn't let any woman take his sister's place. "How will you justify killing me?"

"I'm—" Claude broke off at the sound of tires squealing around the street corner. Rory prayed that it was a police car and this would all end peacefully. But it was a limo. Oh, God! As it rocked to a halt outside

Otto's house she spotted Heinrich in the front passenger seat.

Had Heinrich seen her? She saw his hand reach inside his suit jacket for his gun.

The front passenger door and the rear door flew open simultaneously. Heinrich braced himself behind the door for cover, his weapon drawn. "Release her, Dupont."

"Move a finger and she dies," Claude warned.

A cold blade of terror sliced through Rory as Laurent stepped out of the limo and away from the door. His jaw was set firmly and his inky eyes were calm and determined. He was unarmed.

Rory screamed. His face told her what he was going to do—nobly sacrifice his life for hers. She couldn't let him. "No, Laurent! Don't!"

"Claude," he said with quiet authority, "the princess has done you no harm. Killing her will not bring you peace. If it is retribution that you require, then punish me. I never wanted to hurt Marielle. I loved her, but I was not free to marry her and I respected her by telling her the truth. I bear the guilt of her death with me every day."

Claude's gun hand trembled.

Rory prayed that Laurent was reaching him. She had seen many sides of Laurent since she had met him, but the courage he displayed now, the dignity and the compassion that he offered Marielle's brother, made her realize how much she loved this honorable man. She knew she would always love him, whether he could give his heart to her or not.

Laurent took a cautious step forward. "Is this what you truly want, Claude? Your parents have lost one child. Consider the pain they will experience at losing their only son, too. No one has been harmed. It is not too late to stop yourself from traveling down the wrong path.''

''I do this for them.''

Rory was aware of the precise second when she knew Claude would shoot Laurent. Instinctively she curled her fingers into a fist and threw up her left arm, ramming her elbow into Claude's arm, hoping to knock the gun from his hand or at least deflect his aim. Pain jarred through her arm as she made contact. The gun went off.

Noise exploded in her ears.

Laurent launched himself toward them. Toward the gun. Her heart ricocheted in her breast as she rammed her right elbow back, intending to dig into Claude's ribs—only she hit him in the shoulder. He was falling and dragging her down with him. Had he shot himself?

Laurent went for the gun, deflecting it downward with one hand while his other hand grasped Claude's wrist and twisted it inward. Rory tried to squirm away. Claude was on top of her. The gun discharged again, and Rory panicked. Was Laurent hit?

Suddenly she was jerked up and tossed out of harm's way.

She landed on the grass with a *whoof,* the air knocked from her lungs. Laurent had twisted Claude's arm behind his back and had him pinned facedown.

The gun lay on the grass. Heinrich started for it, but Renald, suddenly appearing with the shepherd's hook in hand, beat him to it. Otto hurried toward Renald.

Rory screamed, ''Stop him. Stop Renald! He's my brother, and he wants to kill me!''

Renald's fingers curled around the gun. His frank blue eyes—a deeper blue than Olivier's—met hers. ''*Non,* little sister. I helped save you. I tripped Dupont with this hook.''

"He did. I saw him," Otto insisted.

Heinrich grimly leveled his weapon at Renald's chest. "*Ja.* We'll debate it once you put the gun down."

Police sirens wailed in the distance like the insistent screeching of gulls.

Renald released the gun—and the hook—and rose stiffly. Rory saw shame and contrition in Otto's age-spotted face. She hugged her knees tightly to her chest and told herself she was not going to throw up. Laurent had Claude subdued and no one appeared to be wounded.

She was overwhelmed. She had no idea what the truth was anymore. Who had hired the assassin? Who had stolen her necklace? Who could she believe? She pillowed her head on her knees and studied Laurent's grief-stricken face.

She felt ten years older.

LAURENT KEPT HIS ARM anchored around Rory as she answered the police detective's questions in the living room of the house on Playa del Norte Street. Concerned that the press would have a field day with this story if any details leaked, Laurent had summoned Odette to manage the media. He'd also called Prince Olivier. Renald's uncle Otto brought in chairs from the kitchen.

Rory had told the police that Claude had confessed to attempting to kill Laurent on Monday night. Laurent could feel her trembling. She'd been so brave. He'd come so close to losing her. He was still not past the shock of seeing Claude Dupont holding a gun to her head.

Nor the shock of discovering that Renald Dartois was Rory's and Prince Olivier's half brother. To Laurent's consternation, Rory had explained that the diamond necklace she'd received as a gift from her father had been stolen from her home a week ago when she had begun her princess lessons. Suspecting that the thief might be working with the assassin, she'd decided to contact Otto who was fluent in German and French to help her order a copy of the necklace that she could use to trick the thief into revealing him or herself.

"Why did you not mention any of this to me or to your brother?" Laurent demanded testily.

"Because the thief was obviously a trusted member of the staff of one of you." She leveled her gaze on Renald. "I didn't want to create an atmosphere of distrust. To report the theft would have been playing into his hands."

Sweat glistened on Renald's angular features. "I did not take the necklace. Nor did I hire anyone to kill the princess. I have been a loyal servant to the Valcourt family—and to Estaire—all of my life. I have been loyal to you, Olivier. And I realized when Claude Dupont seized the princess that I could be loyal to her, even if it meant that Estaire might one day return to Falkenberg rule."

Olivier drummed his fingers upon his thigh, obviously agitated. "All these years we have worked together. Why did you not tell me you were my brother?"

Renald lowered his head shamefully. "Your father did not wish to dishonor my mother's reputation or his own. You were his legitimate heir. It was enough that he wanted me in the palace with him and that I knew the truth."

Olivier clasped Renald's shoulder. "It's important to me, and I believe it's important to Charlotte Aurora that we know we have a brother. My father was a rigid man. Too rigid, I think."

Rory felt her heart warm slightly for Renald. She knew exactly how it felt to have a parent who was supposed to love you make a decision that left you feeling as if you were inferior. Renald hadn't resented Olivier's position. He'd faithfully served his brother as his personal secretary. And although his back-up plan to ensure that Estaire had a Valcourt heir was misguided, it demonstrated a keen desire to protect the country that he loved.

Rory wouldn't reveal what she'd overheard. She'd grant him the dignity of confessing to Olivier in private.

She slipped from the buffering support of Laurent's arm and crossed the cozy living room to kiss Renald's cheek. Then she kissed Olivier. "I'm thrilled to have two brothers. You can take turns telling me what's best for me, and I can take turns telling you that I can figure it out for myself." Gratitude swelled in a hot lump in her throat. "But I appreciate the fact that you want to protect me."

Her remark won strained smiles from both Renald and Olivier. Laurent shifted awkwardly in his chair.

Rory sniffed, trying to pull herself together. Men were always so uncomfortable with emotion! Besides, she was not sure that Renald was completely trustworthy. "How did your uncle come to live in La Jolla?"

"I'll answer that," Otto volunteered from his chair near the entrance to the kitchen. "It was your father's doing, Princess. He wanted someone to keep an eye on your mother and you. I sent him monthly reports."

Rory thought of all the times she'd encountered Otto walking in the neighborhood or down at the beach, and his bi-weekly visits to the Book Nook. "All these years?"

Otto nodded, his watery gray eyes reflecting remorse.

"After his death I continued to give the reports to Renald. They were always glowing, Princess. Your father was very proud."

Yes, Rory thought wryly, considering the other meaning of the word. *Too proud to bend.* "Did my mother know?"

"I'm not sure."

Laurent addressed the police detectives. "Did Claude Dupont hire the assassin?"

"He may confess to it when we interrogate him," Detective Rodriguez, who seemed to be in charge, told her.

"If he'd hired a hit man, why would Claude try to shoot us, then?" Rory asked.

"Frustration, most likely. The accidents the hit man had arranged weren't achieving the desired results. Dupont was getting impatient. He wanted the job done and he didn't care about getting caught, which is why we found fingerprints on the fence and on the envelope."

"Do you think Claude stole my necklace, too?"

Detective Rodriguez shook his head. "No. My guess is it was the hit man. This kind of killer searches a home thoroughly looking for opportunities." He checked his notes. "You told me the necklace was stolen on Sunday while you took your cat to the vet. Or sometime on Monday when the house was overrun by assorted staff."

"Could the hit man be a bodyguard, Heinrich?" Laurent asked gravely.

"Anything is possible if one is offered enough money," Heinrich admitted. "I will make some enquiries."

"I do not believe the stylist is involved," Odette contributed from her post near the living room window where she was monitoring the activity in the street. "I accompanied her at all times. No one is to be left alone with a royal family member's personal belongings. Ms. Allard's references are impeccable.''

Detective Rodriguez noted the information. ''We'll need contact info for the catering company and the butler. We'll check them out.''

Renald produced a personal digital assistant from the pocket of his gray suit. ''I have the information here.''

Rory's heart pinched at the prospect that the grandfatherly butler could be the hit man. ''Pierce is the one who located my vitamins after I couldn't find them.''

''Dupont's been sloppy. We may find something to link us to the hit man once we discover where he's been holing up,'' Detective Rodriguez said confidently.

Laurent rose and took Rory's hand. ''You're staying at the hotel until the assassin is arrested. No arguments.''

Rory caved beneath the concern rife in his eyes and the tantalizing promise of protection in his strong fingers. The same fingers that had stripped a loaded gun from a crazed man's hand. When Laurent looked at her like she was his princess, she wanted to be near him tonight and always.

Even if her heart whispered that he didn't love her.

AFTER THE POLICE were finished with their questions, Rory, Laurent and Olivier were escorted to waiting limos with their heads covered to avoid the cameras. To satisfy the journalists lusting for a story, Detective Rodriguez made a brief statement. Then Otto was interviewed about the gunman's identity, but claimed he had never met the man. He referred to Rory as a friend who had dropped by, but refused to give her name.

Rory gratefully accepted the room that was prepared

for her in her brother's suite. She spent the rest of the day talking privately with Olivier and Renald. Although she still felt miles apart from their world, a fragile bond was forming between them, a sense of belonging that she hoped would grow stronger once she visited Estaire. They had an early dinner as her brothers were taking a private jet the next morning. Over dessert, Rory was relieved when Renald put down his fork and told Olivier of his plan to ensure that Princess Penelope gave birth to an heir.

Olivier's shock was apparent. "You would have done that for us?"

Renald nodded. "I would have considered it my duty. I will understand if you wish me to resign my position."

Olivier sighed. "I will need to give the matter more thought. In fact, I am beginning to reevaluate several of our father's decisions." He paused, his gaze resting pensively on Rory, "Including the marriage treaty with Ducharme. There is no question that the union would be beneficial. But if it alienates one further from one's family, I am not convinced that it is worth the sacrifice."

Rory's heart started to thud. She couldn't believe what she'd just heard. "Really?" she squeaked.

Olivier covered her hand with his. "I do not wish to deprive you of your right to choose your destiny, *ma petite soeur*. If something were to happen to me, I am confident that Renald would assist you in every way possible."

Renald smiled cautiously. "You can count on it."

Rory tried to grasp the thought that she could walk away from Laurent now if she wished. It was the only thing she'd wanted since she'd found out about the ridiculous treaty. But things had changed. Her heart had changed. Did she want to walk away? Could she?

She thought of how she felt when he held her and the way his inky gaze probed her to her soul, stirring up desires. "I'm not sure," she admitted honestly.

"*Bon.* Then I suggest you take time to know your heart. I can reschedule my appointment at the clinic and stay a few days longer until the police arrest this assassin. Or Renald can remain here with you."

"No! This appointment is too important to reschedule and I think you and Renald have a lot to discuss. I'll be fine with Laurent and Heinrich's men."

"All right, then. We will talk again of your feelings for Prince Laurent when you come to Estaire."

Rory forced a smile. Her feelings for Laurent were exactly what she was afraid of.

LAURENT FELT RATTLED about spending an evening alone with his princess. It was their first date, and he wanted it to be an evening that they would remember for the rest of their lives. He wanted to distract her from the fact that the police had not identified or arrested the assassin.

Although the police were strenuously investigating and conducting interviews, Claude Dupont had hired a lawyer and was not talking. The police had not yet discovered where he had been staying.

Rory had awakened early this morning to wish her brothers a safe flight, but Laurent had noticed she'd been subdued during her German lessons and her clothing fittings. He wondered if she was missing her brothers—or feeling trapped in her position, trapped with him.

Whenever their gazes met, he felt the strong pull of

a current, drawing him to her. He wanted their first dinner alone to be as intimate as the conversations they had shared when she thought he was Sebastian Guimond. With the assassin still at large he was reluctant to put Rory at risk by venturing outside the hotel. Instead he had made arrangements with the hotel staff for a private dinner.

Nerves lodged in his stomach as he presented himself at the princess's suite at 7:00 p.m. He had forgone a suit in favor of black trousers and a black knit shirt. He had told Rory that dinner would be informal. He nodded at the bodyguard posted outside the princess's suite.

Chandale Allard opened the door, beaming. "Good evening, sir. The princess will be right out." Her hands spread in front of her. "Prepare to be blown away."

Laurent raised his eyebrows. Americans had such peculiar expressions. "Blown away?"

"She looks incredible."

"Ahh." Laurent stepped into the suite. The last thing he desired was to be reminded that his princess affected his control like no other woman on earth.

Despite the stylist's warning, every muscle in his body ached with a need for release when his princess emerged from the hallway into the salon. She was half-clothed. She wore a virginal, white cotton crocheted top that bared her golden shoulders and her midriff and a white flirty skirt of a diaphanous material that made his fingers itch to peel it up over her thighs and explore her gorgeous body. Delicate sandals accented the slender beauty of her feet, and a fine gold chain studded with seed pearls circled one ankle.

Her eyes were as blue as the mysteries of the ocean, hiding her thoughts, but the hesitancy in her step and the blush of uncertainty in her cheeks was his complete undoing.

He was Crown Prince Laurent Sebastian Wilhelm of Ducharme, and he wanted to be on his knees before this woman, touching, tasting, granting her pleasures that made her tremble.

But they were only supposed to have dinner.

The scented sweetness of her hair enveloped him, sending a fierce hunger pounding to his groin as he kissed her forehead. "Words fail me at your beauty, Princess."

Her eyes leveled on him, frank and clear with a feminine power that made his heart pause. "Not Princess… Rory."

And Laurent knew that he was in more danger than he had ever been in. He knew why his mother had regretted falling in love with his father. He found himself on an emotional precipice and battled for the strength and the wisdom to keep a calm head. "I've been looking forward to this all day," he said, placing his hand lightly on the small of her back and guiding her to the door.

Her skin was temptation tenfold, so satiny soft he imagined it would taste like sun-warmed honey.

They stepped out into the hallway, and he guided her to the right, instead of across the hall.

Rory had intuitively known, from the moment her gaze had met Laurent's in her suite, that they were going to make love tonight. He'd looked at her as if he wanted her naked. Her breasts ached for his touch. Her body was already craving the hardness of his muscled chest and thighs.

"We aren't dining in your suite?" she asked as they walked toward the end of the hallway where she saw Heinrich standing in front of a door.

Laurent ducked his head, his voice caressing her ear. "I have a surprise. For you."

Warmth stole over her. "What kind of a surprise?"

Heinrich opened the door for them.

Rory caught her breath. She was being swept into a fantasy. The balcony doors facing the ocean were opened wide, and a gentle salt-laced breeze stirred the yards and yards of sheer white fabric draped sensuously over wooden Morrocan screens that concealed the room's formal wallpapered walls.

Rose petals and white lily-shaped candles floated in a brass tub nestled in a bed of sand in the open doorway. More candles glowed from tall brass lanterns with ruby-red glass lenses. On the floor was a bamboo mat on which a gold-silk-covered chaise was piled with luxurious pillows in bright sari fabrics of cerise, cobalt and celadon. Two red silk ottomans were placed beside a low table offering platters of cheese, pâté, fruits and other delicacies.

"I couldn't take you to the beach, so I brought the beach to us, *mein* Lorelei," he murmured to her.

"Oh, Sebastian!" Rory turned and Laurent's lips were on hers, hot, demanding and reckless. His fingers splayed through her hair, angling her mouth to fit his. This was a passionate, uncontrolled side of him that made her want to wrap her body around him now and agonize over the decision later. He felt so strong, so powerful.

She ran her hands over his chest. Then, needing to feel his hot smooth flesh, she yanked his shirt from his trousers and explored the rigid muscles of his abdomen.

Laurent groaned and deepened the kiss. Rory joyously continued her exploration, finding the flat circles of his nipples.

She smiled into the kiss as his hands moved from her hair to her breasts to the bared flesh of her midriff. The heat of his palms sent her senses skyrocketing into meltdown mode as he traced her ribs. When his thumbs finally brushed her swollen nipples through her lace bra, Rory whimpered with an urgency that left her thong panties damp with anticipation.

He eased her bra and the cotton fabric aside and suckled her breast, increasing the budding tension locked inside her. The tension built to an exquisite height as he devotedly caressed her other breast with his tongue. "I'm courting you, *mein* Lorelei," he whispered against her damp areola. His warm breath made her shiver with delight.

Rory made a unilateral decision that he was overdressed for the occasion. "I'm courting you, too, Sebastian. You need a wardrobe change."

She tore at his belt, then unzipped his zipper and freed his arousal from a pair of black briefs. The steely soft strength of him in her hand filled her with new love for this man. Laurent could be hard and inflexible, but gentle and sensitive at the same time.

She wanted him, wanted his love more than anything she'd ever wanted in her life. When she was in his arms, her father's abandonment and her mother's lies didn't matter. She felt healed. And she wanted to heal him from his own heartaches.

Laurent broke the kiss. With a fluid motion he pulled off his shirt and divested himself of his shoes and other clothes. His naked body was shockingly beautiful. He was at his most vulnerable—scars and all.

He took her hand and placed it on his chest where she could feel the racing thrum of his heartbeat. "I offer you my devotion and my passion, *mein* Lorelei. And my solemn word that I will treat you always with respect.''

She moistened her lips. ''Does that mean you still won't take off my clothes?''

He muttered an oath in German and picked her up, depositing her in a heap on the chaise. His lips curved with amusement. ''If madame would like her clothes removed, I am her humble servant.''

Rory's heart leaped as he joined her on the chaise.

Laying astride her, he hitched her top up over her breasts and laved her, his tongue tracing a damp path to her belly.

Rory dug her fingers into his hair and squirmed impatiently. ''I thought you were taking my clothes off.''

''All in due time. A man doesn't gorge himself at a feast, he takes his time and savors each bite.'' His tongue dipped into her belly button and a shudder of delight ripped through her. ''You see? I can taste you here. And here.''

His lips and his tongue moved seductively lower. Rory arched her hips toward him, greedily accepting his caresses.

He eased up her skirt as if peeling back the petals of a flower. He ran an appreciative finger over the thin strip of silk that covered her femininity, rubbing her through the fabric. Rory writhed at the incredibly erotic friction. He kissed her inner thigh, then kissed the damp fabric.

Her body quivered. ''Sebastian, please!''

He obligingly moved the tiny band aside, and the rasp of his tongue sent her over the edge. Only, the pleasure didn't stop. He kissed her and caressed her with his clever fingers while she shuddered and cried out his name. She was barely cognizant when he stripped her of her panties and her skirt, and slipped her top over her head.

Time shifted around her. She was only aware that as lovely as this pleasure was, she needed to hold him inside her to fully express the love she felt. She urged him between her parted thighs.

He slid into her, filling her body. Her heart soared at the communion of their souls. He started to move, murmuring words in German she didn't understand, but she knew they were beautiful and they were about her. His handsome features were fixed in concentration. Rory met his every thrust eagerly. Willingly.

The pleasure became too much, and her world fragmented like a wave crushing down on her. She felt Laurent buck inside her as he reached his own climax. She held him tightly into her body. "I love you, Sebastian!"

Laurent collapsed on top of his princess, breathing raggedly, holding himself back. Her words of love rang in his ears, reaching a deep part of him that hadn't been touched by anything in much too long. But he was unable to answer. He saw his mother's face, heard her grief.

He cradled Rory's face in his hands, kissing her delicate brows, her adorable nose and her golden rosy cheeks. "You are so beautiful, *mein* Lorelei," he told her over and over again. But he couldn't look her in her eyes, and he couldn't bring himself to say the words he knew she waited to hear. Duty came before everything, even love.

Chapter Fourteen

Rory stole out of the suite at six o'clock in the morning.
Laurent was deeply asleep. They had made love three
times, each time more incredible than the previous.
They had lain on the chaise naked, eating and laughing.
She felt sated and pleasantly sore, but a growing unease
nagged her.

Even when she had rolled over on top of him and
ridden him until he'd thrown his head into the pillows
and buried his hands in her hair as he begged her never
to stop, he had not whispered a word of love.

Maybe it's too soon, she thought, blushing as she
nodded at the bodyguard who was on duty in the hallway.

Maybe she was only kidding herself, an inner voice
warned. Maybe he would only ever love Marielle.

To her surprise, Odette was sitting at the desk in her
suite's salon, her head bent over the black leather portfolio that no doubt contained Rory's schedule for the
next few days. A cup of coffee was at her elbow.

She lifted her head as Rory entered, a stiff, cautious
smile spread on her coral-pink lips. "Good morning,
Your Serene Highness. How was your evening?"

Rory was aware that her hair was a mess and her

clothes were wrinkled. She wanted a bath and a long nap and some time to think about what had happened between her and Laurent. "Eventful. I'm exhausted."

Odette demurely lowered her eyes to her schedule. "You have an elocution lesson at nine-thirty, followed by a French lesson at eleven. Will you be all right or would you like me to rearrange your schedule?"

Rory was tempted to cancel, but she remembered what Laurent had told her about inconveniencing the staff with last-minute schedule changes. "No, I'll be fine. Just make sure I'm awake by nine."

"Very good. Pleasant dreams, madame."

Rory was almost to her room when it occurred to her that Odette must have known Marielle. She doubled back to the salon, hoping to ask Odette about Laurent's relationship with the heiress, but Odette was on her cell phone.

"I've just reviewed the princess's schedule with her. Everything's continuing as planned…"

Rory told herself she'd ask the press secretary later.

TALKING INTO A MICROPHONE to an empty conference room on three hours of sleep was not a good way to begin the day.

Rory had never liked public speaking. The thought that she would be required to make speeches at public engagements was way beyond her comfort zone. She struggled with the mike for over an hour, trying to read the speech that Odette had prepared and master the art of making eye contact while appearing relaxed and sincere. To her frustration, the elocution teacher Odette had hired reminded her every few minutes to put her mouth closer to the mike or to speak up. Or not to slouch.

By the tenth rehearsal, Rory was ready to tear up the index cards. Her throat was bone dry.

Odette brought her a glass of water and told her she was doing fine. Rory took a grateful sip of the water and put it on the shelf inside the podium. Then she began the speech one more time from the beginning. "Good afternoon, ladies and gentlemen. It is a great privilege to—"

"Confidence. Acknowledge the audience," the elocutionist called from the center of the room.

Rory gave the podium a kick and felt a trickle of water dribble down her knee. Great.

Odette placed her hand over the mike. "Why don't you take a break and finish your water while I have a word with Ms. Johnson about your next lesson."

Rory glanced down. She'd spilled half the water. She drank what was left, then snagged several tissues from her purse and mopped up the mess.

Fortunately, Odette was walking the elocution teacher to the exit. Rory grabbed her purse to tell Odette she wasn't up for a French lesson.

As Rory caught up with Odette near the exit, the press secretary took a call on her cell phone. Odette signaled Franz at the entrance to the conference room. She spoke urgently to the bodyguard.

Shock telegraphed in the blonde's pale features, warned Rory that something was wrong. "What is it?"

"That was Heinrich. Prince Laurent went down to the hotel's jewelry store, and he was shot at close range."

"Shot? Close range? Is he—" Rory's heart sped up, and she had trouble getting a full breath. "Is he all right?"

They'd just made love all night, and now she faced the terrifying possibility of losing him.

Odette slipped a supportive arm around Rory's waist. "Come with me! The bodyguard's gone to get a car. They've taken Laurent to Mercy Hospital."

Rory needed no further urging.

"He's strong. We are not going to lose him," Odette told Rory comfortingly as they hurried out the lobby entrance. A limo pulled up to the curb, and Rory numbly clambered into the back seat.

Odette picked up the phone and told the driver their destination. "Don't waste any time!"

Rory couldn't believe this was happening. A heaviness descended upon her, weighing her down. She closed her eyes, digging deep inside herself for strength. For courage. She could hear Laurent calling her his Lorelei and telling her she was beautiful. A tear slid onto her cheek. They were supposed to have forever together. She wanted to experience the joy of knowing that he loved her. "Who did it? Did they catch him?" she asked, biting back a sob.

Odette patted her hand. "Heinrich didn't say."

Rory silently urged the limo to go faster. It seemed to take forever to drive over the Coronado Bridge. She expected the limo to head north on Interstate 5, but when the driver headed south toward National City she snatched up the phone. "You're going the wrong way—"

Suddenly her arm felt too heavy and it wasn't working right. The phone slipped from her fingers and tumbled to the floor. Her eyelids drooped. She felt odd, drowsy and incredibly tired—like the day she'd passed out during her defensive driving lessons. Had she been drugged again?

Odette serenely bent to retrieve the phone. "Don't worry, Princess. The driver knows where he's going."

Her foggy brain registered a note of triumph in Odette's tone. Oh, no. The water! Odette had drugged her!

Fighting to stay conscious, Rory fell across Odette while reaching for the button that controlled the privacy screen. She had to alert Franz. The screen slid down a few inches. But the front passenger seat was empty.

"Help!" she screamed to the driver.

Odette straightened, squishing Rory against the back of the seat. Then Odette grabbed her arm and yanked her down onto the floor of the limo.

Rory flopped like a dead fish. Odette smiled coldly, not an elegant blond hair out of place. Her gray-green eyes gleamed. "Meet the man who is going to kill you, Princess."

Rory blinked blearily at the press secretary. The drug was too strong. It was overtaking her. The stories Odette had told her of her childhood in the palace jumbled together in Rory's mind along with something Claude had said about the night Marielle had died. Claude had thought Marielle was okay because she was with a girl-friend. Rory had a sick, queasy feeling the shoulder Marielle had cried on was Odette's. She licked her lips. "You killed Marielle."

"Of course I did," Odette replied smugly. "She was planning to trick Laurent into marrying her by getting pregnant. I couldn't let that happen. Laurent kissed me when I was thirteen, and that's when I knew I was des-tined to be his princess. With you finally dead, he'll be free to follow his heart. He will realize that his true princess has always been beneath his nose."

"You stabbed the fashion designer, too?"

Odette shrugged. "He was sleeping with her."

Rory couldn't keep her eyelids open any longer. Regret that she couldn't protect Laurent from Odette's scheming flooded her heart. "He might marry you, but he'll never let himself love you," she mumbled as she lost consciousness.

RORY HAD LEFT HIS BED this morning without waking him. Laurent sat at his desk unable to concentrate, knowing the reason she'd left.

His head jerked up as Heinrich entered the salon accompanied by Franz. Heinrich's face was bone white. His dark eyes carried news Laurent knew he did not want to hear.

"It's Fraulein Schoenfeldt and the princess. They have been lured out of the hotel on false pretenses."

Franz flexed his shoulders, shame reddening his tight jaw. "Fraulein Schoenfeldt received a call she believed was from Heinrich. She was told that you had been shot and were taken to the hospital. She ordered me to get the car."

Disbelief echoed in Laurent's heart. The assassin was still at large. "Can you not call the driver?"

"He's not answering his phone."

Laurent glanced at his watch, horror growing inside him. "When did this happen?"

"It's been seventeen minutes since they were last seen by a doorman. Detective Rodriguez is en route," Heinrich reported solemnly. "They are putting out an APB for the vehicle, and Rodriguez is requesting the assistance of a police chopper." A flush crept over Heinrich's collar. "Sir, if you will forgive me for the impropriety, I fitted the princess's handbags with tracking devices last night. She had already breached her personal protection measures twice. After what happened with Dupont yesterday, I felt the measure justifiable with the assassin still at large.''

Laurent gripped Heinrich's shoulders. They'd address the privacy violation later. ''Can you track her now?''

''*Ja.* If she has her handbag. I would prefer you—''

Laurent cut him off. ''I am coming with you.''

RORY HOVERED between consciousness and unconsciousness. She felt the hot July sun on her face as she was dragged out of the limo and heaved unceremoniously onto the padded floor of a delivery van. Her bones jarred with the impact. Why were people always tossing her around?

She flexed her fingers. She was too weak to move. But at least she was awake after a fashion. Maybe the drug was wearing off. She heard voices: Odette's and a man's.

''What do we do now?'' Odette asked.

''I've found the perfect place to dump her. The police will be looking for the limousine. This will buy us time to get out of the area. I'll drop you off near a gas station on the way to El Centro. The police will believe I intended to dump her in the desert. You pretend you escaped, and I'll expect my final payment within two business days—along with a bonus for the chauffeur. He won't be talking.''

Rory kept her eyes closed as they climbed into the van. They crossed her arms mummy-like over her chest, then tore a strip of duct tape and stuck it on her mouth.

''One more thing,'' Odette said. Rory felt her nemesis attach something around her neck. Her birthday necklace!

"Roll her up now," the hit man directed.

No! It took all Rory's self-control not to scream when she realized what they were doing. Claustrophic panic rioted through her as they rolled her up in a scratchy rug. She couldn't move, could hardly breathe. The sound of more strips of duct tape being torn almost made her sob.

The hit man bound the rug snugly around her with the tape. "That should keep her quiet. She won't last longer than an hour or two in this heat once we leave her in the Dumpster. Best thing is, they'll never find her body."

"Clever man. A garbage dump seems fitting for a trashy American princess. What about her purse?"

"Tuck it inside the carpet with her. I don't want any evidence left lying around."

Rory felt tears of gratitude as her purse was wedged into the roll above her head.

She waited until the van pulled onto the road, then she concentrated on the painstaking task of inching a hand up over her face toward her purse. A princess wouldn't be caught dead without certain essentials.

THE POLICE HELICOPTER had spotted a limousine parked behind an abandoned building two blocks ahead. Laurent sat in an unmarked police car as it raced through the streets of National City with its lights flashing, watching a blipping dot move on a computer screen. He prayed they would find his princess and his press secretary in time.

Detective Rodriguez radioed dispatch for an ambulance. Laurent's stomach felt as if it were being pummeled to dust. "But the dot is still moving east," he protested.

"We'll check the limo first. He may have left Odette there and switched vehicles," Heinrich explained. "We approach Odette with caution. I am finding it suspicious that she mistook someone else's voice for mine."

"I am wondering the same thing," Laurent admitted. "Could it have been a tape recording? She was distraught."

"But to dispatch Franz to get a car?"

Laurent stabbed his hair with his fingers as Detective Rodriguez gunned the police car through an intersection and wove through midday traffic at breakneck speed. "I keep thinking about the theft of the princess's necklace. You know, Odette was on the yacht the night Marielle died. She was a great comfort to me during that time. I secured her a position in the palace press office shortly thereafter and she has done her best to become indispensable to me. I am beginning to see, Heinrich, that we are sometimes blind to the secret ambitions of those around us."

The cruiser whipped into the parking lot of an out-of-business furniture store and drove around to the back of the drab building. Laurent's heart jammed in his throat as the police car screeched to a halt beside the limo.

Laurent and Heinrich bolted out of the car with Detective Rodriguez and his partner.

"There's no one inside the limo," Rodriguez shouted, trying the driver's side door. It was unlocked.

"Pop the trunk," his partner suggested.

Detective Rodriguez worked the trunk lever.

His partner swore. "There's someone in here."

Odette? Rory? Laurent forced himself to remain strong as he looked at the body in the trunk. It was the chauffeur, with a clear plastic bag sealed over his head.

He was dead.

Chapter Fifteen

Princess Charlotte Aurora, contortionist, Rory thought with pride as she squeezed her right hand up past her head toward her purse. She was never going to deride herself for her natural clumsiness. If she hadn't spilled the drugged water, she'd still be unconscious or maybe even dead.

Odette and the hit man were not engaging in chitchat. So far Rory had succeeded in peeling the duct tape from her mouth. Although she was suffocatingly hot and terrified, a sense of calm pervaded her. The night on her patio when Claude Dupont had shot at her and Laurent, Laurent had shown her by example to keep a cool head under fire.

Rory was taking that lesson to heart. She was not powerless. She was a princess of Estaire.

Odette and the man driving the van had killed her mother, and Rory was determined to survive her ordeal to see justice done. Her fingers were damp with sweat as she fumbled with the clasp of her purse. It finally opened.

Sweat pearled on her upper lip as she slid her hand into the purse and found the pepper spray pen that Heinrich had given her.

It took four attempts to flick the cap off the pepper spray with her thumb. Her fingers were so sweaty!

Rory stretched her arm as close to the end of the carpet roll as possible and attuned her senses to the movement of the van. Were they in street traffic or on the highway? Heinrich had warned her that a person's reaction to cayenne pepper spray would be immediate and severe. She didn't want to cause a highway pile up.

Unfortunately the van seemed to be moving smoothly with only the occasional tap on the brakes. She guessed they were on Highway 94 headed east.

"How much longer?" Odette demanded in a strained tone.

"Relax. We're right on schedule. Damn!" The hit man slammed suddenly on the brakes. Rory, bundled in the rug, slid a half-dozen inches closer to the front seats. "Geez, people don't know how to drive. Come on, asshole—" He hit the brakes again.

Rory felt the van's deceleration. She had to act now. Praying for deliverance, she took a deep breath, closed her eyes tight and pressed the button of the pepper spray.

THE TRAFFIC PARTED ahead of them like a school of fish avoiding a predator. They had been joined by several other police cars. Overhead, a police helicopter hovered.

"We're drawing nearer," Heinrich announced. "Just up ahead. The dot shows them merging onto the other highway."

"Watch for a truck or a van with dark windows," Detective Rodriguez said. "Once he sees us, he'll make a run for it."

Up ahead Laurent spotted the sudden erratic movement of a white van. It veered into another lane, side-swiping a silver sedan. ''There, the white van!''

The silver sedan changed lanes to pull over to the shoulder of the highway.

The white van came to a halt, and the driver and passenger doors flew open. A blonde in a pastel-blue suit staggered out of the passenger side. She was bent over double, clutching her face. ''That's Odette.''

To Laurent's shock, the male driver reeled blindly away from the van and was struck by a semitrailer that was braking to avoid him. The man bounced off the truck as if he were made of rubber and landed on the asphalt.

There was no sign of Rory.

Pandemonium reigned. The police cars boxed in the scene and officers spilled out, headed toward Odette and the hit man. Detective Rodriguez tried to hold Laurent back, but he broke free of the detective's hold. The police were shouting warnings about approaching the van, but Laurent ignored them. An officer opened the rear of the van.

''*Mein Gott!*'' Laurent stared in stupefaction at the roll of carpeting, pain tearing his heart. Were they too late?

He heard muffled coughing. ''Help! Please, help me!''

''Lorelei, we're here,'' he shouted, coughing, his eyes tearing up as he helped the officer pull her out of the van. The officer cut the tape that bound the rug. And there was his princess, red-faced and rumpled, and very much alive.

Her beautiful blue eyes opened, filling with tears as he gathered her into his arms.

She buried her face into his shoulder. "That's no way to travel." Then she threw up all over his shoes.

RORY HUDDLED on the floor of Laurent's suite, the balcony doors flung open to the ocean, letting the sound of the surf soothe her.

After a quick trip to the emergency room, she'd returned to the hotel under police escort. Somehow the media had caught wind of her parentage and her title and Laurent's identity, and they had staked out the hotel's entrances. News footage of the accident scene was being broadcast on every station.

The intrusive glare of the cameras had been alarming. She'd been grateful for the protective strength of Laurent's arm. He'd insisted that she stay in his suite. She'd bathed and he'd joined her in the steamy water. He'd washed her hair and they'd made tender, gentle love. Then he'd carried her to bed and held her until she'd fallen asleep. But he didn't tell her he loved her, and although Rory needed to say the words to him as much as she needed to hear them, she bit them back.

A handful of stars shone in a sky that reminded her of the inky depths of Laurent's eyes. It was two o'clock in the morning. The ceaseless energy of the water called to her, tossing answers to her unspoken worries.

Rory had lit a white pillar candle for her mother and wore her birthday necklace in quiet celebration.

Odette was in jail and the hit man was dead. The police had identified him as Elmer Nash. They were searching his home in Long Beach for evidence of his crimes. Rory felt no sorrow for him. Fortunately, the driver of the silver sedan had not suffered any injuries in the collision.

"Mom, I'm okay," she whispered to the ocean's

sympathetic ears. "I survived. And I understand why you left Dad and you couldn't go back. You were right."

"Lorelei?"

Rory turned. Laurent stood in the shadows in a pair of black silk pajama bottoms. His beautiful chest was bare, the muscles gleaming in the flickering candlelight. Her throat ached with love and regret.

She patted the floor beside her. "Come join me."

His lips brushed her hair as he nestled beside her and circled her waist with his arms. "Could you not sleep?"

"No. There's too much to think about."

"You handled yourself magnificently today."

She squeezed his hard thigh. "I had an exemplary teacher. You saved me today."

He shook his head. "Heinrich deserves the honors although he broke several rules with his tracking device."

"I'm naming my firstborn son after Heinrich, but you were the one who taught me not to let fear overtake me."

"I'm flattered."

She leaned her shoulder into his chest and felt the steadying pound of his heartbeat. "I've made a few other decisions." She hesitated. "I'm meeting Olivier and Renald in France on Saturday. I'll be going to Estaire with them. I think it's time Princess Charlotte Aurora returned to her birthplace and faced up to her responsibilities."

"If that is what you wish, my princess."

She lifted her face and admired his dark profile and the tautness of his supple lips. "Do you love me, Sebastian?"

He stiffened, his features wary. "We have talked

about this before. Love serves very little purpose in a royal—''

''Marriage,'' she finished for him. ''I know. I am prepared to make many sacrifices for Estaire, but the one thing I will not sacrifice is the right to be loved by a man of my own choosing. I love you, Sebastian. Not your crown.'' She touched his firm chin. She would miss not having children who bore his aristocratic features.

''I value your friendship and these moments we have spent together more than you'll ever know, but I can't devote my life to a partner who withholds his love from me.'' She sniffled, trying to retain her dignity. ''I'll be asking Olivier formally in writing to release me from the terms of the treaty. I thought you deserved to hear it from me first. I hope that working together as colleagues we can bring an end to the feud between our countries.''

Laurent nodded. He swallowed hard, but he didn't say anything. Frankly, Rory hadn't expected a response. She knew him so well. Her heart ached for his pain, his loneliness, his loss.

She kissed him lightly on the lips, then blew out the candle and walked away. Sometimes a woman needed to take a stand for what she believed in, even at the risk of losing the man she loved.

THE HEADLINES MOCKED HIM. Laurent wished Heinrich would quit leaving the damn tabloids all over his quarters. For the past six weeks, Laurent had found the newspapers and magazines left in chairs, on tables, even in his private car. It was damn irritating to be constantly reminded that he had been royally dumped.

Princess Spurns Royal Proposal. Prince Ducharme

Has No Heart. Princess Takes Palace by Storm. The
Real Reason Rory Dumped Her Prince. Royal Love Tri-
angle.

The flood of bad press had renewed the feud between
Estaire and Ducharme. The world seemed to be cheering
that Princess Rory refused to enter a loveless marriage.

Laurent was not cheering. He was spending long
hours working or trying to find enrichment in books that
no longer satisfied him as they once did. His pride was
bruised, and his father had scolded him for bungling the
treaty and allowing the situation to escalate into a full-
blown scandal. The Schoenfeldt family had left Ducharme in disgrace, creating yet another flurry of headlines.

No matter how frequently Laurent tossed the tabloids
in the rubbish bin, they resurfaced in another location
to taunt him. On the one hand Laurent was incredibly
proud that Rory was spreading her wings and proving
that she could handle her royal responsibilities with confidence and wit. She'd even successfully ridden out the
inevitable rumors questioning her legitimacy.

But he was disturbed to see her smiling picture in the
paper at a Paris nightclub with a movie star. Did she
really think some poorly shaven actor would know the
first thing about raising an heir to the throne?

With each passing day Laurent felt an ache swell beneath his bruised pride—an ache for his beautiful Lorelei. He missed their stimulating conversations and her
adorable faux pas. And the softness in her voice when
she called him Sebastian. He missed her riotous curls
and the impetuous unchecked heat that made him feel
so incredibly alive when he touched her. When he
kissed her.

He missed *her*. The isolation of his position had never

seemed so unbearable. Rory had opened up his emotions like a gutted fish, leaving him with his innards exposed.

Yet, what was he going to do about it?

With a sigh, Laurent helped himself to a brandy from the bar in his private quarters and sank down into his favorite club chair. To his irritation a newspaper had been tucked between the arm of the chair and the seat cushion. Laurent removed the newspaper with a grimace.

The front page headline pushed him beyond restraint: Princess Pregnant with Prince's Love Child.

Laurent swallowed the brandy in one gulp. There was rarely any truth in these trumped-up stories, but it was time to reopen negotiations.

"MESDAMES ET MESSIEURS, it is with great pleasure that I present my sister, Her Serene Highness, Charlotte Aurora, Princess of Estaire," Prince Olivier announced to the guests and dignitaries gathered in the palace ballroom.

Rory beamed and held her head high as she made her grand entrance into the ballroom amid applause in the stunning orange gown that Laurent had picked out for her all those weeks ago. Olivier kissed her, as did her newly pregnant sister-in-law Penelope.

The silver-and-blue rococo ballroom shimmered with light and mirrors and crystal. In well-rehearsed French, Rory told the invited guests how happy she was to be home after living abroad for so many years and that she was honored to serve Estaire and its citizens.

Despite the difficulties of learning what her new position entailed, Rory loved Estaire with its hillsides dotted with wild poppies and daisies and the vineyards of

Riesling grapes sloping down to the ancient village of Auvergne on the banks of the Rhine.

Renald winked at her from the sidelines. In the past eight weeks, Renald had decided that he would like to continue in his position as his brother's personal secretary, and he did not wish to bring scandal upon his mother's name by making the facts of his birth public.

Rory and Olivier had accepted his decision, but had made it clear that they considered him a brother in every way.

Rory's heart froze when she realized who was standing beside him. Laurent.

No, not just Laurent. It was Prince Laurent in formal ceremonial dress of black tailcoat, white piqué waistcoat and tie. He looked even more handsome than he did in her dreams, his inky eyes shielding mysteries that her heart still ached to share. She wasn't over him yet. Like her mother, she'd probably never get over the man she loved.

"*Mesdames et messieurs,* if you would indulge me for a special presentation." Olivier gestured regally. "His Royal Highness, Crown Prince Laurent of Ducharme."

Rory's pulse fluttered and her knees trembled as Laurent made his way up to the dais where she stood with her brother and sister-in-law. She watched him warily.

He acknowledged Olivier and Penelope, then he went down on one knee before Rory. Gasps filled the ballroom.

Her face turned scarlet and her heart plummeted to her stomach as Laurent kissed her gloved hand. Was he going to offer her a public apology?

Her knees threatened to buckle from the warmth of his fingers.

"My darling, Lorelei," he said in his rich clear voice. "I've come here this evening to beg your forgiveness for my arrogance. You offered me the gifts of your love and friendship and demanded the same in return. In my arrogance I thought our union would better withstand the pressures of our positions if we didn't bring false expectations of love into the equation. But there is nothing false about my feelings for you, *mein* Lorelei. I love you, not as a crown prince, but as a man who wants a cherished partner to share his joys and sorrows with. I want your beautiful face to light my days and your wise words to comfort me and make me laugh. I offer you my heart and my devotion with my two hands." His voice shook, and Rory saw tears in his eyes.

That set her off. She started to sniffle.

Laurent smiled at her, his handsome face softening with love. "Will you honor me by agreeing to be my wife?"

Rory beamed at hearing the words she'd longed to hear. "It's hard to resist a man who can admit when he's wrong. I love you, Sebastian. Yes, I'll marry you."

He removed a diamond ring from his pocket and slid it over her gloved finger. "This was my mother's ring." Then he rose and kissed her. The room exploded with applause.

"Champagne!" Olivier ordered.

Laurent laughed, joy dancing in his heart and in his soul. He had never been happier in his life.

Rory was breathless. "What made you change your mind?"

He told her about the newspapers Heinrich kept leaving for him to find. "I read one that suggested you were pregnant with our child."

Her beautiful blue eyes widened. "Is that what your proposal was about? Some kind of misguided duty because you think I might be pregnant?"

He pressed a finger over her lips, unable to keep from smiling. "Shh, *mein* Lorelei. Allow me to finish."

Rory stopped talking, but her eyes sparked her opinion.

"The newspaper article made me think about my mother and the legacy she passed on to me. She spent most of her life pining for my father's love and never having the courage to ask for what she wanted and to expect it as a right. I realized I didn't want to spend my life like that. Life can be very lonely when you do not have love."

The wariness faded from his princess's eyes as Laurent kissed her, losing himself in the lure of her sweet lips.

Love was much headier than the power of the monarchy.

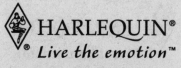

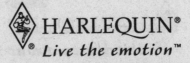

Receive a FREE hardcover book from

H A R L E Q U I N   R O M A N C E®

in September!

Harlequin Romance celebrates the launch of
the line's new cover design by offering you
this exclusive offer valid only in September,
only in Harlequin Romance.

To receive your
FREE HARDCOVER BOOK
written by bestselling author
Emilie Richards, send us four
proofs of purchase from any
September 2004 Harlequin
Romance books. Further details
and proofs of purchase can be
found in all September 2004
Harlequin Romance books.

*Must be postmarked
no later than October 31.*

**Don't forget to be one of the first
to pick up a copy of the new-look
Harlequin Romance novels in September!**

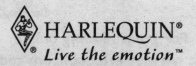

USA TODAY bestselling author

ERICA SPINDLER

Jane Killian has everything to live for. She's the toast of the Dallas art community, she and her husband, Ian, are completely in love—and overjoyed that Jane is pregnant.

Then her happiness shatters as her husband becomes the prime suspect in a murder investigation. Only Jane knows better. She knows that this is the work of the same man who stole her sense of security seventeen years ago, and now he's found her again… and he won't rest until he can *See Jane Die…*

SEE JANE DIE

"Creepy and compelling, *In Silence* is a real page-turner."
—*New Orleans Times-Picayune*

Available in June 2004 wherever books are sold.

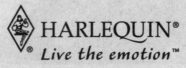